Alternate Personalities of a Cosmic Mind

Leon Isaac Drucker

ISBN: 9798218525842

Disclaimer

This is a work of fiction. Names, characters, businesses, places, events, and incidents are either the products of the author's imagination or used in a fictitious manner. Any resemblance to actual persons, living or dead, or actual events is purely coincidental.

DEDICATION

For Bernardo Kastrup,
whose profound exploration of consciousness and reality has not only reshaped my understanding of the world but also inspired this journey. Thank you for illuminating the path and challenging the boundaries of thought.

Contents

FORWARD

Introduction to "The Spirit Molecule"

DMT (N, N-Dimethyltryptamine) is a powerful psychedelic compound that naturally occurs in various plants and animals, including humans. It is structurally related to serotonin, a neurotransmitter in the brain, and is known for producing intense, short-lived psychedelic experiences characterized by vivid visual and auditory hallucinations, altered sense of time, and profound changes in consciousness.

Currently, DMT itself is not widely used in mainstream medicine. However, there is growing interest in its potential therapeutic applications, particularly in psychiatry.

Some areas where DMT is being explored:

1. Treatment-Resistant Depression: Some studies suggest that DMT might be beneficial in treating depression that does not respond to traditional antidepressants.

2. Psychotherapy Enhancement: DMT is being explored as a tool to enhance psychotherapy. The intense experiences it induces can sometimes allow individuals to access repressed memories or emotions, potentially leading to breakthroughs in therapy.

3. End-of-Life Anxiety: DMT is being studied for their ability to help terminally ill patients cope with end-of-life anxiety and existential distress. The profound, sometimes spiritual experiences reported by users can provide comfort and reduce fear of death.

4. Research into Consciousness: Beyond clinical applications, DMT is also being studied for its effects on consciousness. Some researchers are interested in understanding how it alters perception, cognition, and brain function, which could provide insights into the nature of consciousness itself.

Recently there was a study conducted by researchers at Imperial College London, aimed to prolong the effects of DMT to better study its impact on consciousness and brain function. Typically, a DMT trip lasts about 5 to 30 minutes when inhaled or injected, as DMT is quickly broken down by the body. However, the researchers used a technique called continuous intravenous (IV) infusion to maintain the DMT effects for a longer duration.

By using IV infusion, researchers were able to maintain steady levels of DMT in the bloodstream, thereby extending the psychedelic experience. The goal was to extend the duration of the altered state induced by DMT beyond the usual few minutes.

The extended infusion allows researchers to study the nature of the psychedelic experience in more detail. This includes understanding how prolonged exposure affects the brain, how subjective experiences evolve over time, and what this can tell us about consciousness.

Findings suggest that prolonged DMT exposure allows for a deeper exploration of the "DMT space", a term used to describe the unique and often indescribable experiences reported by users. The extended exposure also enabled researchers to study the brain's response to DMT over a longer period, which may help in understanding the neurobiological basis of consciousness and how psychedelics can potentially be used in therapeutic settings.

Prolonged DMT exposure provides a unique opportunity to explore altered states of consciousness in a controlled environment. This could lead to new insights into the mechanisms underlying consciousness and how psychedelics interact with brain networks.

There is a hypothesis that DMT may be released in the brain at the time of death, contributing to near-death experiences (NDE's).

If DMT is indeed released at death, it could contribute to phenomena often reported during NDE's, such as vivid hallucinations, feelings of euphoria, life review, a sense of detachment from the body, and encounters with otherworldly beings or environments.

Some researchers theorize that DMT might be released during birth, contributing to the dramatic transition from the womb to the outside world. The intense experience of birth could potentially involve shifts in consciousness or awareness facilitated by DMT.

DREAMER'S HEART HEALER'S HANDS

The EMT

The shattered glass glittered like a dusting of frost under the strobe of red and blue lights, each fragment reflecting the urgency etched into Maia Rose's every move. She navigated the mayhem, her green eyes scanning the wreckage with an intensity that belied the dreamer within. The twisted metal carcass of a vehicle lay sprawled across the highway, its form contorted in an unnatural pose of despair.

"Lucas, I need the Jaws over here!" Her voice sliced through the harshness of sirens and frantic shouts, commanding yet tinged with an empathetic undertone that soothed even in the pandemonium. Lucas, moving with polish that spoke of countless hours of shared trials, mirrored her steps, hauling the heavy rescue tool towards the center of destruction.

On the sideline, uniformed figures swarmed, in a controlled flurry, as they tended to the injured scattered like discarded figures around the collision site. The sharp scent of leaking gasoline mingled with the coppery tang of blood, and somewhere, a woman's sobs splashed onto the canvas of this nights haunting picture, a reminder of the human cost at hand.

Maia's focus never wavered, as she and Lucas approached the most grievous scene, a crumpled sedan, its driver's side caved in, trapping the occupant inside.

"Maia, we've got less than five minutes before the gas tank could explode," Lucas said, his voice a low growl grounded in the gravity of their task. His words were few, but they carried the weight of shared understanding between them.

"Understood," Maia replied, her hands steady as she directed the placement of the hydraulic device called "The Jaws of Life" as it whirred to life. Its metallic jaws inching closer to the imprisoned driver, guided by Maia's deft touch.

The sounds of strained metal filled the air as the tool did its work. Jaws bending the body of the car to its will, tearing the mangled steel apart. Other emergency personnel stood ready, awaiting Maia's signal. The once impenetrable barrier yielded, inch by inch, to the relentless force and the collective determination of those whose job it was to pry deaths mouth open night after night.

Maia's heart raced, not with doubt, but with the profound clarity that came from knowing that someone's existence hinged on her actions in this sliver of time. There was beauty in the fragility of life, and Maia, amid the mayhem and the raw cries of fear and strength, found herself at the very center of it all.

Lucas's gaze met Maia's for a fraction of a second, the silent communication between them cutting through the dissonance of sirens and shouting. They had done this dance of life and death so many times before; their movements were now a choreography of efficiency, empathy, and strength.

"Over there," Maia's voice was steady as she pointed to a crumpled SUV on the edge of the scene. The front end was squeezed against a streetlight, the driver's side door ajar but offering no escape. Within, an arm dangled listlessly from the window, offering a stark picture against the darkening sky.

They approached, Maia's intense gaze scanning for the quickest way into the vehicle while Lucas assembled their medical supplies with practiced hands. Time seemed to slow as they worked, each step deliberate and vital. The clamor of the outside world receded until there was nothing but the task at hand and the person who needed them.

"Can you hear me?" Maia called out to the figure inside the twisted metal cocoon. The response came as a weak moan, the sound laced with pain and confusion. A man, young by the look of him, his face smeared with blood that glittered eerily in the flashing lights of the emergency vehicles.

"Lucas, he's got a head wound, looks deep," Maia reported, her tone betraying none of the concern that tightened in her chest. She reached through the shattered window, checking for a pulse, her fingers probing over the cool skin. It was there, strong under her touch, a small victory in the battle they waged every day.

"Keep talking to him, keep him with us," Lucas instructed, pulling out gauze and pressure dressings. He passed them to Maia, who applied them with gentle firmness to the man's temple, staunching the flow of red that sought to drain the life from him.

"Stay with us," she murmured to the injured man, more to herself than to him. "Help is here."

The man's eyelids fluttered, and for a moment, it seemed as if he might slip away into the darkness that edged his vision. But Maia was a champion, her resolve a lifeline thrown into the turbulent sea of his fading consciousness.

"Good work, Maia," Lucas said softly, admiration lacing his voice as the man's breathing steadied. Together, they had turned the tide yet again, holding fast against the storm, preserving a life that might have otherwise been lost amid the wreckage.

"Lucas, we need a C-collar, now!" Maia's command sliced through the noise of sirens and scattered debris.

Without hesitation, Lucas reached into the emergency vehicle, pulling out the requested equipment. They moved as one organism, two halves of a whole.

"Prep him for a spinal board," she continued, her mind racing ahead, assessing, planning. Her hands, steady as rock despite the fluttering pulse of adrenaline. She felt along the man's spine with methodical precision. Maia's intense eyes reflected the tangled metal and glass around them, yet her vision tunneled, focusing solely on the injured before her.

"Breathing is shallow, possible pneumothorax," she murmured, to herself. Her fingers danced over the man's chest, feeling for the telltale signs of trapped air. She glanced at Lucas, who nodded, understanding the gravity of her unspoken thoughts.

"Needle decompression," she stated, voice devoid of doubt. Maia retrieved the appropriate needle from the medical kit, her movements deliberate but swift. The injured man gasped as she punctured his chest wall, and then, instantly, his breathing eased. It was a temporary fix, but it granted precious time.

"Maia, he's stabilizing," said Lucas, relief tingeing his tone.

"Keep monitoring vitals," she instructed without looking up. Her mind buzzed with the next steps, always anticipating the patient's needs. In this orchestrated turmoil, Maia was the conductor, and every action, every decision, spun from her core of calm.

"Another life held in balance," she thought, allowing herself just a fraction of a moment to recognize the day's weight. But there was no time for reflection; not yet.

"Three... two... one..." Together, they lifted the man from his crumpled seat, the world shrinking down to the space between heartbeats. Lucas adjusted the cervical collar around the patient's neck, his actions mirroring Maia's own meticulous care.

"IV is secure," Lucas reported, checking the line as he handed Maia the saline drip. They worked in concert, a duet of calm amidst the storm of flashing lights and urgent voices. Maia felt the gravity of the moment settle in her bones, a weight borne of countless such encounters, each leaving its mark upon her soul.

"Transport's ready," came the call from outside the bubble of intensity they had created.

"Let's move," Maia responded, guiding the stretcher with a steadiness that denied the adrenaline coursing through her veins. They emerged from the wreckage; the injured man now safely installed within the cocoon of their care. The ambulance doors swung open, welcoming them into its white embrace.

As the ambulance doors closed, sealing them within its sterile confines, Maia allowed herself a single, measured breath. It was a brief respite, a momentary stillness before the storm resumed. And though the world outside continued to churn in turmoil, within the small universe of her influence, Maia Yetta Rose was a force unto herself, a dreamer anchored in reality, a philosopher whose musings were etched in the flesh and blood of those she fought to save.

As she secured the stretcher, her fingers worked deftly, buckling straps with an efficiency born of endless repetition. Her eyes never left the man's face, watching for any sign of distress, any flicker of pain that might herald a turn for the worse.

"Vitals are stabilizing," she reported, her voice steady as she monitored the readouts on the portable medical equipment. The symphony of beeps and whirs filled the space, with a mechanical chorus that sang of life hanging in the balance.

"Good job, Maia. He's going to make it because of you," Lucas said, his words heavy with respect and the shared weight of their responsibility.

Maia did not respond, her focus absolute as she administered another dose of medication, her movements fluid and sure. The injured man's breathing steadied, the erratic rise and fall of his chest becoming more rhythmic under her watchful care.

The engine's hum settled into a low purr as the ambulance wove through the city's veins, the siren's cry falling silent. Maia gazed out the window, her reflection a ghostly overlay on the world speeding by. The chaos of the accident scene shrank away in the rearview mirror, yet the echo of adrenaline lingered in her bloodstream.

"Another close one," Lucas murmured beside her, his voice barely rising above the soft clatter of medical equipment secured behind them.

Maia nodded; her eyes still fixed on the shifting landscape outside. She took a deep breath, the air filling her lungs like a cleansing tide washing over the remnants of tension that clung to her muscles. In that controlled exhale, she released the coiled intensity that had driven her movements just moments ago.

She could see it now, the delicate balance between life and death, a scale she tipped with her own hands. Her fingers, still tingling from the exertion, had danced on that precipice, weaving strands of fate with each decisive act. It was a weighty realization, one that grounded her soul firmly in the tangible triumphs and tragedies of her calling.

"Every second counts," she finally said, not so much to Lucas but to herself, affirming the creed that guided her swift response. "Every choice."

Lucas glanced at her, an unspoken understanding passing between them. They were partners in this relentless pursuit, guardians against time's relentless march.

As the hospital came into view, its angular silhouette a beacon amidst the fading light, Maia's thoughts drifted briefly to the dreams that often cradled her restless mind. There, in those vivid adventures during sleep, she explored worlds untouched by the urgency of her reality. Yet even there, amongst the abstract and the otherworldly, her purpose remained clear.

"Maia?"

Her reverie shattered at the sound of her name, squinting eyes refocusing on the present. "Yeah?"

"Ready for the handoff?" Lucas asked, his hand reaching for the door handle as they pulled into the emergency bay.

"Ready," she replied, stepping out into the cool evening air, the scent of antiseptic finally clearing from her nose.

With a final glance at the patient, stable and on his way to recovery, she allowed herself the smallest of smiles, a fleeting tribute to the life they'd anchored to this side of existence. Then, as the hospital doors swallowed them whole, Maia's smile faded, and she readied herself once more.

Emergencies would keep coming; they always did. But tonight, in the quiet theater of her mind, she would replay this victory, savoring the subtle, yet profound impact of her actions. For now, though, there was only the next call, the next chance to tilt the scales, and she stepped forward with unwavering resolve.

Maia Yetta Rose, with her dreamer's heart and healer's hands, would be ready.

The Mailbox Tree

From an early age, Maia had always preferred hiking barefoot. The sensation of the rough terrain beneath her feet was a pleasure she cherished. Her feet had grown tough over the years, resilient enough to handle even the most aggressive trails. She loved the freedom it gave her and the connection she felt with the earth.

Her father, initially skeptical, had come to accept and even admire her choice. "You have tougher feet than anyone I know," he would say with a chuckle.

This day as they navigated the rocky path, Maia reveled in the feeling of the cool stones and soft moss underfoot. Other hikers often stared and made comments about her lack of shoes, but Maia welcomed the attention. She was proud of her strength and abilities, even as a young girl.

"How do you do it?" a fellow hiker asked, his eyes wide with amazement as he noticed Maia's bare feet.

Maia grinned. "Just practice," she said. "I've been doing it for as long as I can remember."

The hiker shook his head in disbelief. "You're something else, kid."

Maia beamed, feeling a sense of pride and accomplishment. Hiking barefoot was more than just a choice; it was a demonstration of her resilience and adventurous spirit.

One of the most cherished traditions of their hikes up Monadnock was the Mailbox Tree. About halfway up the mountain, just off the path, stood a massive oak tree with a fist-sized hole about five feet up its trunk. Her father Mike had a special story about this tree that he shared with Maia.

"That hole," he would say, pointing to the tree, "is where all the animals on the mountain go to get their mail."

Maia would laugh, the sound echoing through the trees. "Really? Do they get bills for acorns and invitations to bear weddings?"

"Absolutely," Mike would reply, his eyes twinkling with mischief. "And don't forget the squirrel's overdue library books."

Each time they passed the tree, her father would ask Maia to check if there was any mail for him. "Go on, stick your hand in and see if there's a letter for me."

Maia would shake her head, feigning horror. "No way! You check if you want to get bitten by a snake or spiders."

It became a regular joke between them, each spinning more elaborate stories about the tree's magical mail system. The Mailbox Tree was more than just a quirky tradition; it was a symbol of their bond, a touchstone of their shared imagination and joy.

As they neared the tree on this hike, Mike paused. "Alright, Maia. Think there's any mail today?"

Maia grinned. "Only one way to find out." She stepped closer, peering into the hole but stopping short of reaching in. "Looks like the animals are behind on their deliveries."

He laughed, ruffling her hair. "Maybe next time."

That night, back at home, Maia's dreams were filled with their day's adventure. She dreamed of the hike, the mountain, and the Mailbox Tree. In her dream, the animals did indeed receive their mail, tiny envelopes addressed in careful script. The squirrels chattered over their acorn bills, and the bears danced at their weddings. She woke with a smile, the joy of the day still warming her heart.

These hikes, filled with laughter, challenges, and shared stories, were more than just physical journeys. They were the threads that wove together the fabric of Maia's childhood, binding her to her father in a web of love and adventure. And as the years went by, the memories of these days on Mount Monadnock would remain a source of strength and inspiration for Maia, a reminder of the unbreakable bond she shared with her father.

Even at an early age, Maia possessed a confidence that belied her years. Her time in the woods with her father had instilled in her a wealth of survival skills. She could build a primitive shelter even in winter, find her way using the moss on trees or the position of the sun and stars, and make a hand drill fire to produce warmth and purify water. She knew which plants were edible and which could be used for medicinal purposes.

Maia's imagination brought the ordinary to life. She would talk to the birds and small rodents, creating stories about their lives and adventures. Often, she would wrap her arms around the trunk of a tree, listening to the whispers of the forest. She felt the universe guiding her, filling her with an unshakable sense of purpose and fearlessness.

Maia could listen to a song and decipher the musician's emotions through the tempo, tone, and melody. She appreciated life and its wonders, a wisdom that seemed beyond her years. Her father Mike often called her an old soul, marveling at her insight and depth. Maia knew that her relationship with her father had given her more than just wilderness craft and imagination; it had forged a deep spiritual connection with the world around her and instilled a faith that she was always exactly where she was supposed to be.

Whenever two people share a bond as strong as Maia and her father, the fear of loss lingers in the back of the mind. It surfaces during moments of happiness or late at night when sleep is elusive. For most, these thoughts are fleeting, retreating to the dark recesses of the mind. But for Maia, in the weeks leading up to her father's birthday on May 13th, this fear became a constant companion.

It nagged at her, a festering wound that would not heal. She could not shake the feeling that something terrible was going to happen, that she was going to lose her father—the light of her life, her hero, and closest friend.

It was knowledge, not just a feeling, that before the end of the next week, her father would be gone from her life forever.

This foreboding sense of doom cast a shadow over her days, turning even the happiest moments bittersweet. Maia tried to ignore it, focusing on her schoolwork, friends, and hobbies. But at night, when the house was quiet and the world seemed to stand still, the fear would creep in, stealing her peace and leaving her wide awake, staring at the ceiling.

Mike, ever attentive, noticed the change in her. "Are you alright, Maia?" he asked one evening as they sat by the fire, the stars twinkling overhead.

Maia forced a smile, not wanting to worry him. "I'm fine, Daddy. Just thinking."

He looked at her, his eyes full of concern. "You can tell me anything, you know that."

Maia nodded; her throat tight with unshed tears. She wanted to tell him, to share her fears, but the words wouldn't come. Instead, she leaned into him, drawing comfort from his presence, silently praying that her intuition was wrong, that they would have many more years of Sundays and adventures together.

These moments, filled with both love and an undercurrent of fear, would stay with Maia. They were a witness to the depth of her bond with her father and the profound impact he had on her life. As the days passed, the sense of impending loss grew stronger, casting a long shadow over the happiness they shared, and setting the stage for the life-changing events to come.

Support

The sirens wailing like a Valkyrie, sliced through the stillness of Boston's night. Maia Rose gripped the steering wheel of the ambulance, her knuckles white as the vehicle sliced a path through the gridlocked panic on Tremont Street. Beside her, Lucas Reed monitored the radio, his calm voice cutting through the discord with practiced ease.

"Unit 42, we're three minutes out," he reported, glancing over at Maia with an assured nod as the adrenaline coursing through them both began to climb.

"Copy that, Unit 42," came the brisk reply from dispatch, the urgency in their tone reflecting the gravity of the situation unfolding.

Buildings blurred past, the city's pulse quickening around them. Maia was focused, her mind clear despite the pace. There was a rhythm to this—a dance she and Lucas had mastered over countless nights like this one. She turned sharply, expertly maneuvering the ambulance into a narrow side street, the siren's cry echoing off the aging brick facades.

"Ready?" Maia asked, her voice steady despite the tightening in her chest.

"Ready," Lucas responded, checking the supplies one last time before they would plunge into the fray.

They arrived at the scene to find pandemonium. Flashing lights painted the darkness as figures moved frantically against the backdrop of an overturned bus. Maia and Lucas stepped into their roles seamlessly, and efficiently within the yelling, screams and sirens blare.

"Let's prioritize—triage by severity," Maia instructed, already assessing the nearest victims with a clinical eye that missed nothing.

"Got it," Lucas confirmed, moving to assist a man clutching his arm, his face etched in pain.

As Maia bent over a young woman trapped beneath a tangle of metal, her hands sure and swift, a flash of something else flickered across her consciousness, an image incongruent with the reality before her. For a moment, she stood under an alien sky, where stars swirled in impossible colors, a landscape of dreams that had been haunting her sleep.

"Maia!" Lucas's voice snapped her back, the nameless woman's pained expression drawing her immediate attention once more.

"Sorry," she murmured, shaking her head to dispel the remnants of the vision.

"Later," Lucas said, understanding without question. His hazel eyes met hers, offering silent support. They were a team, in this world of immediacy and in whatever worlds lay beyond.

Maia refocused, setting a bone with expertise born of countless emergencies, but the dreams lingered at the edge of her thoughts like specters. What did they mean? Were they mere figments of her imagination, or glimpses of something more, something woven into the very fabric of reality?

"Stay with me," she whispered to herself—a plea to keep grounded in the tangible world of flesh, blood, and bone. As she worked alongside Lucas, saving lives under the harsh glare of emergency lights, Maia's mind wrestled with questions that had no answers, at least not yet.

Between the ebb and flow of crisis, Maia found herself adrift in musings too vast for the confines of an ambulance, in dreams that felt as real as the wounded she tended. It was a duality she lived with every day—the healer rooted in the present, the dreamer searching for meaning in the night.

The silence was a stark contrast to the blaring of sirens and shouting that had filled her senses just hours before. Now, Maia lay in the dark stillness of her Boston apartment, the soft hum of the city's nocturnal life whispering through the walls.

She closed her eyes, seeking peace in sleep, but was instead thrust into an all-consuming dream.

It began as it always did, the silver thread of moonlight spilling across the metallic floor, casting shadows that seemed to reach for her. She walked down the narrow aisle between rows of cryo-pods, each one cradling a silent occupant within its frosted embrace. Her heart beat against her ribs with a familiar foreboding, a rhythm that mirrored the pulsing red light bathing the chamber in an otherworldly glow.

"Warning: System failure imminent," a disembodied voice announced, its tone void of emotion yet dripping with urgency. Maia quickened her pace, navigating the maze of pods until she stood before one labeled 'Lucas Reed.' Through the icy glass, she could see his face, serene in suspended animation.

"Maia, don't let go," Lucas's voice echoed, though his lips never moved. The pod began to frost over, obscuring him from view, and a chill ran down her spine—not from the cold, but from the sense of déjà vu that seized her.

With a jolt, Maia woke, gasping for air as if she'd been submerged in the depths of a frigid ocean. Her room felt alien for a moment, the dream's icy grip still clawing at her consciousness. She sat up, pressing a hand to her chest, trying to calm the erratic beating of her heart.

"Another one," she muttered, her voice barely audible. The dreams were becoming more tangible, more insistent, and the line between them and reality blurred with each passing night.

"Lucas," Maia said, her voice steady but tinged with an undercurrent of distress as they sat in the break room, the drone of the dispatch radio a constant backdrop to their conversation.

"Hey," he replied, turning to her with that same attentive gaze she knew so well. "What's going on?"

"Those dreams...they're getting worse." She hesitated, unsure how to articulate the intangible. "I keep seeing this...this place. It's like nothing I've ever known, but at the same time, it feels hauntingly familiar."

Lucas leaned in, his presence a grounding force. "Tell me about it."

"It's always the same, a space station or some kind of facility. There are people in cryo-sleep, and there's always a sense of urgency, as if I'm running out of time. Last night, you were there." She searched his face for any sign of recognition, any hint that the dream might resonate with him too.

"Me?" Lucas's brow furrowed slightly, a mixture of concern and curiosity etching his features. "In your dream?"

"Yes. And it felt so real, Lucas. When I wake up, it takes me a moment to remember where I am. It's starting to affect my days; I'm constantly distracted, on edge, waiting for something to happen." Maia's green eyes shimmered with the weight of unspoken fears. "I can't shake the feeling that these dreams mean something. That they're not just dreams."

The words hung in the air between them, heavy with the gravity of her admission. Lucas reached out, his hand clasping hers in solidarity.

"Whatever it is, we'll figure it out together," he assured her, his voice a grounding melody amid the discord of her thoughts. "You're not alone in this."

Maia nodded, drawing strength from his unwavering support. Together, they had faced the chaos of emergency calls and the unpredictable dance of life and death. But this—this was uncharted territory, a map of the mind and soul that they would have to navigate side by side.

"Lucas, it's like I'm walking through a fog that just won't lift," Maia began, her voice tinged with the frustration of a puzzle unsolved. "Every night, these dreams pull me under, and I wake up gasping for reality."

They sat in the back of the ambulance, the soft hum of the city of Boston enveloping them as a cocoon of normalcy, even though nothing felt normal to Maia anymore.

The dim interior light cast shadows across her face, accentuating the creases of worry that marred her usually composed features.

"Tell me about them again," Lucas said, his tone gentle yet firm, encouraging her to explore the depths of her own mind. He watched her closely, his eyes reflecting a silent promise to wade through this mystery with her.

"It's always different, but the same," she continued, her thoughts winding like the streets they navigated daily. "Places I've never been to, people I don't know, they all feel so familiar. And there's this... this urgency, like I'm running out of time to understand why."

"Maia, you're the strongest person I know," Lucas offered softly, sensing the waver in her resolve. "I can't pretend to decipher your dreams, but I know you. You'll get to the bottom of this."

"Will I?" Her question was not one of self-doubt but of longing, a yearning for answers that seemed as distant as the stars above their city. "These dreams leave traces, Lucas. Emotions that linger long after I've opened my eyes. It's like they're trying to tell me something important."

"Maybe they are." Lucas leaned forward, elbows resting on his knees, embodying the steadfast pillar of support he had always been. "But you can't force clarity, Maia. You got to take this one step at a time."

Maia looked at him, the bright sheen of her eyes in stark contrast to the sterile blues and whites of the ambulance interior. With Lucas's presence, she found a semblance of peace, a momentary reprieve from the chaos that threatened to spill from her dreams into waking life.

"Okay," she whispered, clutching onto his words like a lifeline. "One step at a time."

A tremor passed through Maia's hands, the delicate quiver invisible to anyone but herself.

She pulled her knees up to her chest as she sat on the gurney in the back of the ambulance, the world outside a blur of Boston's nocturnal pulse.

"Lucas," she began, her voice barely threading the hum of the engine and the distant wail of the city's unrest. "I'm scared."

He turned towards her, his eyes a steady lantern in the dim light. "Talk to me, Maia."

Her gaze drifted into the void beyond the ambulance doors, flickering lights casting shadows that danced like specters over her features. "It's like I'm living two lives," she confessed, the words tumbling out with the urgency of a dam breaking. "One here, in this chaos, and another... somewhere else, in my sleep."

"Somewhere else?" Lucas probed gently.

The corners of Maia's mouth twitched in an attempt to smile that never quite reached fruition. "Yes," she exhaled, her breath fogging the cold metal surface before her. "It's this place—luminous and vast. I can't shake the feeling... it's important."

"Go ahead," Lucas urged, sensing the gravity behind her halting speech.

Closing her eyes, Maia let the dream envelop her once more. She spoke softly, her words painting the landscape of her nocturnal sojourns. "There's a field... endless and aglow with a light that doesn't sting your eyes. The sky is a wash of swirling nebulas, colors you've never seen, and can't possibly describe." Her fingers clutched at the fabric of her uniform as if trying to grasp the ephemeral threads of her dream. "There are figures moving in the distance, their forms translucent, shifting like mirages born of heat and light."

"Is it peaceful there?" Lucas asked, his voice guiding her through the fog of her own subconscious.

"Sometimes," she whispered, her voice thick with emotion. "But there's also a feeling of anticipation, as if something monumental is on the horizon. It's beautiful and terrifying all at once."

"Maia..."

She opened her eyes, the dream receding like the tide, leaving her stranded on the shores of reality. "I don't know what it means, Lucas. But every time I wake up, I feel... hollow. As if I've left something crucial behind."

"Whatever it is, you'll face it," Lucas said, reaching over to place a comforting hand on her shoulder. "I got you partner."

Maia leaned into the touch, the simple act grounding her. The fear that had coiled within her loosened ever so slightly, the warmth of human connection reassuring her weary spirit.

"Thanks," she murmured, allowing herself to dwell in the silence that followed.

Maia's fingers trembled as she fumbled with the edge of the ambulance's metallic surface, her gaze fixed on the cold Boston skyline melting into twilight. Her breath formed small clouds in the crisp air.

"Lucas," she said, her voice barely above a whisper yet laden with urgency. "Have you ever felt like the world is trying to tell you something? Like there's a message just beyond your grasp?"

Lucas leaned back against the ambulance door, his eyes reflecting the city lights as they started to flicker on one by one. "Sometimes I think life is full of signs we can't always read," he admitted, his tone even but thoughtful.

She turned to face him, "but what if it's not just life... What if it's something more, something outside of our understanding?" Her pulse quickened with the need for answers, an almost childlike hope that he could offer a lifeline to the meaning she craved.

"Maia, your dreams..." Lucas hesitated, choosing his words with care. "They might be just dreams, or maybe they're your mind's way of processing all we see and do." He looked at her intently, his compassion obvious.

"Or they could be prophetic," Maia interjected, her desperation peaking as the possibility took root within her. "There has to be a reason they feel so real, so important."

He stepped closer, bridging the gap between them, his voice low but firm. "I can't decode the universe for you. But these dreams...they're part of you. And I'm here, Maia. Always." His hand found hers, grip steady and reassuring.

"Is that enough though, Lucas? To just be here?" The question hung between them like a spider dangling from a thread, vibrating with the intensity of her inner turmoil.

"Sometimes being present is the only thing we can offer," he replied, sincerity lacing his words. "I may not have the insight you're looking for, but I'll help you search for it. You'll find clarity I promise."

A long sigh escaped Maia's lips, her body relaxing slightly under the weight of his promise. In the stillness that followed, the chaos of the day's emergencies faded into the background, leaving only the shared space between two souls bound by a common purpose—to heal, to understand, to stand together amid life's enigmatic web.

.Maia leaned against the edge of the ambulance; her gaze fixed on the twinkling lights of Boston's skyline. Lucas stood silently beside her, sharing in the moment of peace from the day's urgencies. The city hummed with life around them, yet within the bubble of their companionship, there was a rare stillness that allowed room for more personal revelations.

"Lucas," Maia began, her voice barely above a whisper, as if afraid to disturb the fragile tranquility, "I've never told anyone about those dreams. Not like I've told you." She turned to look into his hazel eyes, seeking an anchor in their depths.

He nodded, the corners of his mouth lifting in a soft smile that didn't quite reach his eyes. "I know it's not easy, opening up like this. I appreciate your trust."

She exhaled, her breath forming a cloud in the cool air. "With you, it's different. I don't feel the need to build walls. You've seen me at my worst, on the job, when every second counts. Now, you're seeing into the corners of my mind that I don't understand myself."

"Maia, it's because you trust me that I want to help you through this," he said, shifting his weight from one foot to the other, maintaining his stance close enough to offer support yet respectful of her space. "Your dreams... I know their a puzzle now, but we'll piece them together."

"Will we?" she questioned; her curiosity piqued by the uncertainty. "Or will each piece just lead us deeper into the maze?"

"Even a maze has an exit," Lucas countered gently, "and I'm walking it with you, every step of the way." His assurance was as steady as his presence, as reliable as the dawn after a long night.

Maia's lips parted to respond, but words failed her. Instead, she reached out, her fingers entwined with his, a physical manifestation of their emotional bond. In that simple gesture, promises were made without being spoken, pledges of solidarity that transcended verbal contracts.

"Thank you," she murmured, and though the words were commonplace, they carried the weight of shared experiences and unspoken understanding.

"Always," Lucas replied, his tone imbued with a quiet strength that wrapped around her like a protective cloak.

As they stood together, the world around them continued its relentless march. Cars sped by, sirens wailed in the distance, and the night air carried the sounds of a city that never truly slept. But within the cocoon of their connection, time seemed to slow, granting them a brief respite from the inexorable passage of the night.

Despite the comfort found in Lucas's unwavering support, the tendrils of unresolved mystery clung to Maia, coiling around her thoughts, and tightening with each unanswered question.

The shadows cast by the streetlights seemed to stretch longer, grasping, as if echoing her internal struggle.

"Let's head back," Lucas suggested, his voice drawing her attention away from the encroaching darkness.

"Sure," Maia agreed, but her gaze lingered on the horizon where the city met the sky, a line blurred and indistinct, much like the boundary between dream and reality. Her dreams remained a landscape uncharted, a terrain fraught with enigmatic symbols and elusive truths.

The two climbed into the ambulance, the doors shutting with a definitive thud, a period at the end of an unfinished sentence. As they drove through the streets of Boston, Maia rested her head against the window, her reflection a ghostly companion to her thoughts. The evening's conversation had fortified her bond with Lucas, yet it had also amplified the echo of questions unanswered, a haunting refrain that promised the search for understanding was far from over.

Meditation

In the style of the night, where revelations hide just out of sight, Maia journeyed inward, her every inhalation a step deeper into the matrix of her own vast consciousness.

A whisper of something intangible brushed against the edges of Maia's awareness, as if the universe itself exhaled a secret meant only for her ears. The clamor of thoughts that normally thrashed within her, echoes of emergencies, the cries for help that punctuated her days, began to ebb like the tide withdrawing from the shore.

In this chamber of distinction, where only shadows dared to dance upon the walls, Maia surrendered to the weight of her compassion and drive, the burden of being a savior in the tempest of others' despair. Here she was simply Maia, the dreamer, a solitary sojourner through the veils of cognition and reality.

Her breaths, once anchors in the stormy sea of existence, now became gentle gusts ushering her deeper into the realm of stillness. Each exhalation was a release, a letting go of the sharp contours of her daily life in Boston. With each inhalation, the abstract musings that filled her nights took firmer shape, blurring the boundaries between the seen and the unseen, between waking life and the landscape of dreams.

It started as a hum, a low thrumming that resonated within her core before it seeped outwards, permeating the very fabric of the room. The air vibrated with an energy that seemed intimately familiar. It pulsed around her, a living entity that caressed her skin, played with tendrils of her auburn hair, and whispered promises to her soul.

This subtle vibration grew clearer, more insistent, as if it were the heartbeat of the cosmos syncing with her own. The dim light that filtered through the curtains appeared to quiver, casting fluid patterns that swam across her closed eyelids. In this moment, the stark line between Maia and the world beyond blurred, and the air, charged with an inexplicable life force embraced her in its unseen currents.

With the disciplined calm of one who has faced chaos, Maia allowed the sensation to wash over her without resistance. She remained motionless, a statue of serenity amid a world teeming with invisible energies, but within her, a profound shift was taking place. She was not merely in the room, she was becoming a part of it, her consciousness melding with the vibrant, unseen web of life that connected all things.

Maia's breath, rhythmic and deep, became the only sound in the stillness of her modest Boston apartment. Each exhale was a gentle release of her physical form, each inhalation an invitation to the vast unknown. The boundaries of her mind seemed to dissolve, like sugar melting into the warmth of tea, expanding outward in a silent bloom.

She could feel the edges of her consciousness press against the walls of the room, seeping into the cracks of the plaster, sliding over the worn wooden floors, reaching up to brush the ceiling with a delicate touch. Her thoughts had grown tendrils, stretching further and further, seeking connection, not just within the confines of this space, but into the expanse beyond.

The transformation began subtly, the way dawn creeps upon the night. The dim outlines of furniture, the bookshelves laden with medical texts and philosophical musings, the framed photos of old memories, each began to quiver. Maia watched, through her mind's eye, as the solidness of her world started to wane.

Lines wavered, objects trembled, and the sturdiness of her reality became questionable. She watched, fascinated and unafraid, as the walls themselves grew translucent, their firmness betraying them as they shimmered like mirages under a relentless sun. They were no longer barriers but veils, thinning to reveal a spectacle more breathtaking than any dream she had ever conjured.

What once were walls now pulsed with energy, a web of luminous threads weaving through the structure of her home. It was as though the universe had unveiled its skeleton to her, the underlying framework that upheld all of existence, and she witnessed it from the inside, her own being interlaced within the intricate pattern.

The furniture, her cherished possessions, even the very air around her, vibrated with an intensity that suggested they were nothing more than condensed energy—a ballet of particles dancing at the command of an unseen director. Maia, the dreamer, the saver of lives, found herself in a sea of living light, every wave and ripple a note in an eternal melody.

She understood then, with a clarity that pierced the veil of her daily existence, that her role in the vast web of life was both minuscule and monumental.

As an EMT, she had touched the lives of strangers, had held the fragile thread of their existence between steady hands, but now she grasped something greater. She was part of the very fabric that connected those lives.

Breathing in harmony with the pulse of the universe, Maia remained anchored in her meditation, her spirit bathed in the glow of the interconnected energy that bound her to every atom, every star, every soul. And in this sacred moment of revelation, the profound truth whispered to her: she was the cosmos, and the cosmos was her.

DREAMS

On the afternoon of May 13th, 1990, a dark cloud of dread hovered over Maia, thickening with each passing moment. The foreboding feeling that had gnawed at her for weeks had now grown into a full-blown premonition of disaster. Michael, her father, gently broke the news to her that she would be spending the night at her best friend Kimberly's house.

"Maia, sweetheart, you'll be staying with Kimberly tonight. Your mom and I are going out to celebrate my birthday," Mike said, trying to sound cheerful.

"We're going to "Hooked" in Concord," her mother Lee Ann added, her tone impatient. "It's our favorite restaurant, remember?"

Maia's heart sank. She couldn't explain why, but the thought of her parents going out filled her with an overwhelming sense of dread. Instead of the usual excitement at the prospect of a sleepover, Maia burst into tears, clinging to her father as if it were the last time she would see him.

"Please, don't go," she sobbed, her voice breaking. "Stay here with me."

Lee Ann rolled her eyes, exasperated. "Knock it off, Maia. You're being too theatrical. We'll see you tomorrow morning and then we can go out for a pancake breakfast at the diner."

Mirella, Kimberly's mom, came over to lead Maia away, her voice soothing. "Come on, Maia. It'll be fun. You'll see. Happy birthday, Mike. You two have a wonderful time. Don't worry about Maia, she'll calm down once you're gone."

Mike hugged Maia tightly, kissing her forehead. "I love you, Maia. We'll be back before you know it. Be a good girl for Mirella, okay?"

Maia nodded, tears streaming down her face. "I love you too, Daddy."

Mike and Lee Ann waved goodbye as they got into the car. Maia watched them drive away, a sinking feeling in her stomach. Mirella led her inside, trying to distract her with promises of movies and snacks, but Maia's heart was heavy with an unshakable sense of doom.

That night, the worst happened. On their way home from dinner, Lee Ann, who was driving, lost control of the car. It crossed the median strip and collided head-on with a tractor-trailer. The impact was devastating, and both Mike and Lee Ann were killed instantly.

The news came to Mirella's house late that night. The phone rang, and Maia watched as Mirella's face went pale. Tears welled up in her eyes as she hung up the phone and turned to Maia.

"Oh, sweetie," she began, her voice trembling. "There's been an accident..."

Maia's world shattered. She felt as though she were falling into a bottomless pit, the reality of her worst fears engulfing her. She barely heard Mirella's words as the world around her dissolved into a blur of grief and disbelief.

Maia found herself standing at the base of Mount Monadnock, the familiar contours of the landscape stretching out before her like an old, cherished memory. The early morning sun cast a golden hue over the rugged terrain, the light filtering through the trees in delicate rays. She could hear the soft rustle of leaves, the distant call of a bird, and the faint murmur of a stream winding its way through the forest. The air was crisp, carrying the fresh scent of pine and earth, grounding her in a sense of tranquility.

Taking a deep breath, she turned to see her father standing beside her. He looked just as she remembered, his face lined with age but his eyes bright with an enduring spark of life.

He smiled at her, a smile that reached his eyes and spoke of a deep, unspoken love. Maia felt a pang of longing and a rush of unresolved emotions. It had been years since they had shared a moment like this, and the dream seemed to weave together fragments of the past with a poignant clarity.

"Ready to hike, kiddo?" her father asked, his voice warm and familiar, a comforting anchor in the surreal landscape of the dream.

Maia nodded, unable to find her voice. Together, they began their ascent, the path winding upward through the dense forest. The sound of their footsteps mingled with the symphony of nature, creating a rhythm that echoed the beating of her heart. Each step felt significant, laden with the weight of memories and the unspoken words that had always hung between them.

As they climbed, Maia found herself lost in the details of the dream. She noticed the way the sunlight danced on the leaves, the texture of the rocks beneath her feet, and the gentle breeze that caressed her face. It was as if the mountain itself was alive, breathing in sync with her, guiding her toward some elusive truth.

They reached a clearing, a small plateau where they could rest and take in the breathtaking view. The valley below stretched out in a tapestry of greens and browns; the horizon kissed by the early morning sky. Maia sat down on a large rock, her father settling beside her. The silence between them was comfortable, filled with the unspoken understanding that had always been the foundation of their relationship.

"Do you remember the last time we were here?" her father asked, breaking the silence.

Maia nodded; her throat tight with emotion. "It was the week before your birthday," she choked out while holding the tears in. We spent the whole day hiking and talking about everything and nothing."

He smiled, a wistful look in his eyes. "Those were good times, Maia. I miss them."

"I miss them too," she whispered, the words carrying the weight of years of distance and regret.

They sat in silence for a while, the memories flowing between them like an unbroken current. Maia felt a sense of peace, a connection to her father that had been lost in the chaos of life. The dream was to give her a chance to revisit those moments, to find closure in a way that reality had never allowed.

As they prepared to continue their hike, her father turned to her, his expression serious. "Maia, there's something I need to tell you. Something important."

She looked at him, her heart pounding in her chest. "What is it, Daddy?"

He reached out and took her hand, his grip firm and reassuring. "You have a strength inside you, a resilience that I've always admired. No matter what happens, you have the power to overcome it. Remember that."

Tears welled up in Maia's eyes, the words resonating deep within her. She squeezed his hand, a silent promise to hold on to his words. They continued their ascent, the path becoming steeper and more challenging. But Maia felt a renewed sense of purpose, a determination to face whatever lay ahead.

The dream began to fade, the vibrant colors and sounds dissolving into a soft, hazy blur. Maia felt herself being pulled back to reality, the world of the dream slipping away like sand through her fingers. She tried to hold on, to prolong the moment with her father, but it was no use. The dream was ending, and she was waking up.

As her eyes fluttered open, Maia found herself back in her apartment, the morning light streaming through the window. The dream lingered in her mind, vivid and haunting, its message clear and profound.

She lay there for a moment, her heart heavy with the weight of the dream's significance.

The bond with her father, the unspoken words, and the sense of closure it had offered her—these were not just elements of a dream. They were a call to action, a reminder of the strength and resilience her father had spoken of.

Glimpses Through the Veil

Maia's breath came in ragged gasps that echoed oddly, as if she were inhaling the thick, electric air of a looming storm. She stood at the center of a vast, desolate landscape where the sky bled into a palette of bruised purples and sickly greens, devoid of distinction between dawn and dusk. The ground beneath her was a foundation of twisted metal and glass, shimmering like a mirage, while jagged structures spiraled upwards, defying both gravity and reason.

Her eyes scanned the horizon, searching for something familiar, but only found the unsettling shapes that morphed continuously, eluding comprehension. Whispers of wind carried fragmented melodies; harmonies that seemed to be crafted from memories not her own. There was a rhythm in that madness, an otherworldly pulse that beat in sync with her racing heart.

A figure emerged from the fluctuating environment, as if woven from the very fabric of the dream itself. Cloaked in shadows, it stood at a distance, a silhouette against the ever-changing backdrop. Maia felt her gaze drawn to it, inexplicably. The figure's presence was commanding, yet it wore subtlety like an enigmatic veil. Its posture was poised, exuding a sense of timeless patience that one might attribute to a statue or a guardian of ancient secrets.

Neither menacing nor benevolent, the figure simply existed with an aura of inevitability.

It beckoned without motion, pulling at the core of Maia's being, urging her toward a truth she could not yet grasp. As Maia stepped closer, the ground beneath her whispering with every footfall, the figure remained perfectly still, as though waiting for the precise moment to reveal its purpose.

The air around them seemed to hum with anticipation, charged with silent questions and the weight of unspoken understanding. Who was this enigmatic visitor in her dreamscape? What cryptic message did they carry, cloaked in the fabrics of her subconscious? Maia's instincts as an EMT, cultivated in the frantic streets of Boston, trained in clarity and action, now tangled with the ethereal threads of her dreamer's soul, leaving her suspended between two realms.

Her approach halted just shy of arm's reach, and the figure's indistinct features hinted at a knowing smile, or perhaps a frown—a riddle etched in shadow. Maia, driven by compassion and curiosity, found her authoritative voice softened by wonder, her usually decisive words replaced by a whisper, "Who are you?"

But the answer, she sensed, would unfold in its own time, the story hidden within the quiet depth of this surreal encounter.

The figure's voice, a resonant vibration more felt than heard, spoke directly into the essence of Maia's consciousness. "What if I told you that the fabric of your reality is but a patchwork quilt in the mind of the cosmos?"

Maia's eyes narrowed as she tried to ground herself in the dream's shifting landscape. "I don't understand," she said, her voice a blend of skepticism and intrigue.

"Your life, your consciousness," the figure continued, its form shimmering like a mirage, "they are dissociated alternate personalities—fragments of a greater, unified awareness."

A chill ran down Maia's spine. She had always yearned for understanding beyond the confines of her existence, yet now, faced with such an unfathomable concept, her thoughts scrambled for purchase. How could she, Maia Yetta Rose—an EMT from Boston with tangible responsibilities and a life rooted in physicality—be a mere fragment of something else?

"Are you saying we're... parts of a single entity?" Her question emerged as a whisper, a reflection of her internal turmoil.

"Exactly," the figure affirmed. "Like islands in an ocean, each believing itself separate, while beneath the surface, all are connected to the same landmass."

Maia's heart raced; her previous understanding of reality lay in tatters around her. If this was true, then every life she'd touched, every person she'd saved, were they all just... herself? Various aspects of a sprawling consciousness? The thought was both terrifying and exhilarating.

"Think of the moments when you feel most alive," the figure urged, its voice taking on a melodic cadence that seemed to echo through the dream's expanse. "In those instances, the boundaries blur, and you touch the expanse of a shared existence."

"Shared existence..." Maia repeated, her authoritative tone lost in a sea of uncertainty. She felt adrift, unmoored from the solid foundation of her empirical experiences. The very notion spiraled through her, leaving a trail of existential echoes that called into question everything she knew—or thought she knew—about her own self.

"Is this why my dreams are so vivid?" Maia asked, grappling with the implications. "Are they glimpses into this... cosmic consciousness?"

"Perhaps," the figure replied, its ambiguity as tantalizing as it was frustrating. "Or perhaps they are simply dreams. The significance lies in your search for meaning."

"Search for meaning..." she echoed, the words tasting strange on her tongue.

This revelation, if she dared believe it, peeled back the layers of her world, revealing an endless depth she could not yet fathom. Standing there, in the heart of her otherworldly dreamscape, Maia Rose confronted the staggering possibility that her life, her very identity, was part of a grander, more intricate design than she could have ever imagined.

Maia's breath caught in her throat; a silent gasp suspended in the dream's otherworldly atmosphere. The realization unfurled within her like a waking nightmare—or an enlightening dream, she couldn't yet decide. A sense of awe washed over her, tugging at the corners of her consciousness with invisible fingers. The surreal landscape around her morphed subtly, as if reflecting her inner turmoil.

"Who are we, then?" Maia asked, her voice a mere whisper against the backdrop of her cascading thoughts. Her eyes sought the figure's, looking for an anchor in the shifting sands of her psyche.

The figure stood still; its presence enigmatic as ever. "We are both the ocean and the drop," it said, leaving Maia to decipher the riddle wrapped in metaphor.

"An ocean of consciousness?" Maia pressed, her fear wrestling with her curiosity. Her fingers clenched and unclenched as she fought to maintain equilibrium, the ground beneath her feet seeming less solid with every word exchanged.

"Exactly," the figure affirmed with a nod that sent ripples through the space between them. "You stand at the shore, aware only of the waves that lick your toes."

Maia took a step forward, her movements deliberate, her training forgotten in the face of such existential ambiguity. In her line of work, every action had a clear purpose, every decision a tangible outcome. But here, in the dreamscape, reason and logic twisted into new shapes, defying her grasp.

"How can I know this is real? How can I trust these... visions?"

Maia's questions bore the weight of her dedication to saving lives, to dealing in certainties and tangible truths. Her green eyes shimmered with a mix of trepidation and the relentless drive to understand that which defied understanding.

"Trust," the figure intoned, "is not about certainty. It is about opening oneself to possibilities beyond the horizon of one's sight."

"Beyond sight..." She mulled over the words, feeling them resonate deep within her core. They echoed the call of her childhood wonder, the part of her that gazed at the stars sprawled over Boston's night sky and pondered their secrets.

"Tell me more," Maia urged, her resolve hardening amidst the dream's whispers. "I need to understand."

"Understanding comes in fragments," the figure cautioned, "like shards of a broken mirror reflecting an image you must piece together."

"Then help me collect the shards," Maia said, her voice strengthening with the burgeoning need to explore the depths revealed to her—a quest not unlike the emergency calls that summoned her into the unknown, time and again. "Where do I begin?"

"Begin within," the mysterious figure instructed, gesturing toward her own chest. "For that is where the journey to the vast expanse truly commences."

Maia placed a hand over her heart, feeling the steady rhythm that now seemed connected to something much larger than herself. The revelation left her with more questions than answers, yet it ignited a spark of determination, a desire to delve into the mysteries of existence with the same fervor she applied to saving lives.

"Within..." she echoed, her gaze lifting to meet the figure's once more. "I will begin within."

"Consider," the figure began, its voice emanating from a form both indistinct and compelling in the dream's haze, "that every consciousness around you—every person in Boston, every creature on Earth—is but an alternate personality of the same grand, cosmic mind."

Maia's breath caught as she processed the words. "You mean... we're all parts of one entity?"

"Exactly," the figure affirmed, its outline shimmering like a mirage. "Our individual consciousnesses are dissociated aspects of a universal psyche. Separate, yet interconnected—like droplets in an ocean."

"An ocean?" Maia repeated, the metaphor unfolding in her thoughts like a vivid tapestry. She pictured the bustling streets of Boston, each passerby a wave cresting from the same vast sea.

"Each of us experiences reality subjectively," the figure continued. "We are conscious islands, unaware of the depths that connect us beneath the surface."

"Islands..." Maia whispered. The disorientation of the dream began to wane, replaced by a dawning clarity. She had always felt an inexplicable bond with the strangers whose lives she saved, as if their pain and hope were echoes of something much more profound within herself.

"Your dreams," the figure said, as if reading her thoughts, "are glimpses through the veil—flashes of the greater consciousness seeping into your dissociated state."

Maia felt her heart quicken, her palms damp with the realization. Every time she closed her eyes and surrendered to slumber; it wasn't mere fantasy; it was a bridge to an unfathomable truth. Her yearning for understanding, which often left her gazing contemplatively at the stars, now found a new focus.

"Could it be..." Maia started, the seed of a hypothesis taking root, "that my dreams are not just my own but shared experiences of this... this cosmic mind?"

"Perhaps," the figure conceded, its edges blurring with the words. "The dream state is a liminal space where the boundaries between alters can thin."

"Thin boundaries..." Maia mused, the concept resonating with her innate desire to heal and connect.

As an EMT, she worked daily to mend the physical, yet now she wondered about the intangible threads weaving through every interaction, every life she touched.

"Explore these ideas," the figure urged, its presence beginning to fade. "Let your curiosity guide you. The path will be fraught with enigma, but the pursuit of knowledge is a journey worth undertaking."

"Wait!" Maia called out, reaching towards the dissipating silhouette. "How do I find the path? How do I know what's real?"

"Trust in your experiences, Maia Yetta Rose," the figure's voice echoed one last time before vanishing entirely.

The dream's landscape dissolved, leaving Maia suspended in a silent void, alone with her racing thoughts. But even as the vision faded, the intrigue it sparked did not. There was a universe inside her, waiting to be explored—a cosmic puzzle she was now compelled to piece together, one shard at a time.

With a sudden, breath-stealing jolt, Maia's consciousness surged forward, piercing through the veil of her enigmatic dream. She gasped as reality clawed its way back, dragging her from the clutches of the profound revelations she had just witnessed. Her eyelids fluttered open, and she was met with the familiar shadows cast by the early morning light in her Boston apartment.

For a moment, Maia lay motionless, the phantom echo of the mysterious figure's voice still whispering in the corners of her mind. The room around her felt both alien and intimate, as if she were seeing it for the first time through a lens irrevocably altered by what she had learned—or dreamt—about the nature of existence.

She sat up, pressing her palms against the cool sheets, grounding herself. Her heart raced, each beat a reminder that she was back, tethered to the tangible world. But could she truly trust this solidity?

The notion of a single cosmic consciousness, of dissociated alternate personalities, seemed to imbue every object with a surreal significance.

"Trust in your experiences," the figure had said. Maia clasped her hands together, trying to reconcile the vividness of the dream with the stark, quiet presence of her bedroom. The green digits on her bedside clock read 3:47 AM, yet the numbers seemed arbitrary, a feeble attempt to impose order on a reality far more complex than she had ever imagined.

Rising from the bed, Maia padded across the room, her movements hesitant, as though she expected the floor to give way to another dimension at any step. Reaching the window, she peered out at the still, dark streets of Boston, searching for something—a sign, perhaps—that the world outside was part of the same grand, interconnected entity she had glimpsed in her slumber.

A shiver coursed through her as she considered the enormity of her revelation. As an EMT, Maia was no stranger to life's fragility; she had held it in her hands more times than she could count. But now, she faced the fragility of reality itself, the possibility that the lives she saved were mere expressions of a vaster consciousness.

Her reflection stared back at her from the glass pane, those emerald eyes holding a mix of fear, awe, and determination. Maia knew that when morning came, she would step into her uniform, answer the calls, and tend to the wounded. Yet something fundamental within her had shifted, a paradigm that could not be unseen or unfelt.

Maia turned away from the window carrying with her a fusion of questions and the first threads of a purpose that promised to unravel the very fabric of her being.

THE BOOK

Maia Rose paused at the threshold of the antiquated bookstore nestled on a quiet Boston street near Faneuil Hall, letting the soft jingle of the bell announce her arrival. A gentle wave of warmth brushed against her skin, in contrast to the biting autumn chill she'd just escaped. The scent of old books—a mélange of musty paper and worn leather—enveloped her, grounding her in the present moment.

The shop was a haven of tranquility amid the city's perpetual clamor, lined with towering wooden shelves that whispered secrets of bygone eras. Sunlight streamed through the stained-glass windows, casting kaleidoscopic patterns across the floor, and bathing the interior in a subdued yet colorful glow. Maia inhaled deeply soaking in the ambiance that caressed her soul.

As an EMT, Maia had grown accustomed to the harsh sterility of hospitals and the adrenaline-fueled chaos of emergency scenes. Here, however, time meandered lazily, permitting her the luxury to explore without the pressure of ticking seconds that usually governed her life.

She moved through the aisles with grace, her shoulder-length auburn hair swaying gently with each step. Her gaze flitted from spine to spine, seeking a title or author that sparked the flame of her ever-present curiosity. She sought not just a book, but a portal—an escape into the philosophical questions that haunted her dreams and fueled her introspection.

It was here, among these silent sentinels of knowledge, that Maia's compassionate nature intertwined with her insatiable thirst for understanding. Each book offered a promise, a hidden treasure waiting to be unearthed by patient hands and an eager mind. It was not just information she sought, but wisdom—the kind that could make sense of the vivid dreams that often left her feeling adrift between worlds.

Her fingers hovered over bindings, tracing the embossed titles as if they were braille, reading the stories contained within through touch alone. She absorbed the essence of countless narratives, letting her intuition guide her. The bookstore was a microcosm of the universe itself, each book a star whose light reached out to her across the vast expanse of her own yearning.

And then, there it was—a faint pull towards a particular section, an unspoken call that beckoned her closer. Maia's heart quickened in anticipation, the edges of her reality blurring slightly as she neared the source of this subtle magnetism. Something awaited her amongst these shelves, something that promised to resonate with the very core of her being.

The dust motes danced lazily in the narrow shafts of light that penetrated the high windows, swirling in the quiet like tiny, silent galaxies. Maia's steps were soft against the worn wooden floor; each creak a whisper from the past, every groan a story yearning to be told. A gentle hush enveloped the air—this was a place of reverence, a temple to the written word.

The aisles felt alive with possibility, and Maia moved through them with the ease of one who knows their calling. Her gaze, sharp as it was during her night shifts responding to crisis after crisis, swept over the spines with the same discernment she applied to assessing patients—searching for signs, for something that would stand out amid the uniformity.

And then, within the ochres and maroons, her eyes caught hold of an anomaly—a book whose cover gleamed with an otherworldly sheen. It was as though the book itself was illuminated from within, its title etched in silver that seemed to pulse with an inner light. "The Nexus of Dreams" it read, the script flowing like liquid thought across the surface.

A shiver ran down Maia's spine, an echo of the electric adrenaline that surged through her veins when life teetered on a razor's edge under her hands. This was different, yet it stirred a similar sense of urgency within her—a need to understand, to dive into the mysteries that lay just beyond reach in the shadowy corners of existence.

With a steadiness that contradicted her quickening pulse, Maia extended her hand towards the book. The air around her seemed to thicken, charged with the anticipation of uncharted frontiers as her fingers brushed against the binding. The texture was unexpected—smooth but with a subtle vibration, as if the book was eager to be opened, desperate to share its secrets.

She grasped it firmly, pulling it from its resting place among its peers. The shelf sighed, a sound almost imperceptible, and the space the book had occupied felt suddenly colder, an absence where there had been a presence moments before. Clutching the book to her chest, Maia could feel its weight, a promise of the profound journey to come.

For a heartbeat, the world outside—the sirens, the shouted orders, the desperation of loss—faded into insignificance. In this instant, Maia was no longer just an EMT; she was a seeker of truths, standing on the threshold of discovery. With "The Nexus of Dreams" in her possession, the adventure was just beginning, and the anticipation of what lay ahead sent a thrill coursing through her.

Maia's fingers danced over the pages, a whisper-thin rustle accompanying each turn. The air in the bookstore was still, but for the occasional creak of wooden floorboards as invisible patrons meandered through aisles laden with knowledge from floor to ceiling. She caught sight of chapter titles that teased her intellect: "Dreamscapes and Realities," "The Labyrinth of Time," "Echoes of the Quantum Mind."

Her eyes flickered with growing intrigue, each word a steppingstone deeper into the labyrinth she was eager to explore.

The table of contents served as a map, charting a course through territories both alien and achingly familiar. Maia's thumb paused on the edge of a page; breathing halted by a surge of recognition. Here, in black print on cream paper, were concepts that mirrored the elusive thoughts that often visited her in the throes of sleep—ideas about existence, the cosmos, the interplay between consciousness and the physical world.

"Intersections of Infinity" read one title, sending a shiver down her spine. Hadn't she dreamt just last week of standing at the precipice of endless space, the stars whispering secrets meant only for her? And there, "The Paradox of Being" seemed to echo her silent musings during those long nights spent under unforgiving fluorescents, waiting for the next call to action.

She reached into a passage, skimming lines that spoke of parallel lives and the interconnectedness of souls. A thrill ran through her, electric and enigmatic, as if the words reached out, calling to the marrow of her being. Every sentence felt like an answer to a question Maia had been asking since she first looked up at the sky and wondered what lay beyond.

"Could it be?" she murmured, her voice a hushed reverence in the quiet corner of the bookstore. The whisper seemed louder than intended, reverberating off the shelves lined with countless stories. It was as though the universe itself had conspired to guide her to this very spot, to this very book.

"Is this what I've been searching for?" The question was for only herself, a solitary confession in the expanse of her mind.

Without realizing, Maia had sunk down onto the worn Persian carpet, the book cradled in her lap, her jade eyes reflecting a world not seen but felt.

Here was a landscape painted in the hues of her deepest dreams, now given form and substance by the prose that ensnared her completely.

Maia's fingers traced the contours of text as if touching a sacred script, her pulse synchronizing with the revelations unfurling before her. The dim light of the bookstore cast shadows across the pages, but it was as if each word glowed with its own inner luminescence. Theories on the nature of consciousness stretched before her like an uncharted cosmos, each sentence a star guiding her deeper into the vastness.

"Mind before matter..." she whispered, the concept resonating within her, harmonizing with the ambient music that pulsed through Boston's veins outside. Her life, defined by the immediacy of saving others, suddenly intertwined with these loftier ponderings on existence. How could the physical urgency of her work exist alongside this ethereal exploration of being? It was a duality that captivated Maia, demanding reconciliation.

As she turned another page, the notion of 'panpsychism' leapt at her—a belief that all matter is imbued with consciousness. Could the very fabric of reality be aware, from the sprawling city to the tiniest atom in her own body? The thought elicited a shiver that was both unsettling and exhilarating.

"Every decision, every moment, connected..." Maia's voice softened further, her authority yielding to awe. She pictured the chain reactions of her choices, how saving one life might alter countless destinies. Was it possible that her dreams, those vivid nocturnal plays, were more than mere subconscious echoes?

The words wove through her, binding her to a truth she felt had always been there, lurking in the periphery of her cognizance. Maia's soul felt alight, each spark from the book igniting kindling long dormant. Her breath caught; she could no longer separate where Maia ended, and the universe began.

The decision to purchase the book settled upon her with the weight of inevitability. This was not merely an acquisition of paper and ink—it was an embrace of a journey that promised to redefine her essence. Maia stood, her legs stiff from sitting on the carpeted floor, the book now an extension of her hand.

"Consciousness, the final frontier," she mused, echoing the adventures etched into the sci-fi novels lining the shelves around her. But unlike those fictional explorers venturing outward into space, Maia's odyssey would take her inward, towards realms more mysterious and vaster than any extraterrestrial landscape.

With resolve crystallizing in her, Maia walked to the front of the store, the book against her chest like a shield. In her grasp was more than mere literature; it was a key to doors yet opened, pathways yet wandered. And she, Maia Yetta Rose, with her empathy sculpted from countless emergencies and her mind seasoned with questions, was ready to turn the key and unlock that door.

"Find something that speaks to you?" The bookstore owner's voice broke through her reverie, gentle and tinged with the knowing smile of a fellow traveler of fictional realms.

"More than speaks," Maia replied, her gaze never leaving the cover of the book as she placed it on the counter. "It... echoes."

"Ah, Kastrup." The owner nodded sagely, fingers dancing across the worn edges as he prepared the receipt. "He has a way of reaching into your chest and fiddling with your soul, doesn't he?"

"Exactly that." Maia allowed herself a small smile, her eyes meeting his for a fleeting moment before returning to the book. She could hear the unspoken kinship between them, the shared understanding that some books are not just read—they're experienced.

"Will there be anything else?" the owner inquired, handing her the bagged book.

"Nothing else," Maia whispered, clutching the paper bag close as if cradling a newborn dream. "This is all I need right now."

"Enjoy the journey, it's a rare mind that seeks what you're after," he said, his words trailing her as she turned towards the door.

Pushing open the quaint shop's door, a bell chimed softly, heralding her departure. Boston's air greeted her, crisp and laden with the sounds of a city alive with its own rhythm.

Maia felt a surge of energy, an anticipation so intense it seemed to flow through her veins. With the book now a cherished milestone against her heart, she stepped over the threshold and back into the world, her inner sanctum forever altered by the promise of unlocking the enigma of consciousness itself.

The city buzzed around her, but Maia was elsewhere, already adrift in thoughts of existential landscapes awaiting her exploration. Her fingers tightened around the book, as if ensuring its reality, and she allowed herself a moment to bask in the warmth of potential that now swelled within her chest.

"Let the odyssey begin," she murmured to no one in particular, a soft declaration to the universe. The corner of her mouth lifted in a private smile; Maia Yetta Rose had always been one to seek out the depths beneath the surface. And now, armed with the wisdom of Bernardo Kastrup, she was ready to dive deeper than ever before.

The city's harshness enveloped Maia as she navigated the crowded sidewalks, each step punctuated by the echo of a distant siren—a familiar sound that usually demanded her attention. Today, however, it was merely a backdrop to the discourse unfurling in her mind.

The book pressed against her chest became a talisman against the mundane, its unspoken promise igniting a flurry of thoughts that danced like shadows just beyond reach.

Maia's gaze, normally so adept at reading scenes of turmoil and distress, now darted between the lines of an invisible text. What secrets did Kastrup hold? Could his theories unravel the fabric of her dreams, stitch by intricate stitch? A gust of wind whipped through the narrow streets, sending a shiver down her spine. It felt as though the very breath of the city was urging her onward, whispering mysteries only she could perceive.

As she turned the corner onto her street, the thrum of Boston's pulse softened. The buildings here stood closer together, guardians of the quieter life she carved out beyond the rush of her calling. Her footsteps slowed, anticipation simmering within her. She climbed the steps to her apartment building with a reverence akin to ritual; the threshold to her personal sanctuary beckoned.

With a turn of the key, Maia entered the dimly lit space that was uniquely hers. She paused, allowing the door to close with a gentle click that severed her from the world's relentless whir. Here, in this private calm Maia allowed herself a moment to simply be—her existence not defined by the next emergency call or the adrenaline of a life hanging in balance.

She placed the book on the small table by the window, its cover catching the fading light. The room held its breath as she removed her jacket, the fabric whispering to the floor. Her home, usually a place of rest between shifts, transformed into a vessel for a journey of a different sort—a journey inward.

Eager fingers traced the spine of the book, a shiver of connection running through her. With each passing second, the pull of the pages grew stronger, as if they contained a gravity all their own. Maia knew that once she opened it, there would be no turning back. Her world, bound by the tangible, was about to expand into realms of consciousness that defied explanation.

The promise of discovery, of challenging the boundaries of her understanding, was intoxicating. Maia Yetta Rose, the dreamer dressed in the armor of an EMT, stood on the precipice. Taking a deep breath, she reached for the book, ready to plunge into the vast ocean of thought that awaited her.

The chair, a worn relic upholstered in faded fabric, embraced Maia as she sank into its familiar contours. Her apartment hummed with the subtle sounds of the city, a muted symphony that played backdrop to her introspective evenings. She cradled the book, feeling the weight of its bound promise.

As she flipped open the cover, the room's ambient light focused on the crisp, white expanse of the first page. The title etched across the top in bold, enigmatic script whispered secrets and uncharted mental landscapes. Maia inhaled deeply; the air tinged with the musty scent of the paper a portal to the profound odyssey that lay ahead.

Her eyes traced the introductory words, each sentence a bridge leading deeper into the caverns of thought. The text spoke of consciousness, not as a mere byproduct of synaptic firings but as a vast, interwoven fabric that connected every living being. Maia's heart beat in rhythm with the revelations, her empathetic nature attuned to the interconnectedness described.

She leaned closer, her emerald eyes reflecting the depth of her focus as they danced over lines that challenged the very fabric of her reality. The author, Bernardo Kastrup, wove arguments with the grace of a philosopher-poet, his prose enchanting and provocative. With each paragraph, Maia felt as though she were peeling back layers of existence, revealing truths that resonated with the dreams that often visited her in the quiet night.

Maia's thoughts, usually so disciplined in the face of crisis, now cavorted freely among the concepts splayed out before her. The ideas of a collective mind, an all-encompassing 'One' that transcended individual experience, wrapped around her like a cosmic embrace. It was as if her own experiences, the lives she touched daily, were threads in this grand web, each one vital, each one pulsing with shared essence.

The world outside her window, with its honking cars and murmuring pedestrians, faded into obsolescence as Maia journeyed further into the text. Her consciousness, once anchored firmly in the tactile emergencies of flesh and blood, now flirted with the ethereal, skirting the edges of a reality far more expansive than the streets of Boston.

With each turn of the page, Maia Rose, the healer of bodies, became Maia, the explorer of minds, reaching into a realm where questions held more beauty than answers, and the pursuit of understanding was an end unto itself.

The city's rhythmic pulse became a distant, muffled heartbeat as Maia turned another page. Shadows crept across her apartment floor, the sun's descent unnoticed, its farewell kiss to the horizon unseen by eyes immersed in a sea of ink and insight. Time, once her ever-present nemesis during the unforgiving tick-tock of emergency calls, had now dissolved into irrelevance.

Maia's fingers traced the lines of text as if they could physically grasp the wisdom within them. The room around her felt both cavernous and intimate, a sanctuary where the very air seemed charged with revelation. She leaned closer, the words pulling her deeper, her breaths aligning with the rhythm of sentences that challenged reality's fabric.

A question formed silently on her lips, echoing the book's inquiry into the nature of being. Her heart answered in steady beats, harmonizing with the profound dialogue unfolding in her mind.

The familiar comfort of the chair faded; it was no longer a tangible object but an extension of her, a supportive presence on this voyage through consciousness.

Maia's vibrant green eyes, usually so attuned to the physical needs before her, now saw beyond the corporeal. They gazed inward, envisioning the interconnectedness of all life, each soul a star in the vast expanse of a shared cosmic canvas. Every word she devoured wove itself into the dreamscapes that had haunted her nights, giving form to the shadows and light that danced behind closed eyelids.

She was adrift in a stream of concepts, the book her vessel, navigating waters that shimmered with the potential of understanding. The outside world, with its discord and chaos, was a story she had stepped out of, leaving behind a silent protagonist whose journey had taken an inward turn.

An aura of stillness wrapped around Maia, the only movement the flutter of pages and the gentle rise and fall of her chest. In this moment, there was no Boston, no blaring sirens, or urgent voices—only the hush of discovery, the soft whisper of pages promising more than mere words: a gateway to transcendence.

The EMT who had devoted herself to the healing of others found, for a fleeting eternity, her own spirit tended to by the nurturing balm of wisdom. Lost in the labyrinth of ideas, Maia Yetta Rose surrendered to the embrace of enlightenment, her existence momentarily untethered from the ticking clock of the tangible world.

THE SEED

The break room was a small oasis amid the tempest of Boston's emergency services. Maia Rose sat across from Lucas Reed feet up on the table, her work boots crossed with a mug of strong coffee.

"Have you ever considered," Maia began, stirring her coffee absentmindedly, "that every person we help might be... connected? Not just in the societal sense, but on a cosmic level?"

Lucas took a sip from his mug, the steam fogging his glasses momentarily before he wiped them clean. "What do you mean?"

Maia leaned forward, her voice dropping to an excited whisper. "I've been reading Kastrup's latest book, and it's fascinating. He talks about how we, all living beings, could be dissociated alters of a single consciousness. Imagine that Lucas—each life, each soul, just a fragment of a larger, encompassing awareness."

Her eyes danced with the reflection of a new world unfolding within her mind, her hands animated, emphasizing her words. Lucas watched her, the corners of his mouth upturned in a gentle smile. The break room, with its humming refrigerator and ticking clock, seemed to shrink around them, creating an intimate stage for Maia's profound revelations.

"Like pieces of a grand puzzle," Maia continued, "separate but part of something unimaginable when put together. Every patient we save, every life we touch—it's like we're healing parts of this massive, collective existence."

The idea hung between them, weighty yet fragile, and for a moment, the usual sounds of the rushing city outside faded into a hushed backdrop holding its breath to hear more of Maia's theories.

Lucas's gaze lingered on Maia, observing the fervor in her movements, the way her fingertips grazed the air as she traced the outlines of this grand design she spoke of. The break room's fluorescent lights flickered subtly overhead, casting a weird glow on the scene.

"Maia," Lucas began, his voice a soft undercurrent critical of the tide of her enthusiasm. "This is... deep stuff. I mean, it's intriguing, no doubt." He paused, searching for the right words in the silence. "But you have to be careful, you know? Ideas like these can be... consuming."

His concern wound through his words, trailing over the hum of the refrigerator that kept time with the ticking clock. Maia turned to face him, their eyes meeting, a lock of auburn hair falling across her brow.

"Consuming?" She echoed, a hint of amusement in her tone, though she sensed the gravity behind his caution. "Lucas, they're just ideas. Intellectual adventures. It's not like I'm going to get lost in them."

She took another sip of her coffee, the steam momentarily veiling her eyes from his scrutinizing look. The warmth of the cup seeped into her palms, grounding her.

"Besides," she continued, setting the mug down with a gentle clink, "I'm an EMT first and foremost. You've seen me out there. My feet are firmly planted on the ground, even when my head's exploring the stars."

Her laugh was a soft chime that filled the space between them, an attempt to dispel the shadows of worry that had crept into Lucas's expression. She wanted him to understand that her passion for these theories didn't eclipse the reality of their day-to-day lives, the lives they worked tirelessly to save within Boston's pandemonium.

"Promise me you'll stay grounded, Maia," Lucas implored, his tone steady yet tinged with the unspoken knowledge that lines between reality and theory could blur unexpectedly.

"Always," she reassured him, her smile unwavering. Yet somewhere, buried beneath her conviction, the seed of his words found fertile soil. She pushed the thought away, standing up as the break room door swung open, signaling the end of their break and return to duty.

Lucas leaned against the door frame of the break room, his gaze following Maia as she moved with grace to return her mug to the shelf. The lights hummed softly overhead, casting an objective pallor over the room that amplified his thoughts.

"Maia," he began, his voice in a low tone that resonated with an earnestness she couldn't ignore. "Your dreams... they're not just ordinary dreams, are they?"

Her hand paused midair, the ceramic mug an inch from the shelf. She turned to face him, her eyes narrowing in a mix of irritation and intrigue. The subtle furrow on her forehead betrayed her annoyance at revisiting the topic, but she remained silent, prompting him to continue.

"Remember that call last week—the one with the kid caught in the crossfire?" Lucas asked, his hazel eyes reflecting concern. "You said you dreamt it before it happened. And those moments when you zone out, like you're reliving something... It's déjà vu, isn't it?"

A shiver ran down her spine, the memory of the child's bloodied form flashing before her eyes. Maia placed the mug down with a bit more force than intended, creating a sharp clack against the other porcelain vessels.

"Lucas, I..."

"Think about it, Maia." Lucas stepped into the room, closing the gap between them. "These aren't coincidences. Your dreams, this sense of familiarity with events before they unfold—maybe Kastrup's theories have a point. Maybe there's something more."

His suggestion hung in the air, both an invitation and a challenge. The hum of the break room fridge kicked in, filling the space with a low drone that underscored the gravity of his words. Maia felt a knot form in her stomach. She was feeling a touch of fear mixed with her curiosity. Was it possible that the fabric of her reality was more malleable than she imagined?

"Lucas, I..." She started again, her voice softer now, less assured. The certainty she had clung to, the safety of skepticism, was slipping through her fingers like fine sand. "Could it really be true?"

"Maia, look at yourself." Lucas's tone was gentle, a whisper. "You've always known there's something unique about the way you perceive the world. You can't keep dismissing it as mere curiosity."

She looked away, her gaze settling on the window where Boston's skyline cut sharply against the evening sky—a tangible, solid reality. But within her, the tides of doubt rose and fell with increasing intensity. The scenes from her dreams, the echoes of feelings she couldn't quite place; they were parts of a puzzle that refused to remain unsolved.

"Maybe... maybe there is more to these theories," Maia conceded, her voice barely audible over the ambient noise of their surroundings. "Maybe they do explain..." She trailed off, unable to finish the thought.

"Whatever it is," Lucas said, stepping closer, "we'll figure it out together. You don't have to shoulder it alone." His reassuring presence was a relief to her unsettled thoughts.

"Thanks, Lucas," she managed to say, though her mind was already racing ahead, pondering the possibilities he had suggested. As the door swung open once more, signaling another call to action, Maia followed Lucas out, her heart pounding with both trepidation and an unspoken yearning for truth.

Lucas leaned against the cool metal of the ambulance, his gaze intent upon Maia as she rummaged through a cabinet for a fresh supply of IV kits. The urgency of their last call had subsided, replaced by the silence of the garage bay.

"Maia," he began, his voice a steady tone that vibrated through the void between them, "I know your mind is teeming with questions about these theories. But you do have to tread carefully."

She paused, an IV kit in hand, turning to face him. In the dim light of the break room, her energy reflected a world of concern. "What do you mean?"

"Your well-being," he said, stepping forward so that they stood beneath the flickering fluorescent light. "It's... crucial. Diving headfirst into uncharted waters can be dangerous. Have you thought about seeking someone out? An expert, maybe?"

"An expert?" Maia echoed, placing the kit on the counter.

"Someone who swims in these waters daily. A guide of sorts." Lucas's words fell like droplets, each one a ripple expanding across the surface of her thoughts.

"Like joining a consciousness studies group?" Her curiosity sparked, and there was a subtle shift in her posture—a straightening of her back, a tilt of her head—that signaled her engagement.

"Exactly." Lucas nodded, a shadow of relief passing over his features. "Someone who understands the depths you're willing to explore could provide perspective. They could help you make sense of what you're experiencing without losing yourself in the process."

Maia considered this, her fingers absently tracing the edge of the countertop. She could feel the weight of every life she'd touched that day—each one a reminder of her commitment to the tangible world, even as her mind sought to unravel its mysteries.

"Okay," she said finally, her decision firming up like a photograph coming into focus. "I'll look into it. Maybe there's a group here in Boston, or someone at the university who studies this sort of thing."

"Good." Lucas's wide smile was genuine. "It's important to me that you're safe, not just physically but up here, too." He tapped his temple lightly.

"Thank you," she replied, acknowledging the depth of his concern. Her gaze lingered on Lucas for a moment before drifting past him to the window where the city lay sprawled like a circuit board, pulsing with energy.

As she stepped away to join Lucas beside the ambulance, the echo of her own heartbeat filled her ears. It was a rhythm that spoke of life, of existence, and of the unfathomable journey ahead. There was fear, yes, but also anticipation—for in seeking understanding, might she not uncover more of herself than ever before?

The fluorescent lights hummed overhead as Maia emptied the last of her coffee into a potted plant that had seen better days. The break room was empty save for her and Lucas, the quiet creating an intimate space between them. She turned to face him; her expression softened by the weight of their conversation.

"Lucas," she began, her voice steady but tinged with vulnerability, "thank you. Really. It means a lot that you care enough to worry." She tucked a stray lock of hair behind her ear, her green eyes reflecting the sincerity of her words. "I won't go down this rabbit hole blindly. I'll keep you in the loop."

He nodded; his gaze unwavering, protective. The sturdy lines of his frame leaned against the doorframe, a sentinel guarding against unseen threats. "Maia, you have my word—I'm here for you." His voice held the timbre of a lifeline extended without hesitation.

The air hung heavy between them, charged with the unspoken understanding of two souls connected by more than just circumstance. Maia's heart swelled with gratitude, and despite the uncertainties that lay ahead, she felt anchored by Lucas's steadfast presence. She offered a small, hopeful smile—a silent vow to tread carefully into the unknown.

Maia stood motionlessly for a moment, the warmth from Lucas's reassurance still lingering in the air like a comforting embrace. Then, with a deep breath that filled her lungs with resolve, she stepped away from the shelter of the break room. The door swung shut with a soft click behind her, leaving her thoughts to echo loudly in the solitude of the corridor.

She navigated the sterile halls of the Boston emergency medical facility, her footsteps a rhythmic counterpart to the passion of her racing heart. The lights overhead flickered subtly, casting an eerie glow on the walls—a stark reminder of the ordinary world she was anchored in, despite the extraordinary theories that beckoned her mind.

The blend of emotions within Maia churned like a tempestuous sea, excitement and fear melding together until they were indistinguishable from one another. Kastrup's book had planted a seed to possibilities that felt both alien and intimately familiar, stirring a sense of wonder that reached back to the earliest tendrils of her curiosity as a child. Yet, there was a weight to that wonder now, a gravity to her musings that tugged at the fringes of her consciousness, whispering caution.

As she approached the locker room, her hand hesitated over the keypad. A sudden chill traced the length of her spine, causing her to shudder involuntarily. She could hear Lucas's words of encouragement mingling with the shadow of his concern, a call of care that both fortified and warned her.

Inside the locker room, she sat on the cold bench, the metal cool against her skin through the fabric of her uniform. Her mind drifted, unfurling like the pages of Kastrup's book spread across the vast expanse of her imagination. The vivid dreams that had long colored her nights seemed to bleed into her waking thoughts, painting her reality with shades of déjà vu and a yearning for answers.

"Is there more?" she whispered to herself; her voice barely audible above the hum of the ventilation system. The question dangled in the air, unanswered, as her gaze settled on the tiny scratches and imperfections on the surface of the bench—minute details of a world that suddenly felt both incredibly intricate and impossibly simple.

Then, as if the universe itself were responding to her query, the locker door creaked open before her touch. She hadn't even retrieved her key. Staring into the dark cavity of the metal box, Maia's breath caught in her throat. Her pulse pounded in her ears, a drumbeat heralding the arrival of something profound.

"Am I just seeing what I want to see?" Her thoughts took shape, a hesitant dance of skepticism and belief. "Or is the universe truly peeling back its layers, inviting me... no, compelling me to look deeper?"

A small, almost imperceptible movement in the corner of her eye drew her attention. The reflection of her own face stared back from the polished interior of the locker door—an image she knew as well as the lines of her own hands. But there, in the depths of her emerald eyes, something flickered. A glint of something other, a hint of a world beyond the veneer of daily existence, or a trick of the light.

"Lucas might be right," she thought, the notion tightening around her chest. "What if these aren't just theories? What if..."

The locker slammed shut abruptly, cutting off her reverie. Maia jolted, her heart pounding against her ribcage. There was no breeze, no logical explanation for the door's movement. Silence enveloped her, heavy and expectant.

"Consciousness... are you trying to communicate with me?" The question lingered in the stillness, echoing the cosmic inquiry posed by Kastrup's book.

It was the precipice of a cliff Maia found herself upon, peering into the abyss of the unknown. And as she rose from the bench, her decision was resolute. She would step forward, one foot into the darkness, where the line between dreaming and waking blurred into a new reality.

Maia exiting the locker room, her figure swallowed by the shadows of the hallway, the echo of her footsteps a solitary confirmation of her presence—as she walked alongside the whispers of a truth yet to be fully unveiled.

The wail of sirens sliced through the harshness of Boston's rush hour, a discordant symphony that heralded urgency. Maia's hands were steady on the wheel of the ambulance as she navigated the snarled traffic, her gaze focused and alert beneath the flashing strobes. Beside her, Lucas matched the rhythm of his partner's concentration, his eyes scanning for openings as they weaved an intricate race between lanes.

"Left at the next intersection," Lucas said, his voice a calm counterpoint to the blaring horn.

"Got it." Maia swung the ambulance sharply, the vehicle's suspension groaning in protest. Onlookers' faces blurred into smears of curiosity and concern as they parted ways for the hurtling projectile hunting its target.

As they approached the scene, the gravity of their call materialized. A high-rise building loomed above them, its glass façade reflecting the strobe lights with stern, flickering light. People poured from the entrance in a flood of panic, their silhouettes stark against the backdrop of the setting sun. The air was thick with the acrid scent of smoke and the underlying tang of fear.

"Looks like a fire on one of the upper floors," Maia observed, her voice betraying none of the adrenaline that pulsed through her veins. "Crowd control is going to be a nightmare."

"Focus on the ones who need us," replied Lucas, his steady tone grounding her as he reached for the radio. "Dispatch, this is Unit 17 on-site. We have visual confirmation of the situation. Requesting additional support and fire services, over."

"Copy that, Unit 17. Assistance is on the way," crackled the dispatch's reply.

Maia parked the ambulance at a calculated angle, creating a barrier between the milling crowd and their workspace. She grabbed her medical bag, the tools of her trade clinking within, each item a familiar weight in the world of uncertainty they were about to enter.

"Remember, eyes open, stay sharp," Lucas reminded her, echoing the mantra they had lived by since their first day as partners.

"Always," Maia responded, her mind already leaping ahead to the victims they would find within the mayhem.

Together, they plunged into the fray, the fabric of their uniforms their only shield against the unknown dangers that lay ahead, their shared resolve an unspoken pact to bring order to the chaos. The scene before them was a tapestry woven with human threads, each frayed by distress yet bound together by the common thread of survival.

Maia stepped through the sea of onlookers, her eyes scanning for life within the wreckage. The acrid tang of smoke and the coppery scent of blood cut through the autumn air. She moved with practiced precision; her hands steady as she reached down to check the pulse of a motionless figure sprawled across the crumpled hood of a car.

"Got a pulse, but it's weak," Maia called over her shoulder, her voice a calm anchor in the storm. Lucas nodded, already unpacking a neck brace from their kit.

"Keep me updated," he said, trusting her implicitly as he turned his attention to another urgent case.

"Sir, can you hear me?" Maia's question was directed at the semi-conscious man before her. She needed him to focus, to fight through the haze of shock. As she secured an oxygen mask over his face, her mind raced, cataloging symptoms, calculating dosages. Every action was a deliberate step in the dance between life and death.

"Stay with me," she whispered to the patient, as she started an IV line. She was saving lives and trying to preserve the essence of humanity amid chaos.

A sudden shriek pierced the air, yanking Maia's attention away. Her head snapped up, her eyes searching for the source—a child or someone in immediate danger. But there was nothing, no one in her vicinity that matched the urgency of the sound.

It was then that she felt it—a strange, tingling sensation crawling up her spine, as if reality itself had quivered. For a fraction of a second, Maia's focus fractured, her thoughts spiraling away into the realm of her dreams, where echoes of otherworldly whispers sometimes reached out to her.

"Maia!" Lucas's voice sliced through her reverie, sharp and insistent.

She blinked, the world snapping back into place with alarming clarity. Her patient was still there, still struggling for life, and Maia's hand was frozen above the IV bag. How long had she been distracted? Seconds? Minutes?

"Sorry, I—I'm here," she stammered, the certainty in her movements crumbling like ancient ruins. She couldn't afford lapses like this, not when every heartbeat was precious.

Lucas gave her a searching look, his brow creased with concern, but he said nothing. There was no time for questions, only the ever-present demand for action.

"Let's stabilize him enough for transport," Maia said, pushing the unsettling incident to the back of her mind. She plunged back into her work with renewed vigor, her hands once again sure and swift.

But the unease lingered, a shadow at the edge of her consciousness, whispering of things unseen and voices unheard. It was a reminder that, even during life-saving decisions, there were forces at play that defied explanation—and, one day, she would have to face them.

The siren's wail was a distant echo in Maia's ears as the ambulance raced through the labyrinth of Boston's streets, lights painting the darkness with urgent reds and blues. The city blurred past them—a cascade of shadows and fleeting light—as Maia worked to secure the gurney.

"Turn coming up!" Lucas warned, his voice steady despite the urgency that played through the cabin.

Maia nodded, her gaze fixed on the straps that held their patient, a young man whose life teetered on the edge. Her hands moved with precision, yet her mind was not entirely present. Whispers from her dreams tangled with reality, murmuring secrets she could not grasp.

A loud bang exploded from outside, jarring Maia back into the moment. The ambulance lurched violently, throwing her against the interior wall. Metal screamed against metal, a rage of destruction that shattered the fragile bubble of concentrated calm.

"Maia!" Lucas's voice was a lifeline in the confusion. She looked up to see his eyes wide with alarm, his hands grappling with the steering wheel as he fought to regain control.

Panic clawed at her insides. They were spinning, a dizzying whirl of motion as another vehicle—a massive truck—loomed into view, its grill a grimacing maw. Time slowed, each millisecond stretching out as Maia braced for impact.

But the collision never came. By some miracle, Lucas managed to swerve at the last moment, the ambulance skidding to a halt mere inches from disaster.

Silence fell, broken only by the ragged breaths that filled the cabin. Maia's heart thundered in her chest, her body trembling with adrenaline and shock. It was too close, far too close.

"Are you hurt?" Lucas's concern cut through the haze of Maia's thoughts.

She shook her head, unable to speak. Guilt surged within her, a suffocating tide. If not for her momentary distraction, they would not have been in this position. She had almost cost a life—the very thing she was sworn to protect.

As the weight of her responsibility crashed down upon her, Maia's vision blurred with unshed tears. She was supposed to be the one who remained composed, who kept the thread of life intact, not the one who severed it with carelessness.

"Maia," Lucas said softly, reaching out to touch her shoulder. His touch grounded her, pulled her back from the precipice of despair lurking within her own mind.

"We're okay," he continued, his eyes meeting hers. "We're all okay."

But the reassurance felt hollow in the face of what might have been. Maia knew that her lapse, however brief, had endangered them all. The trust placed in her hands felt heavier than ever, and the whispers from her dreams now seemed like harbingers of doom.

She drew in a shaky breath, trying to compose herself. They still had a job to do; their patient still needed them. With effort, Maia pushed aside the fear and guilt, locking it away in a corner of her mind where it couldn't interfere—not yet.

"Let's get him to the hospital," she said, her voice barely above a whisper, but firm. It was a vow, a silent promise to herself and to those she served: she would not falter again.

Lucas gave her a long look, full of things unsaid, before nodding once. Together, they resumed their vital work, the ambulance resuming its journey under a sky that seemed darker than before, with stars that watched over them—indifferent and remote.

Maia's hands moved with a precision born from years of training, the muscle memory guiding her as she worked to stabilize the wounded. The turmoil around her was a blur, the wailing sirens and clamoring voices fading into a distant hum as she focused solely on the task at hand.

"Lucas, I need a C-collar here," she called out, her voice cutting through the din with an urgency that brooked no delay. She didn't wait to see him comply; her attention was already on the next patient—a young man bleeding profusely from a gash on his forehead.

"Stay with me, okay?" Maia said softly, her words intended to soothe as much as instruct. "You've got a head injury. We're going to take good care of you." She applied pressure to the wound, her gaze never leaving his. In his eyes—a clear, frightened blue—she saw a reflection of her own trepidation, a mirror of the fear that clawed at her insides.

For a moment, Maia allowed herself to feel it—the weight of every life in her hands, the terror of what could have been. But then she pushed it down, buried it beneath layers of resolve and determination. She couldn't afford to be paralyzed by what-ifs; not when there were lives to save.

"Maia, backup's on the way," Lucas reported, returning to her side after securing the cervical collar on another victim. His presence was a steadying force, a reminder that she wasn't alone in this.

"Good," she replied curtly, her mind ticking off the minutes until help would arrive. They needed to hold on just a little longer.

As the first responders poured onto the scene, Maia stepped back, allowing them to swarm in with their equipment and expertise. Her part, for the moment, was done. She watched them work, a silent sentinel amid the chaos, her heart pounding a relentless rhythm against her ribs.

It was only now, in the relative calm, that the full impact of the accident hit her. A tremor ran through her body, a shiver of horror at how close they'd come to disaster. She wrapped her arms around herself, as if she could physically hold together the pieces of her fraying composure.

"Hey," Lucas said gently, touching her arm. "You did everything right."

But Maia merely shook her head, unable to accept his reassurance. She had been distracted, lost in a thought that should have had no place in the middle of an emergency. It was a mistake that could have cost more than she dared to contemplate.

"I should have been sharper," she whispered, the confession tearing at her. Lucas wanted to argue, she could tell, but he held back, recognizing that this was a battle she needed to fight with herself.

The air was thick with a silence that spoke volumes, filled with questions that loomed large in her mind. Why had she been so distracted? What were these strange occurrences that haunted her?

With every beat of her heart, Maia felt the resolve harden within her. She needed answers, for the sake of her sanity and for the safety of those she swore to protect. But those answers would have to wait. There were still victims to attend to, still a duty to fulfill.

"Let's finish up here," she said finally, the steely edge back in her voice. As she turned to assist with the triage, a sense of purpose settled over her. The night was far from over, and Maia Yetta Rose would not be found wanting again.

After the turmoil had settled into a grim rhythm of medical protocols and flashing lights, Maia found herself leaning against the cold metal of the ambulance searching the night sky for a steadiness she couldn't find within. Lucas approached quietly, his presence a comforting force amid the residual adrenaline that tingled in her veins.

"Maia," he began, his voice gentle, "you did everything you could."

She let out a breath she hadn't realized she'd been holding, turning to face him, her gaze weary. "Lucas, I... I was distracted, just for a second, but it was one second too long." Her voice trembled slightly, betraying the guilt that gnawed at her. "What if— "

"Hey," Lucas interjected, placing a reassuring hand on her shoulder, his eyes locking onto hers with an intensity that grounded her. "You're one of the best EMTs I've ever worked with. We all have moments, but it's how we respond that defines us."

The corners of Maia's lips twitched, the shadow of a smile, as she met his gaze. But there was more to her distraction, a lingering unease that tugged at the edges of her consciousness.

"Lucas, there's something else," she confessed, her voice dropping to a whisper as if the night itself might overhear. "It's not just today. These distractions...they've been happening more often."

"Distractions?" Lucas's brows furrowed in concern.

"More like...fragments of dreams. They flash before my eyes, unbidden, even when I'm awake." Maia's fingers traced the outline of the ambulance's emblem, a futile attempt to anchor her thoughts.

"Have you talked to anyone about this? A counselor, maybe?" Lucas's question was careful, his tone free of judgment.

"No, no, it's not like that. It feels like..." Maia struggled to find the words, "like they're trying to tell me something. And I need to find out what it is."

"Okay," Lucas said after a moment, his voice steady. "Then we'll figure it out. Together."

"Thank you," she murmured, grateful for his unwavering support. "I need to understand these visions, or whatever they are. If there's something going on with me, I can't risk it happening again during a call."

"First things first, though," Lucas replied, a hint of his usual warmth returning. "You should rest. Whatever this is, it won't be solved tonight."

Maia nodded, knowing he was right, but also knowing that sleep would be elusive. As they packed away the last of their gear, her resolve crystallized. She would dive into the enigma of her mind's intrusions, come daylight. For now, she had lives to save, a duty that wouldn't wait for clarity or peace of mind.

"Let's head back," she said, her voice carrying a new determination. As they climbed into the ambulance, the city of Boston stretched out around them, a maze of shadows and secrets waiting to be unraveled. And Maia Rose was ready to start pulling at the threads.

The ambulance doors swung shut with a definitive thud, encapsulating Maia in the dimly lit confines of their mobile sanctuary. Lucas's presence beside her felt like the tether she needed for the world of logic and reason—a world that was slipping through her fingers like grains of sand.

"Lucas," Maia started, her voice barely above a whisper as the engine hummed softly in the background, "I've been doing some thinking."

He glanced at her; his brow furrowed with concern but his eyes encouraging her to continue.

"Every second counts in our line of work, and today... I almost lost more than just seconds." She paused, gathering her thoughts like fragile pieces of a puzzle. "The distractions—the visions—they're not random. They can't be."

"Okay," Lucas said, his hands on the steering wheel though they remained stationary. The urgency from earlier calls had settled into a low simmer of anticipation for what was to come.

"I need to do something about it, Lucas. If these... episodes are going to keep happening, I must understand them. Before they jeopardize another life," Maia declared, her determination evident in the set of her jaw and the intensity of her gaze.

"Sounds like you've got a plan forming," Lucas observed, a note of admiration threaded through his voice.

"More of a starting point," Maia corrected him. "There's someone I remember from my college days, a neurologist who specialized in sleep disorders and unexplained brain activity. Dr. Evelyn Warren. She might be able to help me make sense of these occurrences."

"Then that's what you'll do," Lucas affirmed, flipping the switch to kill the lingering siren noise, symbolically closing the chapter on their harrowing night.

Maia nodded, feeling the weight of resolve settle firmly onto her shoulders. Tomorrow, she would reach out to Dr. Warren. Tonight, however, the city of Boston might still beckon.

"Let's go home, Lucas. The day's been long enough." Her hands trembled slightly as she reached for the radio, ready to confirm their status with dispatch.

"Home it is," Lucas agreed, bringing the vehicle to life with a turn of the key. As they pulled away from the curb, Maia let her mind drift toward the future—toward answers and understanding.

In the quiet shell of the ambulance, the journey ahead seemed both daunting and necessary. With each passing streetlight that flicked against the tinted windows, Maia felt the pull of an unseen force guiding her towards a destiny she couldn't yet comprehend.

The city faded into a blur as they drove, Maia's thoughts already leaping forward to the challenges of tomorrow. She knew the road wouldn't be easy; the answers she sought could very well change her in ways she couldn't predict. But the promise of discovery, of unlocking the mystery that danced at the edge of her consciousness, was too important to ignore.

Maia Yetta Rose was poised at the threshold, ready to step through the door that would lead her to the heart of the strange occurrences haunting her dreams, and with the first light of dawn, her quest for truth would begin.

MENTOR

The evening air was crisp as Maia Rose navigated the tangled streets of Boston, eventually arriving at a quaint brick building, its windows glowing like lanterns in the dimming twilight. She paused momentarily, taking in the scene - the way the fading light played upon the facade, casting shadows that danced with sentient grace. The hum of the city seemed to ebb away here, replaced by a tranquil energy that emanated from within the community center.

Pushing open the heavy wooden door, Maia stepped inside, scanning the room before her. A circle of mismatched chairs occupied the center of the space, each one cradling an occupant whose face was etched with lines of anticipation and wonder. They were a small constellation of souls, drawn together by the gravity of shared curiosity.

"Ah, you must be Maia," came a voice, warm and infused with a timbre that wrapped around Maia like a comforting shawl. Dr. Evelyn Warren emerged from the periphery, her approach delicate, as she glided across the floorboards. Her curly black hair framed her face in soft tendrils, and her brown eyes held a liquid warmth that was comforting and inviting. Maia knew that their guide tonight was a woman who had spent countless hours exploring the vast landscapes of the mind.

"Welcome," Dr. Warren continued, extending a hand that bore the faintest tremor of excitement. "I'm Evelyn, I facilitate our little gatherings."

Maia accepted the handshake, feeling the firm grip of a woman who had no doubt guided many through the turbulent seas of their psyches. Dr. Warren's presence was commanding yet soothing, a pilot through the uncharted waters Maia found herself adrift in.

"Thank you, Dr. Warren," Maia replied, her voice steady but betraying a hint of awe.

"It's an honor to be here. Your work on interconnected consciousness has been... well, it's been a game changer for me."

"Please," Dr. Warren said with a gentle chuckle, "call me Evelyn. We're all seekers here, there's no need for titles." She gestured towards the circle, where an empty chair awaited. "Come, join us. Your insights as an EMT, your experiences - they'll add invaluable dimensions to our exploration tonight."

With a nod, Maia moved toward the circle, her steps self-conscious, and measured. Each person she passed offered a smile or a nod of acknowledgment, and it struck her that despite their diverse appearances, there was a harmony to this group, a shared resonance that she could feel pulsing in the air.

As Maia took her seat, the community center's walls appeared to recede into the background, and the circle of eager minds became the entire universe. Here, in the heart of the city, they were on the cusp of voyaging inward to realms vaster and more mysterious than the sprawling metropolis outside. And Maia, with her compassionate heart and hunger for understanding, was ready to embark on this journey alongside them, beneath the guidance of Dr. Warren's wise hand.

Maia settled into the empty chair, the soft cushion slightly molding to her form. Beside her sat a young woman whose gaze was fixed on the center of the circle with an intensity that pulled at the very fabric of the room. Maia turned to her, their eyes meeting in a silent exchange laden with unspoken understanding.

"Hi, I'm Maia," she said, extending her hand.

The young woman's grip was firm and her smile, as she took Maia's hand, radiated a warmth that filled the space between them. "Nina Patel," she responded. There was a luminosity to her deep brown eyes, a spark that lit a candle of shared curiosity.

In that brief handshake, an invisible thread wove itself around them—a connection born of a mutual pursuit.

"Your presence feels...familiar," Maia ventured, her voice barely above a whisper, as if afraid to disturb the intimacy of the moment.

"Perhaps our paths were meant to cross," Nina replied, her tone equally hushed, laced with wonder.

Before Maia could respond, Dr. Warren stood, commanding the room with an effortless poise. She cleared her throat gently, and all conversations dwindled into silence. Her eyes held a light, the kind that could ignite souls or soothe them into tranquility.

"Welcome, everyone," Dr. Warren began, her voice infused with the kind of quiet strength that demanded attention without raising its volume. "I am Evelyn, and like each of you, I am a traveler through the vast landscapes of the mind."

She paused, allowing the words to sink in, her gaze sweeping over the assembled seekers. Then, slowly, she started weaving the fabric of her own tapestry, an odyssey into consciousness studies.

"It began with a question," she continued, "a simple query that rooted itself deep into my being: “What lies beyond the veil of our perceived reality?'" Her hands moved with grace, punctuating her speech with gestures that drew the very essence of her tale into the air around them.

"Through years of study and introspection, I've come to appreciate the intricate web that connects us—not just to each other, but to the cosmos itself." Dr. Warren's eyes reflected the stars, galaxies swirling within their depths. "Our minds are not isolated islands; they are bridges to one another, to the universe, to the infinite."

The group hung on every word, as if her story were a mirror reflecting their own innermost yearnings. Maia felt the resonance of Dr. Warren's journey with her own, a chord struck deep within her soul.

"Tonight, we embark together on a quest to plumb those depths, to seek out the threads that bind us," Dr. Warren concluded, her voice now the encouragement calling them to shores of discovery.

In the charged silence that followed, Maia found herself more attuned to the subtle energies around her, to the pulse of shared human endeavor. Beside her, Nina's presence was a comforting reminder that this journey was not a solitary one. Together, with Dr. Warren at the helm, they would navigate the uncharted waters of the mind, seeking the harmonies that connected them to something far greater than themselves.

Dr. Warren's last words lingered, an invitation hanging in the patient hush of the room. Maia leaned forward imperceptibly, a silent admission of her readiness to dive into the vast ocean of the psyche.

"Let us consider," Dr. Warren began, casting her gaze over the circle, "the very fabric of consciousness. Is it not remarkable how we can be both the observer and the observed within our own minds?"

A murmur of assent traveled through the group like a mellow wave. Maia's eyes flickered with the reflection of the dim lights above—a constellation of shared curiosity. She cleared her throat softly, her voice carrying the weight of countless nights spent pondering the enigma of her vivid dreams.

"Could it be," she suggested, her tone steady yet probing, "that our dreams are more than just echoes of our waking life? Perhaps they are language—symbols crafted by the deeper currents of the mind?"

Nina nodded thoughtfully at Maia's side, her expression an open book of fascination. Around them, heads tilted, the question opening channels of contemplation to explore.

"An excellent point, Maia," Dr. Warren encouraged, her approval a warm glow in the coolness of the room. "Dreams could indeed be a bridge to realms within us that remain shrouded in mystery."

The conversation flowed through theories and experiences woven together in a carpet of collective inquiry. Maia listened, her mind alight with possibilities, each new insight a lantern in the dark expanse of her thoughts.

"Let us take a moment," Dr. Warren suggested, voice lilting like the soft turn of a page, "to journey inward through guided meditation. Close your eyes, if you will."

Chairs creaked as bodies shifted, finding comfort in the stillness that settled over them. Maia felt Nina's subtle movement beside her as they both retreated into the sanctuary of their closed eyelids.

"Picture a single thread of light," Dr. Warren instructed, her voice now the sole tether to the world outside. "It starts from the very core of your being and extends outward, connecting you to the essence of all life."

Maia's breath found the rhythm of Dr. Warren's words, her heartbeat syncing with the cadence of instruction. In the darkness behind her lids, she visualized the thread—a silver ribbon originating from somewhere deep within her chest, reaching into the void.

"Feel the energy of this connection," Dr. Warren continued, "the boundless potential that resides within your consciousness. You are a part of something immense, an intricate web spun from the belly of the universe itself."

A profound tranquility enveloped Maia, the borders of her individuality blurring as she embraced the notion of oneness suggested by Dr. Warren's guiding voice. It was like the room, the city of Boston beyond, even time itself, had faded away, leaving only the shared pulse of existence beating within them all.

"Stay with this feeling," Dr. Warren whispered, the sound seeming to come from everywhere and nowhere.

"Explore it, let it guide you to the truths that lie waiting in the corners of your mind."

In this space, suspended between thought and infinity, Maia found herself adrift in the vastness of her own awareness—alone, yet profoundly connected.

Maia's essence drifted, weightless, across a sea of tranquility—a calm so deep it echoed the silence of space. Her heartbeat, once a steady drum in her ears, now synchronized with a universal cadence that pulsed through her, around her, beyond her. She was no longer just Maia Yetta Rose, EMT from Boston; she was a fragment of consciousness, a single note in an eternal symphony.

The boundaries of her mind melted away, and she felt her thoughts ripple outwards, mingling with the collective stream of the meditation circle. Within this sacred communion, a realization dawned: she was not merely within the universe, but the universe was within her.

"Very gently, begin to bring your awareness back to this room," Dr. Warren's voice called, tenderly as a mother's cradle song. "Hold onto the peace you've found, carry it with you."

As Maia's senses reawakened, the ethereal connection thinned but did not break. Her eyelashes fluttered like the wings of a butterfly testing the air, and she opened her eyes to the warm glow of the community center. A shared silence hung over the group, as delicate and profound as the experience they had each traversed.

"Would anyone like to share what they felt?" Dr. Warren prompted; her presence grounded yet still graced with the remnants of their journey.

One by one, voices rose, tentative at first then growing in confidence—a choir of awe, confusion, epiphanies, and mysteries. When it came to Maia, she hesitated, clutching at the myriad fragments of her dreams like scattered pearls.

"Sometimes," Maia began, her voice softer than usual but brimming with a reflective intensity, "I dream of places I've never seen, moments I've never lived.

And when I'm awake, I feel echoes of these dreams in reality—like a déjà vu, but more vivid, almost tangible."

Her gaze, usually so alert and focused, now searched the faces around her for signs of resonance or skepticism. "It's like there are threads in my subconscious weaving together past, present, and future into a design I can't quite understand. But during the meditation... I felt closer to deciphering its meaning."

Nina Patel nodded beside her, her own curiosity alight with empathy. The others listened, their expressions a combination of intrigue and encouragement. For Maia, who spent her days anchored to the harsh realities of emergency response, speaking of her innermost musings felt like peeling back a layer of her soul.

"Thank you, Maia, for sharing," Dr. Warren said, her voice acknowledging and reassuring. "Our dreams can indeed be powerful messengers, gateways to deeper layers of our consciousness."

As the session continued with reflections and support, Maia felt a faint shift within herself—a crack in the door to understanding the enigmatic visions that danced on the edge of her perception. With each word and nod, the circle wove her a little tighter into their fabric, promising that here, she could unravel the mysteries that beckoned her.

The room settled into a hushed stillness, the soft hum of the city beyond its walls a distant afterthought. Dr. Warren's gaze lingered on Maia with a clarity that sliced through the fog of ambiguity surrounding her dreams.

"Maia," Dr. Warren began, her tone gentle yet insistent, "this space—our circle—is a sanctuary for the mind's wanderings. Your experiences, these echoes of another place or time, they are not to be feared."

Around them, the others leaned in subtly, their presence a cushion against the unknown.

Maia felt the weight of their collective focus, a tangible embrace that fortified her resolve.

"Consider," Dr. Warren continued, her eyes reflecting an inner certainty, "that your dreams may not be mere figments but rather insights—whispers from the vast web of consciousness we're all a part of."

Maia could see the words weaving through the air, stitching together possibilities she had dared not voice aloud. Dr. Warren's affirmation was a key turning in a long-sealed lock within her.

"Your déjà vu moments," Dr. Warren said, pausing to allow the idea to breathe, "they might just be glimpses through the veil that separates one reality from another."

A shift occurred within Maia; something primal acknowledged the truth in Dr. Warren's words. The group's faces, once strangers, now mirrored back at her the same hunger for understanding that gnawed at her own soul. Encouraged by this shared communion, Maia found her voice rising from the depths, steady and more confident than she expected.

"Last night, I dreamt of a child lost in a labyrinth of mirrors," Maia confessed, her green eyes glinting with the fragments of the vision. "Everywhere he looked, there were reflections, but none of his own face. It felt so real, as if I were there, searching with him."

The group absorbed her words, their silence not empty but full of the resonance that only true listening can bring. Nina's expression was particularly attentive, her warmth a hearth welcoming Maia to venture further into the revelation of her subconscious.

"And when I woke up," Maia continued, the memory unfurling like a delicate bloom, "I passed by a street mural—of a boy and a maze of mirrors. It was the same child from my dream, down to the very curls in his hair."

Nods and murmurs of awe encircled her, the group's support relief to the chill of isolation that such experiences often brought.

The connection was undeniable, a thread pulled tight between her inner and outer worlds.

"Perhaps," Maia mused aloud, her thoughts emboldened by Dr. Warren's earlier suggestion, "these aren't random firings of my brain but signs... signposts pointing towards something greater?"

Dr. Warren's smile was enigmatic, encouraging. "Exactly, Maia. Our journey here is to trace those signs back to their source—to understand the language of our deeper selves."

In this blanket of acceptance, Maia felt the first stirrings of transformation. Beneath her calm exterior, the dreamer unfurled her wings, ready to soar into the vast expanse of her own psyche—a web of interconnected threads waiting to be explored.

The room hushed as Dr. Warren stood, her presence commanding a natural reverence that stilled the air itself. She clasped her hands before her, fingers adorned with rings that caught the light, casting tiny rainbows across the walls of the cozy community center in the heart of Boston.

"Altered states of consciousness," she began, her voice lacing through the quiet, "offer us doorways to the cosmic mind—the collective that we are all a part of."

Maia leaned forward, her eyes reflecting the dance of colors, her shoulders relaxed but alert. She could feel Nina's presence beside her, the warmth and curiosity that radiated from her like an echo of her own hunger for understanding.

"Techniques like lucid dreaming and mindfulness meditation can serve as keys to these doors," Dr. Warren continued, pacing slowly. Shadows played across her face, accentuating the depth of her eyes. "By mastering these practices, we not only gain insight into our personal psyche but also access to a greater, more universal consciousness."

A murmur of intrigue circled the group, and Maia felt a thrill at the prospect of exploring deeper into the unknown realms of her own mind. The idea of being able to navigate her vivid dreams with intention, to find meaning in the cryptic messages of déjà vu, was electrifying.

"Imagine," Dr. Warren said, pausing to let her words sink in, "being fully aware within your dream, able to explore and interact with the very fabric of your subconscious."

Nina turned to Maia; her eyes wide with excitement. "That sounds incredible," she whispered, the soft lilt of her voice tinged with wonder.

"Doesn't it?" Maia responded; her tone equally hushed. She was used to the adrenaline of emergency situations, the clarity that came with split-second decisions. But this... this was a different kind of clarity, one that promised a journey inward rather than outward.

"Consider this an invitation," Dr. Warren concluded, her gaze sweeping over the circle, inviting each person to embark on their own exploration. "If you're willing, I can guide you through the beginning steps after our sessions."

As the group broke into pairs and trios, discussing the possibilities, Maia felt a gentle tap on her shoulder. Turning, she met Nina's earnest gaze.

"Would you like to try some of these techniques together? Outside of here?" Nina asked, a hopeful tilt to her head.

"Absolutely," Maia replied without hesitation, feeling the bond between them strengthen—a shared quest that had just begun to unfold.

They exchanged phone numbers, the digits a tangible symbol of the connection they were forging. Maia saved Nina's contact with a sense of anticipation. This was more than an exchange of information; it was the opening of a new chapter.

"Let's start with mindfulness," Nina suggested, her thumb hovering over her phone, ready to set a reminder.

"Mindfulness," Maia echoed, the word resonating with promise. As an EMT, she was adept at focusing amid chaos, but this would be a practice of a different sort—focusing within the tranquility of her own spirit.

"Tomorrow?" Nina proposed, locking her eyes with Maia's.

"Tomorrow," Maia affirmed.

They stood for a moment, two seekers at the threshold of a shared journey, the vast expanse of consciousness waiting to reveal its secrets to those brave enough to look within.

The room hummed with the collective murmur of shared revelations as Dr. Warren raised her hands, signaling for attention. Maia watched as the conversations around her tapered off, the group's focus returning to the woman who had guided them through the labyrinth of their minds.

"Thank you," began Dr. Warren, her voice winding through the silence in a firm embrace. "Each of you has brought light to this space with your openness and courage. Remember, the journey within is ongoing, and what we've touched on today is just the beginning."

Maia felt the weight of those words settle in her chest, a soft but immutable truth. In Dr. Warren's eyes—a mirror reflecting their own potential—she found an unspoken promise that the exploration of one's consciousness was not a solitary endeavor.

"Continue to nurture the seeds we've planted here," Dr. Warren continued, her gaze lingering momentarily on Maia, acknowledging her innate curiosity that had been evident in every thoughtful question she posed. "And let the connections you've made become the roots that ground you in your search."

As the group began to disband, a sense of unity remained, its invisible threads weaving through the space, connecting each individual to something greater.

Maia gathered her things, the notebook filled with scribbles of her dreams and déjà vu experiences now cradled against her chest—a bridge to the intangible.

Stepping out into the crisp Boston evening, the city lights danced like distant stars grounded by gravity, a stark contrast to the boundless nature of the mind they had all sought to explore. With each breath of cool air, Maia felt a renewed vigor pulsating through her veins. The night held a deeper stillness now, as if it were aware of the profound shift that had occurred within her.

She walked with purpose, the echoes of Dr. Warren's words accompanying her steps like a mantra. Her eyes, usually so attuned to the tangible emergencies and physical forms she encountered daily, now gleamed with the reflection of an inner emerald fire.

There was a world within her, vast and uncharted, that beckoned with the allure of discovery. And alongside Nina and the others, fellow travelers on this path, Maia knew that together they would venture into the mysteries that lay hidden in the folds of their consciousness.

The faint buzz of her phone signaled a message from Nina—a simple smiley face that represented the camaraderie and anticipation that awaited them. With a small smile tugging at the corners of her lips, Maia pocketed the device and lifted her face to the sky, allowing herself a moment to revel in the possibilities that lay ahead.

"Tomorrow," she whispered to the night, a vow to continue peering beyond the veil of her waking life, into the depths where dreams and reality blurred into one. She was ready to dive deeper, to lose and find herself in the cosmic dance of existence, and she had plenty of company.

The following evening the cool Boston air wrapped around Maia as she stepped out of the community center, a noticeable contrast to the warmth of shared human connection that still lingered on her skin.

Nina emerged beside her, and together they began to navigate the maze of the city streets, their footsteps an easy rhythm against the concrete.

"Where do we even start?" Maia mused aloud; her breath visible in the evening chill. The question wasn't just about the route they would take through the maze of the metropolis, but about the journey inward they had both committed to embarking upon.

"Maybe it's not about starting or finishing," Nina replied, her voice a soothing echo in the quiet street. "Perhaps it's more about continuing. With every step, we're already further than we were."

A smile played at the edges of Maia's lips, her eyes reflecting the flickering streetlights like distant stars caught in green pools. She felt an invisible thread weaving between them, drawing her closer to Nina, to herself, to the heart of the universe that seemed to pulse beneath the city's skin.

"Continuing," Maia repeated, rolling the word across her tongue as if tasting a new flavor. It was a concept that resonated within her—a sense that each moment was a bridge to the next, an unending cycle of growth and discovery.

"Exactly," Nina affirmed, her dark eyes aglow with shared understanding. "And there's so much to explore—lucid dreaming, meditation practices... We could even keep a dream journal to compare notes."

"An exploration of the mind's frontier," Maia said, the excitement building in her chest. She thought of her vivid dreams, those hauntingly familiar scenes that seemed to call out to her from some unknown place. With Nina, perhaps she could decipher their cryptic messages.

"Look at us," Nina chuckled, her breath forming clouds that mingled with Maia's in the cool air. "Two dreamers, walking side by side, yet somehow connected to everything around us."

Maia nodded, feeling the weight of their shared purpose.

They were two souls drawn together by the gravity of their quest, orbiting the same unfathomable mystery that lay hidden within the folds of consciousness.

"Dr. Warren was right," Maia whispered to herself. "About the interconnectedness of all things. I feel it now, more than ever."

"Me too," Nina agreed, her gaze meeting Maia's. In that silent exchange, there was a promise—a tacit agreement that they would chase the horizon of understanding, no matter where it led.

"Let's meet tomorrow, dive into some research," Maia proposed, the leader within her surfacing naturally, guiding them towards their next phase. "There's a small café near here, quiet enough to talk but alive with the city's energy."

"Perfect." Nina's response was immediate, decisive. "I'll text you the details."

They continued walking, the night wrapping itself around them like a cloak, but rather than obscure, it seemed to reveal—the hidden patterns of life, the dance of light and shadow, the infinite potential that lay just beyond the veil of the ordinary.

As they parted ways, the bond they had formed was tangible, a living force that promised to grow stronger with each shared revelation, each step into the unknown. Maia watched Nina disappear into the night, a kindred spirit on a parallel path, and felt a surge of gratitude for this unexpected alliance.

Turning towards home, Maia's steps were buoyant with newfound resolve. There was work to be done, dreams to decode, and a vast cosmos of consciousness to explore. She knew that the journey ahead would be nothing short of extraordinary.

CROSSING THE THRESHOLD

Maia woke abruptly, her heart pounding and her breath coming in short, sharp gasps. The early morning light filtered through the curtains, casting a soft glow on her bedroom. She lay still for a moment, her mind racing to grasp the remnants of the dream. The vividness of the hike up Mount Monadnock with her father lingered, each detail sharp and clear as if she had truly been there.

As her breathing slowed, Maia sat up, the covers pooling around her waist. She glanced around her room, the familiar surroundings grounding her in reality. Yet, the emotional resonance of the dream clung to her, refusing to fade like a typical dream would. She ran a hand through her hair, pushing it back from her face, and closed her eyes, trying to piece together the significance of what she had experienced.

The image of her father's face, lined with age but alight with love and wisdom, was etched in her mind. His words echoed in her ears: "You have a strength inside you, a resilience that I've always admired. No matter what happens, you have the power to overcome it. Remember that." Tears pricked her eyes as she remembered the warmth of his smile and the firm grip of his hand.

Maia swung her legs over the side of the bed and stood up, feeling a sense of urgency. She needed to understand what the dream was trying to tell her. Padding softly to the kitchen, she made herself a cup of tea, the ritual calming her nerves. She took the steaming mug to her small dining table and sat down, her mind replaying the hike, the clearing, and her father's earnest expression.

As Maia sipped her tea, the realization began to crystallize. The dream was more than a simple recollection of the past; it was a message, a call to action. The dream had shown her the strength she possessed, the resilience her father had always seen in her.

It was time to tap into that strength.

Maia knew immediately what she must do. Taking a deep breath, Maia reached for her pen. Her hand trembled slightly as she touched the tip to the paper, the first hesitant stroke forming a curve. "Dear Daddy," she wrote, the letters small and tentative. She paused, her mind racing with thoughts and memories, trying to find a coherent thread to follow. "No matter what you do, please do not go out to dinner with Mom on your birthday, it is a matter of life or death, Love Maia." She carefully folded the letter and placed it inside a plastic sandwich bag.

The next morning, Maia woke early, the sky still a deep indigo as the first hints of dawn began to break. She dressed in layers, donning the flannel shirt she had packed the night before. She moved with a sense of purpose, each action deliberate and mindful. Today was the day she would face her past, confront the memories that had both haunted and sustained her.

With her backpack slung over her shoulder, Maia stepped out of her apartment and into the crisp morning air. The streets were quiet, the city still waking up. She made her way to her car, placing the backpack on the passenger seat and sliding behind the wheel. The drive to Mount Monadnock was filled with a mix of anticipation and trepidation, her mind replaying scenes from the dream and the hikes she had taken with her father.

As she drove, Maia allowed herself to reflect on the significance of the hike. It wasn't just about revisiting a place from her past; it was about honoring her father's memory and finding a sense of closure. The mountain had always been their special place, a symbol of their bond. Returning there felt like the right way to reconnect with those memories and to begin healing.

By the time she reached the trailhead, the sun had risen, casting a golden light over the landscape. She parked her car and took a moment to breathe in the fresh air, feeling a sense of calm settle over her. With her backpack securely fastened, she began the ascent, each step a witness to her determination and her love for her father.

The initial part of the hike was gentle, the path meandering through a dense forest. Sunlight filtered through the canopy, creating dappled patterns on the ground. Birds chirped overhead, their songs intermingling with the soft rustle of leaves in the breeze. Maia felt a sense of calm wash over her, the natural beauty of the surroundings easing her nerves.

As she continued, the trail began to steepen, the climb becoming more challenging. Maia welcomed the physical exertion, using it to channel her emotions. She paused occasionally to catch her breath and take in the views, the expanse of the forest stretching out below her. Each pause was an opportunity to reflect, to let the memories surface.

She remembered how her father would always encourage her during these climbs, his voice a steady presence that kept her motivated. "You're doing great, Maia," he would say, his tone full of warmth and pride. Those words echoed in her mind now, spurring her onward.

The further she ascended, the more vivid the memories became. She recalled the first time they had hiked Mount Monadnock together, her small hand gripping his as they navigated the rocky sections. She had been scared then, but her father's reassuring presence had given her the courage to keep going. Today, she felt that same courage, a resolve to honor his memory.

As she climbed higher, the trees began to thin, giving way to open rock faces and sweeping vistas. The views were breathtaking, the rolling hills and distant mountains bathed in golden light.

Maia paused to take it all in, feeling a deep connection to this place that held so many memories. It was here that she had learned to appreciate nature, to find solace in its beauty.

She reached a particularly steep section of the trail, the rocks slick from recent rain. Carefully, she navigated the slippery surface, her muscles burning with the effort. The physical challenge was a welcome distraction, a way to keep her mind focused on the present. Each step required her full attention, grounding her in the moment.

Further up the trail, Maia came across a familiar spot—a small clearing with a flat rock where she and her father used to rest. She sat down, her legs grateful for the break, and pulled out a water bottle from her backpack. As she drank, she let her mind wander back to the times they had spent here, sharing snacks and stories. The memory brought a smile to her face, a bittersweet reminder of the bond they had shared.

Taking the letter from her backpack, Maia walked over to the mailbox tree. It stood there, a solitary sentinel, its branches reaching out as if to embrace her. She placed the letter protected by the plastic bag inside, her fingers lingering for a moment. It was a symbolic act, a way of releasing her emotions and finding closure.

As she stood there, she felt a sense of peace settle over her. The hike had been more than just a physical journey; it had been a path to understanding and acceptance. She had honored her father's memory, connected with her past, and taken a step toward healing. And as she began her descent, she knew that she carried with her the strength of those memories, the promise of a future built on the foundation of love and resilience.

Maia turned to face the view once more, her heart swelling with a mix of sorrow and hope.

The landscape stretched out before her, a vast expanse that promised endless possibilities. She thought about the future, about the journey that lay ahead. It wouldn't be easy, but she felt a newfound sense of strength within her. The hike had been a test of her endurance, both physically and emotionally, and she had emerged from it with a deeper understanding of herself.

Her thoughts drifted back to the dream that had prompted this hike, the vividness of her father's presence. It had felt so real, as if he were guiding her, encouraging her to take this step. She believed now more than ever that some connections transcend time and space, that the love between a parent and child is eternal. The dream had been a catalyst, a reminder that her father's spirit was always with her, guiding her even in his absence.

Maia took one last look at the mailbox tree, a symbol of the journey she had undertaken. She felt a sense of peace settle over her, a calmness that she hadn't experienced in a long time. With a deep breath, she turned and began her descent, the path ahead clear and bright. Each step felt lighter, her heart unburdened by the weight of unspoken words.

As she walked down the mountain, Maia knew that this hike was just the beginning of her journey. She had faced her past, honored her father's memory, and taken a significant step toward healing. The path ahead was still uncertain, but she felt ready to embrace it, to continue her journey with hope and resilience. The letter in the mailbox tree was a testament to her strength, a reminder that she had the courage to face whatever lay ahead.

The air was crisp and cool, filled with the scent of pine and earth. Maia took in the beauty of her surroundings, the vibrant colors of the foliage, the distant sound of birds singing. Each step brought her closer to the base, but also closer to a renewed sense of self. The physical exertion of the hike was still there, but it was now accompanied by a sense of accomplishment and relief.

She paused at a particularly scenic overlook, where the landscape stretched out before her in a patchwork of green and gold. The view was breathtaking, a reminder of the beauty and vastness of the world. Maia took a deep breath, letting the fresh air fill her lungs and clear her mind. She closed her eyes and allowed herself to feel the weight of the moment, the significance of what she had just done.

Maia reached the base of the mountain just as the sun began to set, casting a warm golden light over the landscape. She felt a sense of closure, but also a sense of beginning. The hike had been a symbolic journey, but it had also been a real one, a physical manifestation of her emotional journey. She knew that there would still be challenges ahead, but she felt ready to face them with a renewed sense of purpose.

When Maia returned to her apartment, the first thing she noticed was how quiet it was. The stillness felt different now, not oppressive, or lonely, but peaceful. She closed the door behind her and leaned against it for a moment, taking in the familiar surroundings. The apartment was just as she had left it, but everything seemed somehow brighter, more welcoming.

She walked through the living room, her footsteps soft on the carpet. The memories of her recent struggles and the nights of restlessness felt distant, as if they belonged to someone else. Maia felt a sense of anticipation, a readiness for change. She had faced her past on the mountain, and now she was ready to face her future.

In the kitchen, she poured herself a glass of water and took a sip, savoring the coolness. She felt a sense of accomplishment, not just from the hike, but from the journey she had been on since her father's death. Writing the letter, hiking up the mountain, and placing the letter in the mailbox tree had been acts of courage and healing. She felt proud of herself for taking those steps.

Maia walked to the window and looked out at the city below. The lights were beginning to twinkle as the sun set, casting a warm glow over the buildings. She thought about the dream that had led her to this moment, the vividness of her father's presence and the message it had carried. It had been more than just a dream; it had been a guiding force, a reminder of the love and support that still surrounded her.

As the days passed, Maia found herself approaching life with a new perspective. The hike up Mount Monadnock had been a transformative experience, one that had given her a renewed sense of purpose and hope. She felt more present, more connected to the world around her, and more at peace with her past.

Walking up the trail it felt like it was only yesterday she was there last. Barefoot, humming and laughing with her father. Life was so innocent and beautiful then.

That night she had another dream. In that dream she saw herself and her father hiking that same trail. The trail with the big tree and the mailbox tree. Her dad said, "Maia check to see if I have any mail." But this time, unlike any time before she said "OK," I bet there is a letter for you, and I am going to get it for you."

As she reached her tiny hand into the hole, she felt something. There was a plastic bag with some paper in it. She drew it out and shouted, "I knew it, I knew it, there is a letter for you daddy."

Handing the plastic bag to her father anticipation and excitement almost too much to bear, she waited for him to open it.

Her father opened the bag and drew out the paper. He put the bag in his pocket and opened the paper. Shock on his face, he began to read out loud. Then the alarm went off and woke her from her dream.

The evening air in Boston carried a brisk chill, as Maia Rose navigated her way through the maze of cobblestone streets. Her jade eyes flickered with anticipation beneath the city lights as she approached the old Victorian building where the consciousness studies session was being held.

Maia paused momentarily at the entrance, gathering her thoughts. Inside, a group of individuals, each absorbed in hushed conversation. Maia took a deep breath, her skeptical mind temporarily suspended and stepped into the room.

The space was intimate, lined with shelves overflowing with books that held tales of the human psyche. Dr. Evelyn Warren stood at the helm, a port in a sea of mental explorations. With a gentle smile she welcomed Maia with a nod, her curly black hair bouncing slightly as she gestured toward an open seat.

"Tonight, we embark on a journey," Dr. Warren began, her voice edging through the attentive silence. "A journey not through space, but through the intricate warren of our own consciousness." She paced deliberately in front of a large, antique chalkboard, her fingers lightly touching the frames of various images depicting the evolution of consciousness studies.

"Think of the mind as an uncharted territory," she continued, her words painting pictures more vivid than the images behind her. "Throughout history, pioneers of psychology have dared to map its contours, to understand its enigmatic landscape." Maia leaned forward, her curiosity pulling her closer to the heart of Dr. Warren's narrative.

"From the early works of Freud and Jung to the modern-day marvels of neuroimaging, we've come a long way," Dr. Warren said, pausing to allow the gravity of the subject to settle over the room. Maia felt a tingle of excitement. The skepticism that had been her shield for so long began to chip away, piece by piece, revealing a burgeoning intrigue beneath.

"Each discovery," Dr. Warren emphasized, "brings us closer to answering the age-old question: What is consciousness?" Her brown eyes locked onto Maia's, a silent invitation to plunge deeper. Maia responded with a slight nod, her driven nature recognizing the call to unravel the mysteries that had danced at the peripheries of her dreams.

As Dr. Warren spoke of groundbreaking research - theories woven into the fabric of reality itself - the participants listened, absorbed. Maia found herself among them, no longer just an observer but a participant in this collective odyssey towards understanding.

"Let us consider the possibilities that lie ahead," Dr. Warren concluded, the finality of her statement hanging in the air like a challenge. "Not just to learn, but to experience."

In that moment, with the soft hum of Boston life continuing beyond the walls, Maia knew she had crossed a threshold. This was more than mere intellectual fascination; it was the beginning of a profound exploration into the very essence of what it meant to be alive.

Maia leaned forward, the cool metal of the chair pressing against her palms. Dr. Warren adjusted her glasses, a subtle shift that heralded the deep dive into the invisible currents of consciousness.

"Consider," Dr. Warren's voice flowed gently, "the mycelium network beneath our feet, vast and unseen, connecting plant life across distances. This is but one example of nature's intrinsic interconnectedness."

The room held its breath, and the air was charged with anticipation. Maia felt her heartbeat synchronize with the cadence of Dr. Warren's speech.

"Similarly," she continued, "there exists a hypothesis within consciousness studies that suggests all living beings are linked by a cosmic consciousness. A shared mind, if you will, that transcends individual experience."

A flicker of recognition danced in Maia's eyes. Her nightly dreams, vibrant tapestries of interwoven narratives, suddenly held new weight. Could there be threads in her own subconscious linking her to this grand cosmic web?

"Imagine," Dr. Warren proposed, and Maia's imagination unfurled like a flower to the sun, "that you could tap into this reservoir of collective wisdom."

The thought was at once exhilarating and daunting. Maia's fingers tightened on the chair; her role as an EMT had always been about substantial, immediate connections. Now, she pondered the possibility of bonds far more profound.

"Let us embark on a journey inward," Dr. Warren said, her presence a lantern in the dimly lit room. She instructed the group to close their eyes, and to breathe deeply.

Maia obeyed, her breaths forming a rhythmic soundscape with the others. The city's distant din receded, leaving only the shared sanctuary they had created within these walls.

"Picture your consciousness as a drop of water," Dr. Warren's words flowed, "merging with the ocean of collective existence."

In her mind's eye, Maia saw her drop—a vibrant, shimmering green—join an iridescent sea. The sensation was one of returning home after a lifetime away.

"Allow yourself to expand beyond the confines of your physical form," Dr. Warren coaxed. "There are no boundaries here, only limitless horizons."

Maia felt a gentle loosening, like tuning down a higher note on her guitar. Her skepticism, once a fortress, now seemed a distant shore rapidly fading from view.

"Embrace the connection," Dr. Warren murmured, "feel the unity with all things."

A warmth enveloped Maia, a comforting embrace from the universe itself. In this space, she found permission to let go, to explore the vastness without fear.

"Open up," Dr. Warren whispered, "to new possibilities."

And so, Maia did. She allowed herself to drift within this cosmic consciousness, her sense of self both diminished and magnified. For the first time, she understood the true scope of her curiosity—not a mere hunger for answers, but a quest for communion with the infinite dance of existence.

In the tranquil refuge of Dr. Warren's session, nestled in the heart of Boston, Maia Yetta Rose, the compassionate EMT and perennial dreamer, discovered a gateway to worlds unseen but deeply felt. She emerged from the guided meditation with a mind stirred by new concepts, and a soul awakened to the unexplored depths of her own being.

The room eased back into the physical as the last reverberations of Dr. Warren's soothing voice faded, leaving a profound silence that hummed with newfound understanding. Participants stirred, like divers resurfacing, blinking against the harshness of reality's light. Maia remained still, her breathing slow and deliberate, savoring the lingering embrace of interconnectedness.

"Let's bring our journey into words," Dr. Warren suggested softly, her gaze sweeping across the circle of awakening souls. "Who would like to share their experience?"

One by one, individuals spoke, their voices tentative but growing in conviction. A man with salt-and-pepper hair recounted an overwhelming sense of unity, as if for a moment, he was the breath of the city, the pulse of every heart within it. A young woman with eyes bright as the moon whispered of a clarity that cut through life's noise, revealing strings of synchronicity weaving their days together.

Maia listened, her green eyes reflecting a quiet storm, thoughts tumbling like leaves caught in an unseen current. Each story was a thread, and she felt them entwining around her, pulling her deeper into the web of shared human consciousness.

"Thank you for your openness," Dr. Warren's words were a gentle tide, drawing them back to shore. "These experiences are glimpses into the profound depths of our minds. To explore further, there are practices we can adopt."

She moved gracefully to the whiteboard, her hand sweeping across it as she listed methods—tools for the seeker. "Journaling," she began, "is a powerful way to document your inner landscape. It can capture the fleeting moments of insight that often fade as quickly as the morning dew."

Maia reached for her notebook, the empty pages crisp beneath her fingers. She scribbled passionately, each word a promise to herself.

"Then there's dream analysis," Dr. Warren continued, her curls catching the light as she turned to face them again. "Our dreams are often the mind's way of communicating what we consciously overlook. Record them, study them—they are maps to hidden chambers of your psyche."

A knowing smile touched Maia's lips. Her dreams, vibrant stories of chaos and revelation, had always been a source of mystery. The prospect of decoding them sparked excitement, a challenge to unravel the threads that had long woven through her nights.

"Lastly," the doctor's voice pulled Maia from her reverie, "mindfulness exercises. Simple, yet profound. They teach us to be present, to observe without judgment. In this awareness, you'll find a wellspring of wisdom about yourself and the world around you."

Maia nodded, the notion resonating within her. As an EMT, presence was her anchor amidst the tempest of emergencies, yet she had never considered its profound impact on understanding consciousness. She imagined integrating these exercises into her routine, a steadfast companion to guide her through the cacophony of the city.

"Start with these," Dr. Warren encouraged, her warm brown eyes holding each participant in turn. "And see where they lead you."

In the quiet that followed, Maia felt a shift—a subtle realignment of her inner compass. The skeptic in her had not drowned in the sea of collective consciousness; rather, it had found a new direction, buoyed by the possibility that these practices might illuminate paths yet untraveled in the labyrinth of her mind.

As the session adjourned, the room filled with the rustle of notes being gathered and chairs sliding across the floor. Maia rose, her movements deliberate, her mind alight with the promise of exploration. She held her notebook close, a repository of the knowledge imparted and the discoveries yet to come.

Maia wove her way through the cluster of participants, each lost in their own thoughts and revelations. The hum of quiet conversations provided a soothing backdrop to her determined approach. Dr. Warren stood near the windowsill, bathed in the soft glow of afternoon light filtering through the Boston skyline. Maia's green eyes held a newfound spark as she neared the woman who had opened a door within her that she never knew existed.

"Dr. Warren," Maia began, her voice steady yet permeated with a softness reserved for moments of true revelation. "I can't express how much this session has shifted something in me. Thank you."

The doctor turned, her warm brown eyes meeting Maia's. A gentle smile played on her lips, the kind that acknowledges a shared understanding without the need for many words. "Maia?" Dr. Warren said, her tone inviting, "I'm so glad to hear that. Our minds are intricate universes waiting to be explored."

"I want to learn more," Maia confessed, her earnestness evident. "The meditation, the theories... I feel like I've only just glimpsed the surface."

"Ah, the pursuit of knowledge is a never-ending journey." Dr. Warren reached into the folds of her colorful scarf and produced a small, intricately designed card. "Here are some resources—books, articles, even virtual forums where you can connect with others on similar paths."

Maia accepted the card, her fingertips brushing against the textured paper. It felt like a key, a tangible symbol of the doors waiting to be unlocked.

"Keep that curiosity alive," Dr. Warren advised, her eyes twinkling with the same intensity that colored her lectures. "It will guide you well."

As they rejoined the group, the air seemed charged with the collective energy of minds seeking deeper truths. Dr. Warren resumed her place at the forefront, her presence commanding attention without demanding it.

"Let's delve into the fabric of our reality," she began, her voice playing through the room like an invitation. "Consider the cosmic mind—the interconnected web that binds us, not just to each other, but to the very essence of existence."

A murmur of agreement rippled through the participants, and Maia found herself leaning forward, eager to catch every word.

"Has anyone here experienced a moment that felt larger than themselves? A moment when the boundaries of individual consciousness seemed to blur into something greater?"

Hands tentatively rose, and Dr. Warren nodded encouragingly. As stories were shared, Maia absorbed them, each narrative a voice in the chorus blending into the symphony of collective experience.

"Once," Maia spoke up, her voice clear and resonant, "in the rush of saving a life, time slowed. I was both myself and part of a larger story. Every action, every breath felt orchestrated by something beyond my comprehension."

"Beautifully said, Maia," Dr. Warren acknowledged. "In those moments, we touch the cosmic mind. We become acutely aware of the delicate symphony of life."

The room settled into contemplative silence, each participant reflecting on their own encounters with the profound. Maia's heart swelled with a sense of kinship and purpose. Here, among these seekers of truth, she had found asylum —a place where her questions were not burdens but portals to infinite possibilities.

Maia scribbled furiously, the pen in her hand dancing across the paper with a will of its own. The air in the hall was still, heavy with the collective concentration of every participant hunched over their journals. Dr. Warren's assignment had unleashed a torrent within Maia—a cascade of dreams and moments that now flooded the pages before her.

"Consider this an exploration," Dr. Warren had said with a gentle smile, "a journey through the landscape of your subconscious."

Maia paused her writing for a breath, her gaze lifting to meet Dr. Warren's eyes from across the room. There was a silent understanding between them, a mutual recognition of the depths they were about to explore.

"Remember, there are no mundane moments," Dr. Warren continued, her voice soothing against the harshness of scribbling pens. "Every dream, every coincidence, may hold a key to understanding the greater tapestry of consciousness."

The session faded into a quiet drone. Maia felt the others' presence around her—kindred spirits seeking meaning in the metaphysical. She returned to her task, documenting a recurring dream: an ancient tree, its branches sprawling into the cosmos, leaves whispering secrets of lives past and futures unfolding.

As the group dispersed, Maia lingered, her heart beating with anticipation. Dr. Warren approached, her presence calm and reassuring. They settled into a secluded corner, the world beyond their conversation fading into obscurity.

"Tell me about your dreams, Maia," Dr. Warren prompted, her voice a warm lantern in the dimly lit space.

"Always the same tree," Maia confessed, her voice a mere whisper. "It feels...significant, like it's calling out to me, but I don't understand why."

"Symbols in dreams often represent something much larger than ourselves," Dr. Warren explained, her tone permeated with the wisdom of one who has traversed these realms many times. "They can be doorways to our deepest intuitions, our connection to the cosmic mind."

Maia considered this, her thoughts a whirlpool of skepticism and wonder. Each dream she recounted brought forth more questions, more knots to untangle in the intricate web of her subconscious.

"Deja vu," Maia said, shifting topics. "There are moments on the job when I feel certain I've lived them before, down to the smallest detail. It's unsettling."

"Such experiences can be jarring," Dr. Warren acknowledged, nodding solemnly. "Yet they serve as reminders that time is not as linear as we perceive. These moments are gifts, Maia—they encourage us to look deeper, to consider the interconnected nature of all things."

"Trust your intuition," Dr. Warren advised, her gaze piercing yet kind. "It's a powerful ally in navigating these waters."

Maia absorbed her words, feeling the weight of their truth settle within her. She wasn't merely an EMT saving lives; she was a seeker, a dreamer, tapping into a vastness that transcended her everyday reality.

"Thank you, Dr. Warren," Maia said, her voice steadier than she felt. "This...it's more than I expected. But I want to explore further."

"Then let's continue this journey together," Dr. Warren replied with an encouraging smile, the promise of discovery shimmering in her eyes.

The room's ambiance shifted as Dr. Warren ushered in the next phase of the workshop.

"Mindfulness is about anchoring yourself in the now," Dr. Warren said, returning to the center of the circle where a single candle flickered. "It's the art of observing without judgment, embracing the current moment with acceptance."

Maia felt the weight of her own breath, the steady rise and fall of her chest. The sound of her heartbeat was a drumbeat, grounding her to the present.

"Close your eyes," Dr. Warren continued, her voice a tranquil current in the silence. "Focus on the sensation of being alive—the air on your skin, the earth beneath you, the fire within you."

As Maia complied, her senses heightened. She could hear the soft hum of the city beyond these walls—an ambulance siren in the distance, its urgency a stark contrast to the serenity within. She envisioned herself as part of a larger organism, each cell, each person, interconnected in an intricate design.

"Let the thoughts come and go," Dr. Warren instructed, pacing slowly around the circle, her steps barely a whisper. "Like leaves on a stream, observe them as they drift by. You are not your thoughts; you are the observer, timeless and boundless."

Maia imagined her worries as those leaves, watching as they floated away on the water's surface. She was here, now, in this space of learning and unlearning, tethered to the moment.

"Good," Dr. Warren affirmed after several minutes, her tone filled with confidence. "Let's bring our awareness back to the room."

When Maia opened her eyes, she found Dr. Warren gazing at her, a knowing smile playing on her lips.

"Balance is key, Maia," Dr. Warren said, her expression solemn yet encouraging. "You have a gift for healing, for being a beacon of hope in the chaos of emergencies. Embrace it and remember to also embrace this journey of self-discovery."

Maia nodded, feeling a sense of duality within her—a lifesaver clad in the armor of practicality, and yet a dreamer, a philosopher of the cosmic mind.

"Your path as an EMT is noble," Dr. Warren added, gathering her notes as participants began to stretch and murmur amongst themselves. "But do not neglect the exploration of your inner world. One will feed into the other, creating a wholeness that is greater than its parts."

"Thank you," Maia whispered, her voice barely audible over the sounds of chairs scraping and bags zipping. Dr. Warren simply touched her shoulder in response, an acknowledgment of the unspoken understanding between them.

As the session concluded, Maia remained seated, allowing the others to file out. Her mind was a whirlpool of thoughts and emotions, yet she felt an undeniable clarity. The city awaited her return, its rhythms a backdrop to her newfound quest.

She would don her uniform, attend to the wounded, and navigate the unpredictable streets—all while nurturing the seed that Dr. Warren had planted. The balance of saving lives and delving into the enigma of consciousness was her new reality, a delicate dance on the edge of existence.

Maia stood; her legs unsteady as if the gravity in the room had shifted. A silent thank you hung in the air, directed at the retreating backs of fellow seekers who'd shared this sacred space with her. Their stories and vulnerable explorations had woven a tapestry of human experience that now hugged Maia's shoulders like a comforting shawl.

"Dr. Warren," she found herself saying, the words catching the tail end of the meditation's serenity. "I can't express what this... it's been transformative."

The doctor's eyes met hers, soft and understanding. "You're beginning to see, aren't you?" Dr. Warren's voice was low, a soothing hum in the emptied room.

"The layers of our existence, they're more permeable than we've been led to believe."

Maia nodded, her thoughts ablaze with possibilities. "I feel like I've only just opened a door that I didn't even know was there."

"Keep stepping through, Maia," Dr. Warren encouraged, a gentle firmness in her gaze. "And remember, the door never really closes."

As she stepped out into the cool Boston evening, the city sounds wrapped around Maia—a symphony of life playing its relentless tempo. She paused, taking a deep breath, feeling the rush of traffic and the pulse of distant sirens syncing with the rhythm of her own heart.

Instead of walking towards the subway station she chose the winding path of a nearby park, her sanctuary within the urban commotion. The canopy of trees whispered from above, their leaves shimmering under the touch of streetlights. With each step, Maia contemplated the blend of voices from the session, the shared moments of awakening that seemed both personal and universal.

A bench invited her to sit, and she obliged, gazing up at the patchwork of night sky visible through the branches. There, amidst the twinkling stars and the dark expanse, she felt the profound interconnectedness Dr. Warren had spoken of—the cosmic mind that cradled her own consciousness.

"Embrace the interconnectedness," she murmured, a vow to the night, to herself. Maia drew her notebook from her bag, the one she'd begun to fill with dreams and musings. She etched into its pages a promise. She would weave these teachings into her life, a thread of intentionality among the fabric of her daily routines.

Closing the notebook, Maia sensed the alignment of her two worlds—the urgency of her duties as an EMT and the tranquility of her inner exploration. They were not at odds but in harmony, each giving depth to the other.

With newfound resolve, she rose from the bench, her footsteps light against the gravel path. Tonight, she carried more than her equipment bag; she carried the wisdom of the cosmic mind, ready to serve as both healer and seeker.

WE ARE THE COSMOS

Maia Rose settled into the stillness, her form a solitary silhouette against the sparse furnishings of the dimly lit room. She perched cross-legged atop a cushion that had known the contour of her thoughts more intimately than any confidant ever could. The faint glow from the narrow window traced the outline of her determined face, casting shadows that danced with the rhythm of the city beyond—Boston, ever restless, ever breathing.

Her eyes remained closed, veiling the vivid green that often reflected a world unseen to others. Her hands, those conduits of life and healers of sorrow, lay in repose upon her knees, fingers unfurled like the petals of a Lily in bloom.

Maia's breath, a witness to the pulse of existence, cascaded through her with the depth of an ocean's embrace. Inhale, the rise of her chest a gentle swell; exhale, a serene tide receding into the depths of her being.

The cadence of her breathing a lullaby to the commotion of her daily encounters—the sirens, the urgency, the grip of life and death that clasped her heart as an EMT.

Each breath was a deliberate step away from the precipice of, a descent into the present. There, within the sanctum of her meditation, Maia found the tranquility she sought, the equilibrium that so often eluded her during the harsh reality of her working life.

With each cycle of air that filled her lungs, the walls of the room seemed to inch further apart, granting her spirit the expanse it yearned for. Maia's focus honed sharp as a scalpel, yet as tender as the touch required to coax a trapped soul back from the brink. It was here, in this liminal space between breaths, that Maia navigated the delicate balance of her existence, tethered to the tangible yet ever drifting towards the ethereal dreams that whispered secrets in the language of the subconscious.

A cascade of colors unfurled before Maia's inner gaze, painting the dark canvas of her closed eyelids with a brilliance that defied the natural palette of Boston's greys and browns. The luminous web spun around her pulsed with iridescence, each thread woven from the spectral light of beings not bound by flesh or time.

Azure strands shimmered with the calm wisdom of ancient trees whispering secrets to the wind. A vibrant scarlet streak throbbed with the collective heartbeat of every creature that had ever drawn breath. Swirls of emerald green twisted into patterns reminiscent of DNA helices, encoding the very essence of life itself. And there, laced between them all, were filaments of soft gold, glowing with the gentle touch of human kindness—each one a memory, a gesture of compassion, an echo of laughter.

Maia's breath hitched at the beauty of it. Here in this space, removed from the urgency of sirens and the clamor of city life, she could see the infinite connections that her mind had always sensed but never fully grasped. Her dreams—the ones that set her apart since childhood—had been preparing her for this revelation. The idea that her hands, which had so often worked to save lives, were now reaching out to understand the very essence of existence left her awestruck.

The vast interconnectedness embraced her, accepting her presence without judgment. In its embrace, she felt a unity that transcended individuality; her own consciousness melded with the greater whole. She, Maia Yetta Rose—the dreamer, the healer—was no longer just a single entity moving through a crowded world but an integral part of a grand cosmic fabric.

The realization was a warm wave washing over her, comforting yet exhilarating. She belonged here, within this intricate network of energy, where every life was a vital thread, and every action a stroke of the artist's brush across the universe's boundless canvas.

She understood now that her empathy, her drive to aid those in distress, was not just a professional calling but a fundamental aspect of her being—one that connected her to every living thing.

In this spectral realm, where the physical borders of her body dissolved, Maia's spirit soared. She was a drop in the ocean, yet the ocean itself, small but infinite. And as she hovered in this state of wonder, the knowledge settled deep within her: the cosmos whispered its secrets not to the mind but to the soul, and hers was listening intently.

The pulsation continued, a gentle rhythm that echoed the beat of Maia's own heart. The vibrant colors and patterns that swam before her eyes grew more vivid with each throb, the web of energy that surrounded her quivering as if alive. It synchronized with her breaths—deep and rhythmic—but as the moments passed, the vibrations intensified, building into a crescendo that resonated through her very essence.

Maia tried to steady herself, to cling to that sense of wonder she had felt only moments before. But it was slipping away, replaced by an overwhelming surge of energy that threatened to sweep her consciousness away like a leaf in a storm. Her breath hitched, the harmonious in-and-out becoming jagged, disrupted by the force that now seemed to pulse from every strand of the cosmic web encasing her.

She fought to keep her focus, to remain the observer within this expanded state. But the pulsing grew stronger, a relentless tide against the shores of her mind. It demanded her attention, pulling at her senses, urging her to let go, to surrender to the tide. She could feel it trying to consume her, to dissolve her identity and scatter it across the vast expanse of interconnected existence.

"Stay grounded," she whispered to herself, the words almost lost in the thrumming that filled the room. Her voice, usually so calm and authoritative, wavered with the strain of maintaining her composure. It was a struggle, a battle between her disciplined training and the raw power of this unseen force.

She drew upon every ounce of her resolve, every memory of steadying her hands while suturing wounds or comforting panicked victims, to remain whole.

"Breath is life," Maia recited the mantra that had become her lifeline in countless emergencies. She closed her eyes tighter, shutting out even the phantom light that danced behind her eyelids, and focused inward. She imagined her breath as a steady flame flickering in the tempest. With each inhale, she visualized drawing the chaotic energies into this flame, taming them, transforming them into something she could withstand. With each exhale, she pushed back, reinforcing the boundaries of her self.

The room—her entire reality—continued to tremble and shift around her. Yet, inside, Maia built a fortress around her core, brick by brick with each measured breath. The vibrant web still pulsed eagerly, seeking to overwhelm her, but she held firm, a solitary rock against this torrential sea.

"Center. Focus," she commanded herself, her internal voice adopting the tone she used to bring order to scenes of panic and peril on Boston's unpredictable streets. This was her domain, she affirmed internally, as a sentient being connected to the fabric of all things. The tumultuous energy would not claim her today.

There, in the quiet sanctuary of her mind, Maia found the eye of the storm. The roar receded to a murmur, the pulsating web dimmed, and she remained, resolute and undiminished. The tension ebbed away, leaving her enveloped in a newfound silence—a silence profound and full of secrets yet to be explored.

The profound silence cradled Maia, a respite from the storm that had raged just moments before. Within this tranquil void, her senses sharpened, attuning to the subtlest of vibrations that now whispered to her across the gossamer threads of existence. It was then that it surfaced—an aberration in the silence.

A disturbance fluttered through the web, like a dark ripple on a still pond. Before Maia could brace herself, a vision flashed within the intricate lattice—a face, or the suggestion of one, distorted and fleeting. Its features were stretched grotesquely, as if molded by unseen hands of anguish. Eyes, hollow and deep-set, bore into hers with an intensity that bordered on malice.

This specter, a smear against the backdrop of cosmic harmony, brought with it a chilling familiarity. Maia's breath hitched, and her fortress of calm quivered. Was this contorted visage a reflection of her own psyche, a shadow aspect birthed from the depths of her being? The thought clawed at the edges of her identity, seeding doubt where there had been conviction.

She fought to look away, but the vision clung to the periphery of her awareness, a persistent echo. It seemed to pulse with the erratic rhythm of a distressed heart, its chaotic swirls of energy resonating with the cadence of emergency sirens that she knew all too well.

"Steady," Maia whispered, her voice barely a thread. She sought the anchor of her breath once more, clinging to it as a lifeline back to herself—to the Maia who navigated life's tangible crises with unwavering composure.

The vision faded as swiftly as it had appeared, leaving behind a trail of cold dread that lingered in its wake. Maia's heartbeat thundered in her ears, a stark contrast to the returning serenity of the room. The web of energy, once again docile, hummed softly, indifferent to the turbulence it had harbored.

With measured breaths, Maia coaxed her spirit back from the precipice of the unknown, her thoughts untangling from the enigmatic tapestry. As the last tendrils of otherworldly perception slipped away, she felt the familiar weight of her body anchored to the cushion beneath her.

Her eyes flickered open, revealing the dim outlines of her Boston apartment.

The shadows cast by sparse light seemed mundane now, yet they whispered of mysteries just beyond the veil. Maia's fingers curled into the fabric of her jeans, grounding her further, pulling her away from the vastness she had touched.

Disoriented, she rose unsteadily, her limbs heavy with the gravity of both worlds. The experience left her trembling—not with fear, but with a profound sense of awe. The essence of life, its interconnectedness and boundless depth, clung to her consciousness like morning dew.

"Was any of it real?" she murmured to the empty room, her voice soft and reflective, betraying none of the authority it held in the harsh light of day. Her green eyes, now wide with wonder, scanned the quiet space as if seeing it for the first time.

Maia Yetta Rose, EMT and dreamer, remained motionless, allowing the enormity of her journey to wash over her. She stood as a bridge between two realities, each calling to her with equal fervor. And though the unsettling vision had shaken her, it also reminded her that there were still infinite realms within herself left to explore.

The wind whispered to Maia Rose as she navigated her way through the maze of Boston's streets. Her jade eyes, wide with anticipation and curiosity, reflected the glow of flickering streetlights. She was not merely walking to a meeting; she was stepping closer to unraveling the mystery that played at the edge of her consciousness—synchronicity.

As she entered the small community center, a refuge within the urban expanse, the room hummed with the low, expectant murmurs of fellow seekers gathered within. Dr. Evelyn Warren stood at the podium, her presence a port of calm in a sea of eager minds.

"Good evening, Maia," Dr. Warren greeted, her voice carrying the gentle weight of knowledge. Each syllable settled over the room, commanding silent respect. "We're about to begin."

"Evening, Dr. Warren," Maia replied, her calm tone belying the flutter in her chest. She took her usual seat, tucking a stray auburn lock behind her ear, her body remembering the contours of the chair from sessions past.

To her left sat Theo, an older gentleman whose silver hair contradicted his youthful excitement towards the metaphysical. He leaned toward Maia, his eyes gleaming with unspoken stories. "You ever feel like you've lived this moment before, Maia?" he asked, a whisper meant for conspirators.

"Deja vu?" she queried softly, the idea spiraling into her thoughts.

"More than that," Theo insisted, tapping the side of his temple. "Like there's a pattern we're all following, but only some of us see the stitches holding it together."

"Perhaps that's what brings us here," Maia mused, her fingers tracing the edges of her notebook. She knew the sensation well, the pull of unseen threads weaving through her life, tying her dreams to her waking world.

Nearby, a woman named Priya—a software engineer by day, philosopher by night—chimed in, her voice tinged with analytical precision. "It's not just a feeling. There are events in my life that statistically shouldn't coincide, yet they do. It's like the universe is calculating our paths."

"Or maybe we're calculating it," suggested a young man named Micah, his dreadlocks falling over earnest eyes. "What if our collective consciousness influences more than we realize?"

Maia listened, her gaze drifting among the faces, each alight with the possibility of understanding something greater. This was no ordinary gathering; it was a convergence of souls seeking answers to questions most feared to ask aloud.

"Could it be," Maia ventured, finding her voice within the collection of theories, "that synchronicity is not just a personal experience but a universal language? A way for the cosmic mind to communicate across the veil of illusion?"

Heads turned, eyes fixed on her as she spoke, her words revealing shared thoughts and silent acknowledgments.

In this space, every uttered theory wove deeper into their collective quest for truth, their individual stories becoming part of a grander narrative stretching beyond the confines of their own lives.

In the intimate safety of the community center, surrounded by kindred spirits beneath the watchful guidance of Dr. Warren, Maia felt the barriers of isolation dissipate. Here, in the heart of Boston, she was no longer an EMT with vivid dreams; she was a seeker, connected by invisible strings to a world pulsating with mysteries waiting to be understood.

The room hushed as Dr. Evelyn Warren stood and approached the projector, her shadow stretching across the screen like a challenge. Maia leaned forward from her chair, a notebook balanced on her knees, pen poised for revelation. The soft click of the projector cut through the anticipation, bathing the room in a pale blue light signaling that threshold between worlds.

"Consider," began Dr. Warren, her voice steady in the dimmed room, "the intricate web of existence, where a single thread pulled might resonate through the entire fabric." On the screen, images flickered—a butterfly's wing, a clock stopped at precisely the right moment, a pair of strangers locking eyes across a crowded subway—and with each slide, she wove a narrative of cosmic coincidence.

Maia scribbled notes, her handwriting a hurried script that attempted to capture the essence of each example. There was the psychologist who dreamt of a golden scarab only to have one tap against his window during a patient's session; the spiritual leader whose lost keepsake was found by a child halfway across the world; the grieving widow who received a call from her husband's disconnected phone number on the anniversary of his death.

As the case studies spilled into the room, Maia's mind raced, connecting dots that formed constellations of thought.

She felt the gentle pull of something greater, a force that defied simple explanation or dismissal as mere chance.

"Who here has felt the universe whisper to them in these uncanny moments?" Dr. Warren asked, her gaze sweeping the circle of faces now turned towards her, reflecting a spectrum of wonder.

Maia's throat tightened; her heart beat a nervous rhythm against her chest. She hesitated, her glance skimming the room, meeting eyes that held stories untold. With each second of silence, the weight of her own experiences burgeoned within her until it was too heavy to carry alone.

"Um, I have," Maia's voice emerged, softer than intended but carried by a resolve that grew with each word. "There was this one time, after a particularly rough shift on the ambulance." She paused, gathering the fragments of memory like shards of glass. "I saw a street artist painting a scene—it was exactly like the dream I had the night before. The same colors, the same strokes of chaos and calm."

Dr. Warren nodded, encouraging Maia to continue. "Then there was the call," Maia said, her voice gaining strength. "We were dispatched to help a man who'd collapsed. His address—451 Hawthorne Street—it was the exact number of my childhood home. And Hawthorne... that was the name of the street artist."

A collective breath was held within the room, the air charged with the energy of shared understanding. Maia's words hung suspended, a bridge spanning the gap between personal revelation and universal truth.

"Thank you, Maia," Dr. Warren said, her tone filled with genuine appreciation. "These moments are markers, signposts that guide us toward a greater comprehension of our place in the cosmos."

Maia sank back into her chair, her heart still racing but enveloped in the warmth of acceptance. She had voiced her truth, and rather than being met with doubt or ridicule, she found connection—a reflection of her own curiosity and longing mirrored in the eyes of those around her.

In that moment, the walls between them seemed to dissolve, leaving only the profound sense of unity that comes from sharing in the mystery of existence. Maia realized then that the synchronicities she experienced were not just random occurrences, but a language spoken by the universe, a language she was only beginning to understand.

As Maia's confession tapered off into the thick murmur of the room, there was an imperceptible shift in energy beside her. Nina Patel leaned closer, the subtle scent of jasmine from her hair mingling with the mixed aroma of the meeting space. Her deep brown eyes, usually alight with spirited curiosity, now shimmered with a layer of solemn understanding.

"Maia," Nina said softly, ensuring only her neighbor could hear. "Your story—it totally resonates with me. I've had my own experiences with synchronicity."

Maia turned to face Nina, her eyes reflecting the fluorescent lights overhead that cast an otherworldly glow on their quiet corner of the room. The initiative was hers; she prompted the young woman with a simple tilt of her head, encouraging Nina to continue.

"Last week," Nina began, her voice barely above a whisper, "I was reading about the migration patterns of monarch butterflies, marveling at how they journey thousands of miles with such precision. The very next day, a patient in the hospice where I volunteer gave me a bookmark adorned with—you guessed it—monarchs."

"Patterns," Maia echoed thoughtfully, her gaze drifting toward the window where Boston's skyline played hide and seek between the blinds. "Patterns that guide us, perhaps?"

"Exactly," Nina agreed, twisting a strand of her black hair nervously. "It's as if these occurrences are threads, weaving together the fabric of a grand tapestry we're only seeing snippets of."

"Snippets that hint at something larger," Maia mused, her fingers tracing the edge of her notepad, where words like 'cosmic mind,' and 'interconnectedness' were scrawled in hurried handwriting. "Do you think, maybe, it's the universe nudging us? Showing us that everything is... connected?"

"More than connected," Nina replied, her tone saturated with a reverence that transcended the room's confines. "Interdependent. As if every action, every thought, has its place in a vast, conscious network."

The two women shared a glance, a silent acknowledgment of their mutual journey into the unknown. Around them, the consciousness studies group continued to buzz with discussions, but Maia and Nina found themselves enveloped in a bubble of introspection, the ambient noise fading into insignificance.

"Dr. Warren speaks of the cosmic mind," Nina continued, her hands gesturing as though she could pluck the very concept from the ether. "But what if we are more than just passive observers? What if we're active participants in its unfolding narrative?"

"Participants who can influence the plot," Maia added, her voice steady, a stark contrast to the tumultuous thoughts racing through her mind. "By recognizing these synchronicities, maybe we're learning to speak the language of the cosmos."

"Learning and listening," Nina said, nodding slowly. "And, perhaps, through understanding, we might even rewrite our own stories within it."

Their conversation flowed as seamlessly as the tide, each woman finding consolation and stimulation in the exchange. The idea that they were both solitary and united—that their individual experiences of synchronicity were but singular notes within a grand symphony—was both humbling and exhilarating.

As the meeting wound down, Maia and Nina remained seated, reluctant to sever the connection that had formed between them.

They were seekers on parallel paths, brought together by the enigmatic force of synchronicity, eager to dive deeper into the mysteries that bound them—not just to each other, but to the entirety of existence itself.

The room was a microcosm of the universe, each person a star with tales of cosmic coincidence. The murmur of shared stories swirled around Maia, stitching her into the tapestry of voices. A man with salt-and-pepper hair leaned forward to speak, his voice tinged with awe.

"Once, by mere coincidence, I met a stranger who shared my mother's rare maiden name," he began, as the group leaned in. "Turns out, our great-grandfathers were brothers."

A woman across from him, draped in a shawl that held the colors of twilight, chimed in. "I painted a scene from a dream once, only to find myself standing in that exact place, years later—halfway across the world." Her eyes sparkled with the magic of her story.

Each narrative thread wove itself around Maia, pulling her further into the fabric of this collective phenomenon. The coincidences they described transcended mere chance; they seemed to be whispers from the underlying structure of reality.

Dr. Warren observed the group, her warm brown eyes reflecting the spiral of conversation. She stood gracefully, and the room naturally quieted, all eyes turning towards her. "Consider the implications," she prompted gently, her voice a guiding light through the fog of wonderment. "What if synchronicity is not just serendipity? What if it is a signpost, pointing toward a more profound interconnectedness?"

Her words lingered, and Maia felt them resonate within her like a bell struck upon the truth. Dr. Warren moved among them, her presence calming and curious. "Might these experiences challenge what we perceive as the boundaries of our individual selves?" she continued.

"Could they hint at a collective consciousness we are only beginning to understand?"

Maia sat, rapt, as Dr. Warren facilitated the flow of ideas. The notion of individuality being an illusion in a vast, interconnected cosmos sent shivers down her spine. Each story became a piece of evidence, a fragment of a puzzle that suggested a grander picture she had always sensed but never seen.

"Perhaps," Dr. Warren posed, her tone shifting to encompass both the room and realms beyond, "we are all windows into the cosmos, our lives woven together by a force that defies time and space. Synchronicity might well be the language of this design—subtle, yet powerful in its ability to reveal the unseen connections."

Maia felt a revelation unfurling within her mind, like the blooming of a flower that had been waiting for the kiss of dawn. The stories around her, the insights of Dr. Warren—all were converging into a singularity of thought. In this hushed room in Boston, amidst seekers and scholars, Maia found herself on the cusp of understanding something vast, something that bridged the gap between science and spirit, between her solitary existence and the cosmic whole.

Maia's fingers hesitated above the smooth surface of her iPhone, the glow of its screen casting a soft light on her face. She lifted her gaze to Nina's, where an unspoken understanding lingered with the quiet hum of anticipation. "Can I have your number?" Maia asked, her voice steady but laced with the excitement of finding kinship in this quest for answers.

"Of course," Nina replied with a smile that acknowledged the gravity of their shared experiences. She rattled off the digits as Maia's thumbs danced across the screen, committing them to memory and technology.

"Let's meet at the Arboretum next weekend?"

Nina suggested, her eyes reflecting the myriad possibilities that lay ahead. "It's peaceful there, away from the city's pulse. A perfect place to talk about... well, everything."

"Sounds perfect," Maia agreed, saving Nina's number with a soft chime. She tucked it into the pocket of her jacket, feeling the weight of her phone knowing it was now a portal to deeper connections.

As the group began to disband, the chairs scraping softly against the floor, Maia stood up, stretching her limbs which had grown stiff from prolonged sitting. The energy in the room was dissipating, yet within her, a vibrant current surged, spreading warmth through her veins.

She glanced around the room, watching as people exchanged farewells and lingering thoughts. Dr. Warren was folding her notes, her expression one of contentment. Maia approached her, gratitude shaping her words. "Thank you for today, Dr. Warren. It has been... eye-opening."

"Keep exploring, Maia," Dr. Warren encouraged, her voice inspired with the wisdom of years spent traversing the mind's landscape. "What we discussed here is just the beginning."

Stepping out into the cool Boston evening, Maia drew in a deep breath. The city lights blinked like distant stars, each one a story, a life in motion, a synchronicity waiting to be discovered. She felt a sense of validation envelop her, the realization that she was not alone in her quest, that others too were tracing the delicate webs of meaning that bound them together.

As she walked, the echoes of the meeting resonated within her, blending with the rhythmic heartbeat of the city. Every person she passed, every whisper of wind, seemed to speak of interconnectedness, of a cosmic dance in which they were all partners. She was part of a community now, seekers united by the thirst for understanding the language of the universe whispered through synchronicity.

Maia paused at a crosswalk, the traffic lights cycling from green to yellow to red.

She watched the cars stop, their passengers cocooned within, oblivious to the profound discussions that had unfolded just blocks away. Yet even here, amid the mundane flow of urban life, Maia sensed the undercurrents of something greater, something that connected them all.

With each step toward home, her mind buzzed with newfound ideas and connections, a ballad of thoughts harmonizing with the city's night song. Boston, with its storied history and bustling streets, was more than just a backdrop; it was a living, breathing entity that held secrets and serendipities in its very bones.

The city's pulse throbbed through the soles of Maia's boots as she made her way down the dimly lit street, her mind still awash with the evening's revelations. The consciousness studies group had been a launch pad where her swirling thoughts and questions found an echo in the voices of others. Now, alone, she felt the weight of those shared stories pressing upon her, urging her to look deeper, to dig beneath the surface of what she knew—or thought she knew—about reality.

A soft mist began to fall, casting halos around the distant streetlights. Maia turned her face skyward, letting the cool droplets kiss her skin, each one a tiny affirmation of connection. Synchronicity was not just a concept discussed in the safety of Dr. Warren's conference room; it was alive here, in the mist, in the rhythm of stoplights changing, in the gaze of a stranger.

She reached her apartment building, its facade a blend of brick and memory, and climbed the stairs to her third-floor apartment. Once inside, she didn't bother with the lights, drawn instead to the large window overlooking the mesh of alleyways and rooftops. The city spread out before her—a tangle of lives intersecting and diverging in patterns too intricate to discern without looking from just the right angle.

Maia pulled a notebook from her bag, the words of Dr. Warren echoing in her head. “Synchronicity is the language of a larger consciousness,” she’d said, and Maia could almost hear her now, that calm, assured voice cutting through the chaos.

The bookshelf beside her desk held the usual medical texts, manuals on emergency care that spoke to the tangible, the immediate. But tonight, they seemed like relics from another life. She reached for the list she had scribbled during the meeting, her fingers brushing over titles that promised to open doors to understanding: "The Coincidence Conundrum," "The Cosmic Web: Ties That Bind," "Quantum Threads: The Fabric of Intention."

Her phone buzzed—a message from Nina, no doubt a continuation of their earlier exchange—but Maia resisted the impulse to respond. This moment was for introspection, for allowing the seeds planted by the group to take root in the fertile soil of her curiosity.

She selected a volume on the recommendation of Dr. Warren, its cover worn from use, the spine cracked from the countless times it had been opened and studied. It felt like a sacred text as she cradled it in her hands, a guidebook to the unseen currents that flowed through all things.

Settling into the armchair that faced the window, Maia flipped to the first page. The words leapt out at her, each sentence a quiet revelation. With each paragraph, the world both expanded and contracted, becoming at once more complex and more intimate. The boundaries between her inner and outer experiences blurred, the barriers erected by years of scientific training and practical work dissolving in the face of something as immeasurable as the soul.

Hours passed; the city's nocturnal sonata was a backdrop to her deepening journey. Maia read, reread, and annotated the margins with her own insights, her thoughts branching out like the neural pathways that defined her very essence. Here, in the quiet of her apartment, surrounded by the sleeping city, she was more than a student.

She was a disciple.

As dawn approached, painting the horizon in hues of pink and gold, Maia finally set the book aside. Her eyes were heavy with fatigue, but her spirit was ablaze with possibility. She knew that come morning, she would return to the demanding rhythms of her job, to the immediacy of life and death decisions. But something fundamental had shifted within her.

She closed her eyes, breathing in the promise of the new day, feeling her place within the infinite expanse of the cosmic mind. In this space between night and light, she understood that her search for meaning was not a solitary quest, but a shared odyssey—one that connected her to the hearts and minds of seekers everywhere.

Synchronicity was not only a thread weaving through her life; it was the loom upon which the very fabric of reality was spun. And Maia, with her heart wide open to the mysteries of existence, was ready to weave her part in its grand design.

Maia stepped out of the building, and the city greeted her with its dissonance of sounds and pulsating energy. Boston's streets lay sprawled before her like veins of life, carrying the essence of countless souls in a grand symphony of existence. Her meeting at the consciousness studies group had ended, but within her, a dialogue of epic proportions was just beginning.

The chill air brushed against her skin, a physical whisper that contrasted with the internal warmth she felt. As she navigated through the throng of pedestrians, her eyes captured snapshots of their lives—each person an enigma, each face a story untold. Maia's thoughts raced as she contemplated the invisible threads connecting these strangers, wondering if they too experienced the strange dance of synchronicity that now occupied her every waking thought.

The hum of the city rose around her, a living entity that pulsed with the very heartbeat of the cosmic mind she sought to understand. Her footsteps carried her rhythmically, a steady beat grounding her swirling thoughts.

Maia felt a connection deeper than any she had known. The concepts Dr. Warren and the others had discussed now wove themselves into her perception, coloring her view of the world with new hues of meaning. Synchronicity was not merely a curiosity; it was a call to explore the uncharted territories of the mind and soul.

The familiar sound of an ambulance siren in the distance brought a sense of clarity. That was her domain, where her compassionate heart and skilled hands worked in harmony to save lives. Yet the pull of the unknown beckoned her with equal force, promising answers to questions that lingered at the edge of her consciousness.

A smile touched Maia's lips as she recognized the interplay of her two worlds—the immediate and the infinite. Each step she took was a deliberate movement toward a destiny intertwined with the enigmatic concept she yearned to decode. Maia knew that soon she would return to her vital work as an EMT. But right now, she was a seeker walking the streets of Boston, her mind alight with the mysteries of synchronicity and the whispers of the cosmic mind.

DOWN THE RABBIT HOLE

Maia's voice quivered with a mix of exhilaration and reverence as they huddled over the cluttered kitchen table, Nina's tablet glowing between them, casting eerie shadows across their faces. Her gaze was locked on the screen, absorbing the details of the research that caused her breathing to catch in her throat.

"Imagine," Nina began, her words plummeting out in an enthusiastic rush, "a realm where you dissolve completely, where your very essence is untethered from the corporeal anchor we call the self." Her fingers danced across the tablet, bringing up diagrams and dense text that spoke of Dimethyltryptamine (DMT)'s ability to unlock doors within the human mind.

"Harvard's study...it's like they're cartographers, charting the inner cosmos, Maia." Nina's eyes shone with an intensity that matched the significance of what she was saying. "They're seeking to understand Ego death, not just as a concept but as a tangible experience. This could be the key, Maia. The key to the universe inside us."

Maia leaned in closer, her athletic frame tensed with anticipation, her practical ponytail swishing as she nodded thoughtfully. She understood the gravity of the moment, the weight of the study's potential revelations pressing down upon her chest. They were perched on the edge of a precipice overlooking an expansive, unknown landscape.

"Think about it," Nina pressed on, her infectious smile betraying her excitement. "Ego death, cosmic consciousness - these aren't just ideas anymore. They could become visceral truths we can visit, explore, maybe even map out for others."

"And if we can truly understand that" Maia added, her voice steady but awash with wonder, "perhaps we'll finally grasp what it is to exist beyond the physical, to connect with the universal energy that binds everything together."

Nina nodded vigorously, her long dark hair cascading over her shoulders as she leaned back, considering the enormity of such a prospect. "Exactly! And who knows what else we might uncover about the mysteries of existence? Harvard's breakthrough could be the dawn of a new understanding, a new era of enlightenment!"

The atmosphere was electric, charged with a sense of adventure and the allure of the unknown. In this small kitchen, amid the routine of daily life, Maia felt a pull towards the vast and uncharted territories of the mind, beckoned by the call of unraveling the fabric of reality itself.

Maia's fingertips trembled slightly as they reached out to trace an invisible arc in the air before her, a gesture that felt like drawing back the veil on a realm she had only dared to ponder in abstracts. The idea of Ego death, of merging with a cosmic consciousness that could stretch infinitely beyond the confines of her own mind, sent an exhilarating shiver through her spine.

"Imagine it," she whispered to herself, more a mantra than a statement. Her eyes, those deep green wells of empathy and wisdom, were burning with the fire of curiosity that had shaped the contours of her life—a passion to heal, to understand, and now, to transcend.

As an EMT, she had stood sentinel at the threshold of life and death, bearing witness to the fragile boundary that separated the two. Yet, this was a different kind of liminality—the beckoning horizon of human understanding itself. To participate in this study wasn't just a leap of faith; it was an odyssey into the very essence of being.

"Decades within hours..." Maia mused, the thought more tantalizing than any siren's song. The potential to live lifetimes within the space of a single day, to converse with the universe's wisdom etched into the fabric of existence itself—how could she turn away from such a promise?

"Knowledge is the vessel, and I am ready to sail," she affirmed, her voice a steady timbre that reverberated through the stillness of her kitchen. With a decisive nod, Maia reached for her laptop, her fingers no longer trembling but purposeful, filled with resolve.

"Dr. Jameson Brooks," she said, rehearsing the introduction in her mind. "I believe my experiences, my understanding of cosmic consciousness, can contribute meaningfully to your study. And I am prepared to embrace the unknown."

The decision was made. As she hit send on her email, initiating contact with the lead researcher, there was no turning back. Maia Yetta Rose had chosen to be a pioneer on this most profound voyage, driven by her desire for direct experience, through the transformative power of DMT, and her unwavering determination to unlock the secrets of the universe.

Her laptop's screen glowed softly in the dim light of Maia's living room as she wrote another email, her fingers pausing over the keys with reverence. Addressed to "Dr. Evelyn Warren", a totem heralding wisdom and guidance. Maia felt an echo of her mentor's tranquil presence, a calming force against the whirlwind of excitement swirling within her.

"Evelyn," she began, "I seek your counsel on a matter of some significance. Harvard Medical School is conducting a DMT study— "

Before she could finish typing, her phone rang interrupting her thoughts. Dr. Warren's voice beckoned with her familiar cadence.

"Maia, my dear, I just had a feeling that something momentous was going on in your life and had to call. Tell me what stirs your soul this evening."

Maia couldn't help but smile at the intuition of her mentor and being able to share her excitement with her close friend.

"I've decided to volunteer for a study that explores ego death through DMT. It's... it's a chance to delve into the very heart of cosmic consciousness, Evelyn. To experience directly what we have been lecturing about for the last year." Her voice was a whisper of awe, laced with a zealous need to understand the mysteries that had long captivated her mentor and herself.

"Ah, the spirit molecule," Dr. Warren speculated, so you are going to visit the nebulous realms beyond ordinary perception. "To dance among the stars within one's own mind—it's a journey you were destined for, Maia."

"Destiny" echoed in Maia's mind, a concept they had dissected under countless starlit skies during their philosophical sojourns. Yet now, it took on a tangible form, as if the universe itself had scripted this moment into being.

"Your insights have always pierced the veil between known and unknown," Dr. Warren continued. "You possess a rare blend of empathy and intellect, a guiding light that will show you the way even in the darkest expanses of inner space."

"Thank you, Evelyn. I feel as though every step I've taken, every life I've touched as an EMT, has been leading me here—to this precipice where knowledge and existence intertwine."

"Remember, Maia," Dr. Warren said, her voice dipping low, filling each word with gravity, "that even as you traverse the boundless, you are not alone. You carry within you the torch of all who have shaped you, all who have believed in you. My dear, I believe in you, unequivocally."

Tears touched the corners of Maia's eyes, gratitude and resolve swelling within her chest. "I will hold onto that torch, and when I return, I hope to share it with you."

"Go forth, and soar my dear," Dr. Warren whispered, a huge smile and a hint of envy in her breath. "Discover what awaits us in the expanse of infinity."

After the call Maia remained still, letting her mentor's words settle upon her like stardust.

She stood up slowly, stretching out the tension that anticipation had woven through her muscles. With each breath, she felt herself becoming better grounded, ready to embark on the voyage that lay before her—a voyage into the furthest reaches of the human psyche, a descent into the abyss with the promise of enlightenment shimmering just beyond the void.

Maia's fingers paused above the keyboard of her laptop, suspended in a moment of silent reverence. A conversation with Dr. Evelyn Warren had left her mind teeming with celestial possibilities. The soft glow of her laptop screen bathed her face in pale blue light, casting shadows across the desk cluttered with notes and open journals. Her eyes, wide with wonder, reflected an inner cosmos expanding beyond the confines of her apartment in Boston.

She clicked through digital archives, her curiosity blazing as she probed into the depths of research papers on dimethyltryptamine - DMT - its structure a simple key to unlock profound realms within the human psyche. The articles unfurled before her; each paragraph, each sentence, a step closer to understanding the enigmatic experience so eloquently explored in her recent dialogue with Dr. Warren.

"Breakthroughs in Consciousness: The Harvard DMT Study" - the title of one paper stood out like a constellation among the academic stars. Maia's heart drummed in her chest, her breaths becoming shallower with anticipation as she absorbed the text. Complex interactions of neurotransmitters and receptors spun a tale of transformation that promised more than mere alteration of thought - it hinted at transcendence.

Images accompanied the dense blocks of text, diagrams of the brain lit up with activity, vibrant as if the neural pathways themselves were alive with electric currents from another dimension.

Maia envisioned the molecule, its simplicity belying the complexity of the doorways it opened within the mind. She could almost hear Dr. Warren's voice, a calm current beneath the surge of excitement, reminding her of the potential for enlightenment resting dormant in every synapse.

"Imagine," Dr. Warren had said, "a substance that could dissolve the barriers between self and universe, allowing you to commune with the universe."

The concept was intoxicating. Maia pictured herself adrift in the cosmic ocean, her sense of 'I' dissipating like mist under the morning sun. The idea of time stretching, folding upon itself until decades could be lived in mere hours, seemed both fantastical and within reach. Maia continued to navigate through the sea of knowledge, each click bringing her closer to the voyage of her soul.

Her athletic frame leaned forward, muscles tensed with eagerness, her expressive eyes scanning line after line, her mind already dancing at the edge of the universe. With each new revelation, her resolve solidified; she was ready to embark on this odyssey, to explore the farthest reaches of cosmic consciousness and return with the knowledge etched into the very fabric of her being.

Outside, the city buzzed with life, unaware of the silent threshold that Maia was poised to cross, where twelve hours in the world of matter could unfold into lifetimes within the infinite expanse of the mind. She felt a kinship with explorers of old, charting unknown territories not of earth or sea, but of the boundless human spirit. The night awaited, and with it, a journey beyond the veil of reality, into the heart of existence itself.

She leaned back in her chair, an orbit of thoughts whirling around her. The possibility of experiencing Ego death—of standing at the precipice of her own consciousness and peering into the vast cosmic mind—exhilarated her.

A shiver ran down Maia's spine, both from anticipation and the sudden wave of trepidation that washed over her.

It was like standing at the edge of a celestial cliff, the abyss below both inviting and formidable. The unknown beckoned her with a siren call, its melodies woven from the very stars themselves.

"Decades..." she murmured to herself, contemplating the subjective eons she might spend in communion with entities beyond mortal kind. Her practical nature warred with her longing for transcendence. Would the wisdom gained be worth the gamble?

Maia urged her own reflection in the darkened windowpane, "the rewards... they could redefine everything."

Maia stared into the quiet room, her heart a pendulum swinging between eagerness and apprehension. The chasm of cosmic consciousness awaited, a realm where decades could pass in the span of a day, where the soul could dance with the divine or lose itself in the eternal expanse.

The room around her seemed to pulse with silent anticipation. She pictured herself adrift in an ocean of stars, each wave a decade of discovery cresting beneath her. There, time would unravel, and she would swim through centuries in pursuit of answers that had eluded humanity since the dawn of thought.

Maia's fingers hovered over her phone, trembling slightly with anticipation. She gathered the courage to dial the number that could bridge her reality with the unknown. She pressed the call button; the line rang once, twice, "Dr. Jameson Brooks speaking," came the voice, clear and resolute, slicing through the static of Maia's thoughts.

"Dr. Brooks, this is Maia Rose. We haven't met, but Dr. Warren mentioned your DMT study at Harvard, and I'm very interested in participating."

"Ah, yes, Dr. Warren speaks highly of you," Dr. Brooks replied, his tone acknowledging the weight of her mentor's endorsement. "Your curiosity about cosmic consciousness aligns with the focus of our research."

Maia felt her resolve strengthen. "I've been exploring the concept for years, and it seems your study might provide the insights I've been seeking."

"Very well, let me outline what you'd be undertaking," Dr. Brooks said, pausing as if to arrange his thoughts into precise, clinical sentences. "We're investigating the effects of an extended twelve-hour IV drip of DMT on the human brain. This has never been done before. All our previous studies have only lasted for one hour. This isn't a light affair, Ms. Rose. The risks are real."

"Risks?" Maia echoed, the word hanging between them like a shadow.

"Indeed. The experience can be... expansive, even overwhelming. Subjects report profound encounters, perceptions of alternate realities, and interactions with entities we've termed 'Ascended Beings'. Time dilates profoundly under the influence - decades can pass in the mindscape within mere hours of our time."

Maia's breath caught at the mention of the Ascended Beings, her intuition resonating with something primal, a truth buried deep within the fabric of the cosmos. "And through this, one could gain insight into the nature of self, the universe?"

"Potentially," Dr. Brooks continued, his voice steady, betraying none of the excitement that was mounting within Maia. "Our subjects have experienced ego death, merging with what they describe as a cosmic mind. It's as if their individual consciousness expands to touch the edges of the universe itself."

"Participants have reported profound shifts in perspective, an intensified sense of interconnectedness with the universe. Many describe it as a rebirth of consciousness—a dismantling of the ego that allows the self to reform without the boundaries we take for granted."

His words painted strokes of possibility across the canvas of her mind.

Images fluttered in her consciousness: figures of light and energy, landscapes undulating with the breath of creation, the echo of a cosmic symphony that promised to untangle the very fabric of her being.

"Imagine, Ms. Rose, the opportunity to converse with Ascended Beings, entities that dwell in realms our science is only beginning to grasp. It's not just about personal growth; it's a voyage into the heart of existence itself."

"Think of it, Maia," he continued, his words lacing through her hesitation like threads of certainty, "to navigate the expanse of cosmic consciousness—not as a fleeting dream, but as decades of lived experience. What you learn could change everything."

The words painted a vivid panorama in Maia's mind, a landscape where the boundaries of existence were not merely pushed but shattered. A place where every atom of her being could dance with the stars, sing with the void, and whisper secrets with the fabric of space-time.

"Are you prepared for such a journey, Ms. Rose?" Dr. Brooks asked, his question slicing through the reverie.

With a conviction birthed from the depths of her soul, Maia responded, "More than you know, Dr. Brooks. More than you know."

"Dr. Brooks," Maia's voice was steady, though it carried the weight of her anticipation. "Before we proceed, I need to understand the specifics of what I'm walking into. Can you walk me through the study protocol and what safety measures are in place?"

"Of course, Ms. Rose," Dr. Brooks replied, his tone clinical yet not without a tinge of respect for her diligence. "We've established a comprehensive protocol. The 12-hour duration of the infusion is segmented into stages, each meticulously monitored."

Maia leaned forward; her gaze fixed on the soft glow of her laptop screen as if the answers might manifest there.

"And the risks? Side effects are inevitable in a trial like this."

"Indeed," he acknowledged. "Subjects report varying degrees of disorientation post-infusion, often accompanied by mild nausea. We take every precaution to mitigate these side effects. Your vitals will be closely watched by our medical team, ready to intervene at any sign of distress."

"Your assurance is comforting," Maia noted, her fingers tracing the edge of her desk, grounding herself. "But what about psychological aftereffects? A prolonged exposure to DMT could profoundly alter one's psyche."

"True, the psychological landscape can shift," Dr. Brooks said, the faintest hint of fascination creeping into his otherwise detached delivery. "However, we've found that proper integration therapy post-experience aids participants in reconciling their journey with their daily lives. You'll have access to our therapists specializing in psychedelic aftercare, and of course Dr. Warren will be an invaluable support."

"Integration therapy," Maia repeated thoughtfully. "That suggests you've anticipated profound changes. I trust your team is prepared for any outcome?"

"Absolutely," Dr. Brooks reassured her. "We've assembled professionals skilled in emergency response, psychiatric support, and holistic care. No participant is left to navigate the aftermath alone."

"Good," Maia said, a single word encapsulating both her satisfaction with his answers and her readiness to face the unknown. Her mind already grasped at the edges of that otherworldly expanse, yearning to unravel its mysteries.

"Excellent," Dr. Brooks concluded. "We pride ourselves on the caliber of our personnel and our commitment to participant well-being."

"Then I'm ready," Maia affirmed, the decision resonating through her core. The path lay open, a conduit to realms uncharted, and she, a willing voyager to the very brink of consciousness.

"Let's move forward with the practicalities," Dr. Brooks said, his voice a tether of clarity amidst the anticipation humming through Maia's veins. "We'll need to schedule your sessions and conduct a thorough medical evaluation to ensure you're fit for the study."

She nodded, though he couldn't see her affirmation. "When do we begin?" Maia asked, poised at the edge of her seat, her hand hovering over her laptop taking notes as if ready to encode her destiny.

"Firstly, you'll come in next week for preliminary screenings—blood tests, a physical examination, and a psychological assessment. Assuming all is well, we'll schedule your first DMT session," Dr. Brooks outlined with meticulous care.

"Understood. And preparation? Is there anything specific I should be doing?" Her question was a lifeline cast into the ocean of unknowns.

"Abstain from alcohol, maintain a healthy diet, and try to meditate or engage in any practice that centers you. The clearer your mind before the infusion, the more profound your journey may be."

"Thank you, Dr. Brooks. I'll follow those guidelines closely." Maia's fingers danced across her laptop, each word an engraved intention.

"Excellent. I'll have my assistant send over the consent forms and additional information. Review them carefully. We prioritize safety above everything," he continued. "Our medical team will be present at all times during the administration. You're in good hands, Ms. Rose."

"Thank you for ensuring this path is paved with care," Maia responded, her heart buoyant with trust and resolve.

"Indeed," he affirmed, the finality in his voice punctuating their conversation. "Welcome aboard, Maia. We're on the cusp of something extraordinary."

"Looking forward to it, Dr. Brooks," she breathed out, her gaze fixed on the unseen horizons unfolding before her.

The chime of an antique brass bell heralded Maia Yetta Rose's arrival into Dr. Evelyn Warren's sanctuary, a study that breathed with the essence of countless spiritual journeys. Walls lined with towering bookshelves cradled volumes upon volumes on cosmic consciousness, their spines a mosaic of gilded letters and worn leather. Between them, artifacts whispered tales from beyond—the glint of Tibetan singing bowls, the muted colors of Aboriginal dot paintings, and the intricate geometry of sacred mandalas.

Maia paused, taking in a slow breath as if to absorb the room's tranquil energy, her athletic frame casting a slender shadow upon the Persian rug that adorned the hardwood floor. The air felt alive, charged with an unseen current that hummed through her veins, heightening her senses. Her gaze lingered on a particularly ornate text, spine cracked, and pages yellowed, evidence of its journey through time and thought.

"Maia," came the voice, as serene as the garden breeze, "please, come and take a seat."

Dr. Warren stood by the large window, its panes framing a living portrait of stillness. The garden beyond bloomed in defiance of the urban sprawl of Boston, a patch of Eden where even the city's clamor bowed to the whisper of rustling leaves and the soft symphony of bird calls. With the grace of one who has mastered the art of presence, she beckoned Maia toward a chair bathed in the afternoon sunlight, its cushion an invitation to repose.

"Thank you, Evelyn," Maia responded, her voice filled with reverence for this mentor who had become her guide through the intricate pathways of the mind. She settled into the chair, its embrace familiar and comforting against her back, and faced the verdant expanse that stretched beyond the glass.

Dr. Warren returned the smile, her eyes reflecting a wisdom born of years spent exploring the inner cosmos. She joined Maia, claiming her own seat, their shared silence a prelude to revelation.

Each breath they drew was a silent ode to the moment, a sacred pause before the odyssey that lay ahead—an odyssey not of space and stars, but of the boundless realms within.

And as they sat there, mentor and mentee, two souls bound by the quest for enlightenment, the study seemed to recede, giving way to something far more profound—a sense of connection with all that is, was, and ever could be. It was here, in this very room, that the gateway to Maia's DMT journey would swing wide open, propelling her into the vibrant fabric of the universe where decades would pass like dreams within the span of a single Earthly day.

The silence in Dr. Warren's study was a living entity, a serene presence that wrapped around Maia like a shroud. She could feel the weight of her recent experiences as a substantial force within her chest, tethering her to a reality vastly expanded by her newfound insights.

"Evelyn," Maia began, the words rippling through the still air, "lately, I've felt the fabric of my being interwoven with something... grander. During my shifts, when life teeters on the brink, I sense a profound unity. It's as if every heartbeat I strive to save echoes through me, reminding me that we are all but fragments of a single consciousness."

Dr. Warren's eyes shimmered with understanding. "That sensation is the whisper of cosmic consciousness. You're feeling the pulse of existence itself, Maia. With each life you touch, you become more attuned to the symphony of the universe."

There was a deliberate pause, a moment for the gravity of those words to sink in before Dr. Warren continued, her voice carrying the ethereal quality of someone who had transcended mere academia.

"Many years ago," she said, her gaze drifting towards the mountains of memory, "I found myself perched in silent meditation amid the snow-kissed peaks of the Himalayas.

I sat there, enveloped by a silence so profound it roared in my ears, and that's when it happened." A faint smile graced her lips. "My self—this construct of Evelyn Warren—dissolved into the ether, and I became one with the web of life. It wasn't just about losing the ego; it was about realizing that the energy which animated me was the same that sparked stars into being."

Maia listened, rapt, as Dr. Warren painted a picture with her tale, the imagery so vivid that Maia could feel the chill Himalayan wind on her skin. The idea that this woman beside her had touched the ineffable and returned with such clarity filled Maia with a mixture of awe and yearning.

"Imagine," Dr. Warren whispered, as though confiding a sacred secret, "realizing that time is but an illusion, that decades can unfold within you while outside, seasons change in the span of a breath. That is the gift of true consciousness, the promise of your journey with DMT."

Maia absorbed the magnitude of what lay ahead, her mentor's words etching themselves into her soul, she knew with crystalline certainty that her own odyssey was not just about exploration—it was about coming home.

Maia leaned forward, an orb of golden light from the study's antique lamp dancing in her eyes. Dr. Warren's voice wove through the air as she elucidated mysteries that, until now, had danced just beyond Maia's grasp.

"Evelyn," Maia began, her voice a steady stream flowing into an ocean of inquiry, "when you speak of consciousness expanding beyond our physical form, is it akin to the sensation of waking from a dream? One where we're both the dreamer and the dream itself?"

"An astute observation, Maia," Dr. Warren responded, the corners of her mouth curving upwards with approval. "It's that very realization—that we are the architects of our reality—which is so liberating."

The room pulsed with the rhythm of their dialogue; each question Maia posed unfurling like a petal reaching for sunlight. With each answer, Dr. Warren planted seeds of wisdom deep within Maia's fertile mind.

"Let's begin," Dr. Warren suggested after a pause that held the weight of eons. She rose gracefully and gestured towards two cushions positioned before the large window. The garden outside was a tableau of serenity, its blossoms and leaves swaying gently, as if to the cadence of an unseen conductor.

Maia settled onto her cushion, mirroring Dr. Warren's cross-legged posture. A beam of sunlight found its way through the glass, casting a warm glow on the scene. As she closed her eyes, the world faded, leaving only the sound of their synchronous breathing—a whisper shared between the walls of infinity.

"Focus on your breath," Dr. Warren instructed, her words no louder than a brush of wings. "Feel the life force that enters you, animating your being, connecting you to the vast expanse of creation."

The air became a river of tranquility flowing through Maia, her chest rising and falling in gentle tides. Thoughts ebbed away as if carried off by a cosmic breeze, leaving her anchored in the present moment.

"Visualize your consciousness expanding," Dr. Warren continued, her voice now a distant echo. "With each breath, push the boundaries of your awareness further into the universe."

Within her mind's eye, she became insubstantial, her essence stretching outwards, touching the edges of galaxies, whispering across the surface of distant planets. Time dilated, stretched, contracted—became irrelevant.

There, in the silent communion with all existence, Maia touched the face of eternity. Her heart, a drumbeat in harmony with the cosmos, knew this was but the prelude to the symphony awaiting her.

This the grand voyage through the corridors of her own psyche with the aid of the "Spirit Molecule."

She would travel not merely as an observer but as an integral note in the universal melody. Maybe even resonating with the Ascended Beings whose wisdom spanned the ages. Though the journey might last decades in the timeless expanse of her mind, she would emerge only half a day later, reborn into the world she left behind, armed with insights that transcended the temporal shell of her existence.

Maia's consciousness rippled like a serene lake touched by the breath of dawn. The meditation had taken her deep within, to spaces uncharted and serene. Dr. Warren's study, an earthly sanctuary of knowledge and spirit, seemed to dissolve around her, replaced by the vastness of space. The quiet rustle of pages from ancient texts became the distant whispers of stars.

The boundaries of Maia's self began to blur, edges softening until they were indistinguishable from the cosmic fabric surrounding her. The particles of her being mingled with the stardust, and she felt a profound peace that eclipsed all prior understanding. She was no longer merely Maia Yetta Rose; she was a continuum, part of the endless expanse, a child of the cosmos.

"Let this feeling guide you," Dr. Warren's voice beckoned from somewhere far away, "as you journey further."

In the afterglow of the meditation, Maia's senses remained heightened, attuned to frequencies beyond the ordinary spectrum. Dr. Warren's presence now felt like a gentle gravitational pull, guiding her through the next phase of exploration.

"Imagine," Dr. Warren instructed, "that you are a beam of light. Radiant, pure, boundless."

Closing her eyes again, Maia obeyed, her imagination unfurling like sails in a cosmic wind.

She envisioned herself as a brilliant thread of luminosity, weaving through all of existence. Her light connected with the essences of others—past, present, and future. She saw luminaries that outshone constellations, their wisdom etched into the very fabric of the universe.

She danced among them, a radiant entity moving with grace through astral planes. Their knowledge sang to her, a celestial chorus that filled her with ecstasy. Each note vibrated through her essence, teaching, enlightening, transforming.

Maia experienced lifetimes of love, loss, creation, and discovery. She drank deeply from the well of the cosmos, each sip more intoxicating than the last.

When Maia finally opened her eyes, the garden outside the window bloomed in silent affirmation of her transcendental odyssey. Dr. Warren's study embraced her return, its serenity a gentle cradle for her expanded soul. The talisman in her hand—a tangible anchor to the physical realm—pulsed with the energy of her journey.

"Welcome back," Dr. Warren said, her smile a knowing crescent. "You have traveled far."

Maia nodded, her voice a tranquil murmur. "I have seen the interconnection of all things, felt the pulse of the universe itself."

"Remember this feeling," Dr. Warren advised, her eyes reflecting pride and empathy. "It will be your compass on the journey ahead."

Maia stood; her movements deliberate yet imbued with a new fluidity. The DMT experience awaited her, but she already carried within her the wisdom of eons, a gift from meditation and visualization that had so vividly bridged her spirit with the cosmic mind.

Maia reached out, her fingers grazing the textured spines of the ancient knowledge that lined Dr. Warren's shelves. Each book was a vessel of sacred knowledge, their pages worn by the touch of countless seekers before her.

With a reverence that bordered on the ceremonial, she withdrew a volume bound in leather that whispered tales of the eternal and the infinite.

"Within these writings," Dr. Warren's voice held the weight of history, "you'll find the threads that weave the tapestry of the universe."

Maia turned the pages delicately, as if each leaf might crumble under the weight of its own profound wisdom. Prose that spoke of worlds within worlds danced before her eyes, igniting synapses with sparks of understanding. She had read of mystics who had traversed the astral planes, of philosophers who had dissected the fabric of reality with nothing but the scalpel of their intellect.

"Reality is not merely what we perceive with our senses," Dr. Warren continued, her tone grounding yet expansive. "It's interconnected in ways that defy our conventional understanding. It's the pulsating energy beneath the still waters of perception."

Maia absorbed the words, her mind stretching to encompass the vastness of the concept. Ideas of interconnectivity resonated within her, harmonizing with the lingering vibrations of her meditation journey.

"Embrace the unknown, Maia," Dr. Warren encouraged gently. "The path you're about to walk in this study will illuminate the spaces between stars, the silence between notes. The universe speaks in many voices; you must simply learn to listen."

Nodding slowly, Maia felt the last remnants of trepidation dissolve into a sea of tranquility. Her mentor's assurance was the lighthouse guiding her toward a horizon brimming with the unexplored, the mysterious, the transformative. The adventure that loomed was not one of fear but of discovery - an odyssey through the inner cosmos where time folded upon itself, where decades were mere heartbeats.

"Thank you," Maia whispered, her gratitude enveloping the room. "I'm ready to listen."

"Good," Dr. Warren said, her smile echoing Maia's. "Because the cosmos has been waiting to speak to you, Maia. Since the beginning of everything."

Dr. Warren rose from her chair, the soft fabric whispering a farewell as she moved gracefully across the room to an intricately carved mahogany cabinet. Maia watched, her breath caught between curiosity and anticipation, the air in the study thick with the scent of old books and sandalwood. The elder woman's hand paused on an ornate handle before pulling open a drawer with deliberate care.

"Throughout your studies, you've shown remarkable courage and commitment, Maia," Dr. Warren said. She turned back to face Maia, holding a small object nestled in the cradle of her palm. "I believe this will serve you well on the journey ahead."

It was a talisman, ancient and mysterious, its metallic surface etched with symbols that danced and shimmered in the dim light. As Dr. Warren extended her hand, Maia reached out, her fingers trembling slightly as they brushed against the cool metal. The moment their skin touched, an electric charge of connection sparked between mentor and mentee.

"Carry this as a reminder of the bond we share," Dr. Warren whispered.

Maia clasped the talisman tightly, feeling its weight tying her to this moment, to this reality. A surge of gratitude swelled within her chest. With the talisman came a flood of determination, a readiness to dive into the depths of consciousness and emerge reborn.

"Thank you," Maia breathed out, standing to face Dr. Warren. Her eyes glistened with a world of emotions—appreciation, reverence, and an unspoken promise to honor the wisdom imparted to her. "For everything."

"Be brave, my dear," Dr. Warren replied, her arms opening in an invitation as warm as the sun breaking through the morning mist.

Maia stepped into the embrace, their connection a tangible force that transcended the physical space around them. In this silent communion, words were superfluous; everything that needed to be said resonated in the two hearts aligned in purpose.

As they parted, an ineffable understanding lingered in the air, a shared acknowledgment of the profound odyssey upon which Maia was about to embark. The talisman, now warm from their touch, pulsed with an energy that promised revelations of the universe's deepest secrets—a bridge between the seen and unseen, the known and the mystery yet to unravel.

With a final nod, Maia tucked the talisman close to her heart, where it lay hidden but fiercely alive against her skin. Each step she took away from Dr. Warren, away from the sanctuary of the study, was one step closer to the vast expanse of cosmic truth awaiting her discovery.

Maia's hand hovered over the doorknob, a lingering warmth from Dr. Warren's touch still imprinted on her skin. The talisman pressed against her chest was a reminder of what lay ahead, its weight light yet profound. She turned the knob and stepped over the threshold, leaving the steady cadence of ticking clocks and the scent of aged parchment behind. The world outside seemed to pause, acknowledging the gravity of her departure.

The garden greeted her with an explosion of life that contrasted starkly with the solemnity of her decision. Bees danced in the air, their buzzing a symphony for the vibrant blossoms they courted.

She closed her eyes, inhaled deeply, and let the garden's essence fill her lungs. The air was crisp, laden with the earthy aroma of damp soil and the sweet tang of ripening fruit. The sun's rays caressed her face, a gentle kiss that ignited every cell within her.

With each breath, she drew in strength and exhaled trepidation, her spirit swelling with eager anticipation.

Around her, the garden was alive with the hum of nature's persistence, a reminder of the continuous cycle of transformation. She imagined herself as part of this eternal rhythm, her being resonating with the pulse of all creation. Every leaf, every droplet of dew, every whisper of wind was a note in the grand symphony of existence, and she, too, was ready to contribute her verse.

Maia's mind painted vivid strokes across the canvas of her imagination, conjuring images of transcendent landscapes where time held no dominion. In her mind's eye, she stood at the precipice of infinity, gazing into an abyss teeming with celestial wonders.

Opening her eyes, Maia took one last look at Dr. Warren's study, the fortress of wisdom from which she had emerged. The garden, now imprinted in her memory, would be a light through the tumultuous voyage that awaited. With a heart brimming with courage and a mind thirsty for enlightenment, she turned towards the path leading away from the sanctuary.

The city's gray palette was punctuated by bursts of life—a child's laughter, a street vendor's call, a fluttering bird—that seemed to resonate with the newfound frequencies humming within her.

Her apartment awaited, its familiar contours now housing the anticipation of transformation. As she turned the key, the click of the lock was not just an audible confirmation but a harmonic chime in tune with her readiness. Inside, Maia moved with purpose, each gesture deliberate and unhurried. She prepared her space with ritualistic precision, laying out comfortable clothes for her physical vessel and arranging cushions as if they were the foundation stones of a sacred temple.

She showered, letting the water cleanse away any remnants of doubt or hesitation. With every droplet that cascaded down her skin, she envisioned impurities dissolving, her intention rinsing clear and pure. Wrapped in a towel, Maia caught her reflection in the fogged mirror—her eyes, those windows to cosmic realms, sparkled with an inner light that foretold the journey ahead.

Maia Yetta Rose stepped through the glass doors of Harvard Medical School, her pulse quickening as the clinical symphony of beeping monitors and clicking keyboards enveloped her. The air carried a faint antiseptic tang that mingled with the undercurrents of excitement buzzing from the cluster of participants. She scanned the room, noting the gleam of medical equipment that stood like silent sentinels awaiting their patients.

Her gaze landed on the two familiar figures. Samantha "Sam" Spencer, a whirlwind of vibrant energy encased in a kaleidoscope of fabric, and Vivian Lang, whose presence was like a still lake—calm and deep. Maia smiled as Sam caught her eye, giving a small wave. Vivian's nod was more reserved, a gentle acknowledgment steeped in the quiet solidarity they shared.

They exchanged a moment—a triad of smiles and nods, each gesture weaving them into an unspoken bond of support and curiosity. Maia felt the nervous flutter in her stomach settle, replaced by a burgeoning sense of camaraderie. Here, in this sterile space, they were pioneers on the cusp of a great unknown, their individual quests for understanding about to unfold within the mind's vast expanse.

The anticipation was a tangible force that hummed beneath Maia's skin as she took a steadying breath, readying herself to step beyond the veil of reality and into the realm of the extraordinary.

Maia's fingertips grazed the edge of the paper, crisp and cool, as she reached for the consent form at the registration desk. The words were a ballet of legal jargon and scientific terminology that did little to quell the fluttering in her chest. She skimmed over the paragraphs, a rapid scan punctuated by the pulsing rhythm of her heart.

"Everything is going to change," she whispered to herself, the sound barely audible above the chorus of soft murmurs and the occasional clink of medical instruments being prepped for use.

Folding the document with deliberate care, Maia turned and found herself enveloped in the waiting area's hushed expectancy. Sam's green eyes sparkled with an artist's hunger for the unknown, while Vivian exuded a serene sense of searching, her gaze holding the patience of trees.

"Hey," Sam greeted her, voice filled with warmth as her curls bounced with an eager nod. "Ready to dive into the cosmic ocean?"

"You betcha," Maia replied, settling next to them. Her athletic build contrasted with the softness of the chairs, yet she eased into the support.

"Think we'll find what we're looking for?" Vivian's question, soft-spoken but laden with depth, hung between them.

"Seek and ye shall find," Maia said, offering a smile that carried the weight of planets—a silent reassurance that they were bound by more than just their presence in this room.

"Or maybe it'll find us," Sam mused, her eyes glinting with the potential of an empty canvas.

"Either way," Maia added, "we're stepping through a doorway. What lies beyond...it's as much within us as it is out there."

Their conversation gently flowed, the kind of small talk that was anything but small—each word a drop in the vast pool of their collective anticipation. They shared stories of past experiences, each tale a tape and texture to the rich fabric of their expectations.

Hopes of enlightenment, fears of the abyss, all woven together in a patchwork quilt.

"Twelve hours on the clock," Sam said, glancing at the wall where time ticked away, witness to the odyssey about to unfold within their minds.

"Decades, perhaps, in our perception," Maia added thoughtfully, her voice steady beneath the surface of her nervous excitement. "An entire lifetime distilled into a single day."

"May we live it fully," Vivian intoned, to the universe whispered from the sanctuary of their shared vulnerability.

They sat in camaraderie, three souls perched on the cusp of infinity, each beat of their hearts a countdown to the moment when the veil would be lifted and the journey within would begin. And as they waited, the reality of the sterile room around them seemed to fade, giving way to the promise of realms unseen.

"Maia Yetta Rose," the voice cut through the murmur of the room, clear and clinical. Maia inhaled deeply, her chest rising with a promise to herself. She turned to Sam and Vivian, her gaze lingering on her friends and kindred spirits.

"See you on the other side," she said, her words tinged with the gravity of what lay ahead. Their smiles were brave, their nods filled with an understanding that transcended spoken language. With a final squeeze of hands, she rose from the comfort of their shared anticipation and crossed the threshold into the unknown.

The preparation room was a stark contrast to the world she had just left. Fluorescent lights hummed overhead, casting a clinical glow over the space. A hospital gown lay folded at the foot of a bed that seemed more like a vessel for a space flight than a piece of medical equipment. Maia's movements were deliberate as she exchanged her clothes for the uniform of the experiment, her skin prickling with the cool touch of the fabric.

With each step towards the bed her heart pounded harder in anticipation. Reclining, she allowed the plush contours of the mattress to cradle her body. The researchers' hands were gentle yet purposeful as they affixed electrodes to her scalp, a constellation of connections mapping the terrain of her thoughts. The cold gel squished beneath the sensors, sending a shiver down her spine—a physical echo of the enormity of her decision.

"Relax, Maia," one of the researchers murmured, their voice both a suggestion and a comfort. Her eyes tracked their movements, each instrument a herald of the deep dive into her psyche. She focused on her breathing, the rise and fall of her chest, a mantra grounding her to the moment.

The last electrode clicked into place, a tether linking her to the realm of waking analysis while her spirit prepared to soar beyond the veil of illusion. Maia's eyes fluttered closed, her face a serene mask that belied the whirlwind of emotions within. In her own mind, she stood at the precipice of discovery, ready to embrace the cosmic truth.

The lead researcher leaned forward, her voice a steady stream of information that flowed over Maia's heightened senses. "Once we begin, the DMT will take you on a journey much longer than any clock can measure. Your perception of time will be profoundly altered," she explained, her words punctuated by the soft hiss of the IV machine.

Maia drew in a deep breath, her eyes tracing the sterile geometry of the room—the squareness of the cabinets, the perfect circularity of the electrode pads affixed to her body. She exhaled slowly, feeling the clinical chill of the air mingle with the warmth radiating from her core. A nod was her silent assent, her heartbeat a steady drumroll against her ribs.

"Are you ready?" the researcher asked, her eyes providing her unspoken encouragement.

"Ready," Maia affirmed, her voice resolute in the sea of uncertainty.

With a practiced motion, the researcher initiated the IV drip. Maia watched the liquid travel along the clear tubing, the fuel for her journey into the vast unknown. Then, the first drop entered her bloodstream, and a tingling sensation blossomed at the site, sending ripples of electricity dancing across her skin.

She closed her eyes, the darkness behind her eyelids becoming a screen for the spectacle to come. The initial prickling grew into a warm, spreading flush that promised to unlock doors within her mind. Maia surrendered, her body relaxing into the bed as her catalyst coursed through her veins, a river charting new pathways through the landscape of her consciousness.

Outside, the world would continue its relentless march forward, but inside, Maia had all the time she needed to explore the depths of existence. The tempo of her heart slowed, each beat fading into the distance as she drifted away from the physical realm, embarking on an odyssey that would span lifetimes within the span of half a day.

The fabric of reality buckled, twisted, and unfurled around Maia as the "Spirit Molecule" seized her senses. She was a solitary voyager, sailing across an ocean where time flowed not in streams but in ripples and waves. Each heartbeat, once so distinct, now blended into an endless symphony of rhythm, the tempo of life itself stretched thin and played over aeons.

Colors erupted before her closed eyes, dazzling and intense; they pulsed with the very essence of existence. The sterile white walls of the preparation room dissolved into an iridescent spectrum, each hue singing its own melody. The air itself began to vibrate with this energy. Maia felt it resonate within her core, harmonizing with the molecules of her being.

She was no longer lying on the bed or even tied to the physical plane. Her consciousness soared, expanding beyond the confines of her flesh, reaching out to embrace the infinite.

The vastness of the cosmos cradled her, a child once more, in the arms of a universe teeming with wonders unspoken and unseen.

Lights appeared, guides composed purely of luminescence and vibrancy. They were the architects of realms that defied the laws she had known. With a serenity that echoed the stars, they beckoned her forward, their forms shifting—now geometric, now fluid, always perfect.

"Maia Yetta Rose," they whispered, a chorus of energy rather than voice, "witness."

Through dimensions woven from the threads of potentiality, through landscapes that breathed and danced with a logic all their own, they led her. They revealed secrets inscribed in the fabric of space-time; truths that resonated with the wisdom Dr. Warren had only glimpsed through the lens of academia and her own meditations.

Each revelation was a lifetime, a chapter in the cosmic narrative she was now part of. With every insight imparted by these celestial guides, Maia understood more profoundly the interconnected web of existence. She saw how each soul's thread contributed to the grand design, a tapestry of incalculable beauty and complexity.

There was no fear, no hesitation, as she traversed the astral planes. The entities instilled within her a sense of purpose, a sense of belonging to something far greater than herself. The woman who had once grounded her life in the tactile, in the immediate pulse of emergency and response, now embraced the ethereal, the eternal pulse of universal truth.

Decades passed in the blink of an eye, a mere breath in the lifespan of the cosmos, yet for Maia, they were rich with growth and understanding. She lived a thousand lives among the stars, each one painting another stroke on the canvas of her soul.

Time had unfurled like a ribbon in the wind, infinite and ever-changing. Maia, propelled by an unseen force, journeyed through realms where nebulous concepts took tangible form. Galaxies spiraled within her grasp, stars pulsed to the rhythm of her heartbeat, and she danced along the edge of black holes that hummed with the secrets of existence.

She soared across an astral sea, each wave a different shade of consciousness. The dance of particles and waves, the very essence of quantum mechanics, played out before her eyes—a ballet of possibility choreographed by the universe itself. Maia, the perpetual student, had watched with rapt attention, her mind expanding with each revelation.

"Everything is connected," she whispered, her voice a mere vibration amidst the celestial harmony. "The cosmos is a symphony, and we are notes in an exquisite composition."

In that boundless expanse, time was not a line but a dimension to explore, its layers filled with profound introspection. She delved into the past, witnessed civilizations rise and fall, understanding that their legacies were woven into the fabric of now. Every action, every thought rippled through the cosmic tapestry, leaving an imprint for eternity.

While Maia was basking in the awe of interconnectivity, a figure emerged from the luminescence. It was a being of indescribable beauty, composed of pure energy, its presence resonating with the wisdom of ages. It approached her, its form shimmering as if it were both there and not there, a paradox made manifest.

"Maia Yetta Rose," its voice heard directly in her soul.

"Who are you?" Maia asked, her composure steady despite the crescendo of uncertainty rising within her.

"I am a guide," it replied, "a reflection of your innermost self."

The entity reached out, and where its hand should have been, Maia saw the countless strands of her own life.

It intertwining with those of others, a complex web of interactions and experiences.

"Your perception shapes your reality," the guide continued. "But what if your perception is limited? What if there is more beyond the veil of your understanding?"

Maia felt a jolt of doubt. Her beliefs, the foundation of her cosmic exploration, wavered under the scrutiny of this entity. Had her pursuit of knowledge been a chase after shadows, an illusion crafted by her own mind?

"Question everything," the guide urged, its form dissipating into a haze of light. "Doubt is the beginning of a deeper knowing. Embrace it."

Maia stood at the precipice of uncertainty; her prior convictions challenged. Yet, within that doubt, a seed of determination took root. She would not falter; she would seek the truths hidden behind her questions.

The realms continued to unfold around her, offering no respite, no easy answers. She was adrift in a sea of wonders and mysteries, each one beckoning her closer, whispering promises of enlightenment. And Maia, the healer, an EMT who had comforted countless souls in their darkest hours, accepted the challenge. She would navigate this odyssey of the mind, where every moment held the weight of eons, and emerge with the light of understanding she so fiercely sought.

Maia, the essence of resilience, stood firm amid the cosmic tempest. Her heart, a steady drumbeat, resonated with the pulsating energy of the realms she traversed. The guide's words, an echo in the vast expanse, ignited an inferno of resolve within her. She drew breath, a breath that spanned galaxies, and with it, she summoned the fortitude from the very fabric of her being.

"Uncertainty is not my enemy," she whispered to herself, her voice a gentle ripple that somehow permeated the infinite void. "It is the crucible in which truth is forged."

The echoes of her mentor, Dr. Evelyn Warren, resounded like ancient hymns in her mind. Maia imagined their shared moments, the late-night discussions under a canopy of stars, each one a beacon in her current odyssey. Those memories were her allies, her companions in the solitude of exploration. With every insight gleaned from her mentor's wisdom, Maia fortified her spirit, weaving a shield of philosophy and love against the barrage of existential questions.

As if responding to her inner light, the entities of energy that had been mere observers now converged around her. They pulsed with an otherworldly glow; a kaleidoscope of colors too profound for mortal eyes. Their presence bolstered her courage, a tangible reminder that she was not alone on this journey through the enigmatic fabric of consciousness.

"Show me," she implored, her voice steady, emboldened by the silent support of these luminous entities. "I am ready to bear witness to the truths that lie hidden in the folds of reality."

The voyage had reached a zenith, and the boundaries of understanding stretched beyond their limits. Maia embraced the expanse, her identity diffusing into the grandeur of all existence. What were moments or millennia passed as she danced with revelations, each step a deeper communion with the universal dance of life itself.

Then, as subtly as the onset of twilight, the vibrancy began to wane. The brilliant hues dimmed, and the once-majestic vistas gently retracted their embrace. Maia felt the pull of her physical form, the tether to her earthly vessel growing stronger. A cascade of sensations returned—the softness of the bed beneath her, the whisper of air across her skin.

Her eyelids, heavy with the weight of eons, fluttered open. The sterile room materialized before her, the machinery and electrodes that anchored her to this plane a stark contrast to the ethereal realms she had roamed. Yet, there was no jar of re-entry, no sense of loss.

Instead, a profound peace enveloped her, a tranquility born from the acceptance of the great journey's end.

A tear, a single, crystalline droplet, traced the path down her cheek—a testament to the awe that filled her soul. Maia took a deep, grounding breath, her chest rising and falling with a rhythm that spoke of life's simple beauty.

"Thank you," she murmured, her gratitude a prayer to the universe. For the wisdom gained, for the challenges faced, and for the incredible odyssey of the mind she had been privileged to navigate. The experience, though fleeting in temporal terms, was etched into the very core of her being—an indelible mark of transformation that she would carry with her always.

Maia's skin shivered under the gentle touch of the researchers' hands as they peeled away the adhesive pads, disconnecting her from the web of wires that had mapped the journey of her mind. The low hum of medical equipment faded into the background like a distant echo as the electrodes were lifted one by one, freeing her from their cold grasp.

"Maia, can you hear me?" A voice soft and reassuring cut through the haze of her transition. "We're going to sit you up slowly now."

Her head felt weightless as they eased her into a sitting position, her body reflecting the languid pace of a dream. The room was still a blur, its edges softly merging into one another, but with each passing second, the clarity of reality sharpened its focus.

"Take your time," another researcher encouraged, a note of admiration threading his words for the strength she'd shown. "The experience was intense, and it's important to reorient yourself at your own pace."

She nodded, though the gesture required a monumental effort, as if her neck bore the burden of the cosmos she had traversed.

Her breaths were deliberate, each inhale drawing in the sterility of the room, each exhale releasing fragments of the celestial splendor she had witnessed on her odyssey.

As the last electrode was removed, Maia's tactile senses flooded back, grounding her. The crispness of the hospital gown against her skin, the subtle give of the mattress beneath her, the air's cool kiss—all conspired to anchor her back to this dimension.

"Here, have some water." A plastic cup pressed against her lips, and she sipped, the liquid a lifeline trickling down her throat, soothing her parched insides as if she hadn't drunk for years, decades even.

"Thank you," she whispered again, but this time her voice found strength, reverberating with the echoes of otherworldly wisdom gleaned from her communion with the beings of light. The simplicity of the cup, the purity of the water—everyday miracles, she now understood, as potent as the revelations that had unfurled before her like an interstellar tapestry.

Her eyes darted around, reconnecting with the familiarity of the room. She noticed the precision of the instruments, the dedication etched on the faces of the researchers, the embodiment of human curiosity and endeavor. How small these pursuits seemed, yet how vital to the mosaic of existence.

"How long," Maia asked the nurse who had offered her the water, "Has it really been only 12 hours", amazed at the temporal dissonance she had experienced. "Oh no Maia, sorry this was just a short trip I am afraid." "We wanted to see how you would handle the DMT. You have been receiving the drip for about 20 minutes and your vitals were perfect", the nurse cheerfully replied.

In the stillness that followed, Maia gathered the threads of her expanded consciousness, weaving them into the fabric of her present being.

The insights came in waves, memories of a lifetime spent in the company of ascended guides, lessons learned not in hours but across aeons.

Now, as the temporal dissonance settled, Maia contemplated the significance of what she had experienced in only 20 minutes. The journey within had shattered her perception of time, had shown her the vast expanse of her own potential. With every choice stretching out like a constellation of possibility, she felt the weight of her new knowledge and profound responsibility to integrate and share this experience.

"Are you feeling alright?" one researcher asked, a hand resting lightly upon her shoulder, grounding her further.

"Yes," Maia replied, meeting the researcher's gaze. Her eyes, once windows to a soul seeking, now shone with the luminescence of one who had found. "I'm more than alright. I've been given a gift, and I intend to use it well."

With resolve fortifying her spirit, Maia rose from the bed, each movement an affirmation of her renewed purpose. There would be time to articulate the intricacies of her transcendence, to distill wisdom from the phantasmagoria that had enveloped her essence.

But for now, Maia stood reborn amidst the machines and white walls, her heart beating to the rhythm of a universe forever changed by the voyage she had braved—an explorer returning home, carrying the starlight of discovery in her soul.

GATHERING ALLIES

Maia closed her eyes, the sterile coolness of the Harvard Medical School study room fading away as the second phase of the DMT study began. Coursed through her veins, the Spirit Molecule's key began to unlock her consciousness. Her pulse quickened, anticipation tingling at the edges of her awareness. The world within began to blossom in vibrant bursts as if each thought she had nurtured was now blooming into a vivid flower of swirling hues.

The colors danced before her, streaks of neon green and electric blue tangling with deep purples and fiery reds, coalescing into a tapestry that pulsed with the rhythm of the cosmos. Shapes emerged from the chaos, landscapes stretching out in all directions, ethereal and shrouded in a mist that was both alien and intimately familiar. Floating islands adorned with crystalline structures hung suspended in a sky that was not a sky, a void that was not empty but brimming with unspoken possibilities.

Beneath her, the ground—or what served as ground in this place—shimmered like a lake kissed by the dawn. Each step Maia took sent ripples across its surface, sending reflections of herself scattering into the infinity that surrounded her. It was here, in this starlit expanse, that she first sensed them—the beings of pure energy and light.

They encircled her, their presence both formidable and gentle. They did not speak; they resonated, each one a different note in a cosmic chorus that vibrated through Maia's very soul. The beings moved with purpose, their light casting prismatic patterns that narrated truth from the beginning of space time.

One being drew nearer, a cascade of luminous particles that whirled around it in a delicate storm. Its aura was a soft, luminescent gold that hummed with the secrets of the universe and the meaning to all things.

Maia felt a connection to it, a recognition that transcended her human experience. She knew without knowing that this entity held answers to questions she hadn't yet formed, truths that stretched beyond the confines of her mortal understanding.

"Who are you?" Maia whispered, her voice a mere breath in this boundless domain.

The being's radiance intensified, a silent affirmation that transcended language. Here, in this convergence of energy and enlightenment, Maia stood at the precipice of discovery, ready to dive into the depths of cosmic knowledge, to swim in the oceans of collective consciousness that beckoned with a promise of untold revelations.

And so, amidst these Angels, these Ascended Beings, Maia embarked upon her journey—one that would span the equivalent of decades within her mind while only hours passed outside. In this realm, time bowed to experience, and understanding was the currency of existence. Maia surrendered to the voyage, her heart ablaze with the fervor of a seeker poised on the brink of the infinite.

A shimmering silhouette approached Maia, its edges blurring and reshaping like a reflection on rippling water. The entity, composed of an incandescent light that pulsed in harmony with the cosmic backdrop that cradled them both. Its voice, if it could be called that, resonated within Maia's mind, a symphony of harmonics that carried clear intention.

"I am without name but recognize me as Illumination," the presence communicated, its vibrational tone permeating Maia with a sudden influx of warmth and recognition. "I am the Guardian of Knowledge. My essence is to guide those who seek to traverse the vastness of cosmic understanding."

Maia absorbed the communication with every fiber of her being, as if Illumination's message was meant for her soul's comprehension alone. She nodded; her physical gestures unnecessary yet instinctual.

"Lead me," she responded, her thoughts intermingling with the ambient energy around her, becoming part of the majestic dance of universal wisdom.

Illumination extended what might be perceived as a hand, though it morphed into streams of light that entwined with Maia's own essence. Together, they embarked upon an odyssey through the celestial tapestry.

The first realm they entered shimmered with the iridescence of potential. Here, ideas bloomed like nebulae, their gaseous colors painting possibilities onto the canvas of Maia's mind. She witnessed concepts taking form, theories crystallizing from the ether, and felt her understanding deepen with each ephemeral vision.

"Behold the birthplace of thought," Illumination intoned, gesturing toward the cosmic display. "Within these folds lies the raw material of creation—unshaped and unrestrained."

Maia's eyes, though no longer confined by corporeal limitations, widened in awe. She could sense the unbridled power of unfettered imagination, the seeds of innovation waiting to be sown across the dimensions.

They moved onward, seamlessly transitioning into another realm where the fabric of reality twisted and turned upon itself. It was as if space folded, allowing distant corners of existence to touch, to commingle. This was the nexus of connection, where disparate ideas found unity, where diversity merged without losing distinction.

"Here, we witness the convergence of differences, the harmonious coalescence that forms the basis of consciousness," Illumination explained, the light of their combined presence casting prismatic reflections against the undulating expanse.

Maia drank from the wellspring of Illumination's guidance, her intellect intertwining with the essence of the realms they traversed. Through this tutelage, she began to grasp the intricate web of existence, the delicate balance of cosmic interplay.

Each subsequent realm unveiled further insights. One realm hummed with the resonance of empathy, another throbbed with the pulse of creativity. A different sphere echoed with the silent strength of resilience, while another radiated the pure clarity of truth. With each transition, Maia's perception expanded, her inner eye opening to the interconnectedness of all things.

As they journeyed deeper into the heart of the cosmos, Maia became aware of the ebb and flow of the universe's breath, its cyclical nature mirroring her own inhalations and exhalations. She realized that each realm was not merely a place to visit, but a state to embody—a facet of the gemstone that was her very existence.

With Illumination's guidance, Maia navigated the complex architecture of the multiverse, her spirit soaring on the wings of newfound understanding. Each revelation etched itself indelibly upon the core of her being, a mosaic of enlightenment that would shape her understanding of the meaning of life.

As the brilliant array of realms danced before her, Maia embraced the cosmic odyssey laid out before her.

Maia stepped forward, or at least she believed she did. There was no ground beneath her, yet she felt a sense of movement—an inward dive into the luminous embrace of the realm of Unity. Here, the borders that once defined her melted away like mist under the morning sun. A gentle warmth spread through her essence, and in this place of iridescent light, Maia experienced the profound sensation of merging with a collective consciousness.

Around her, there were no individuals, only an endless sea of energy that pulsed with the rhythm of shared existence. Each wave of this cosmic ocean carried echoes of thoughts, emotions, and memories from countless beings. Maia's mind expanded, touching upon the living network that connected all forms of life throughout the universe.

She was a drop in an infinite ocean, yet she was also the ocean itself—boundless and eternal.

The love she felt was unconditional, saturating her being with a compassion so vast it transcended words. In this unity, she saw the link between the heartbeats of lovers, the silent understanding between friends, and the unspoken bond of families. She could feel the very pulse of the universe—a heartbeat resonating with a love that knew no boundaries, encompassing all in its tender, infinite embrace.

Transitioning from this realm, the scenery shifted once more. Timelessness unfolded around her, an expanse where stars hung motionless in a sky that was not a sky, and the concept of 'when' held no meaning. Chronos emerged before her, an entity of indeterminate form, its presence both ancient and ever new. It spoke without speaking, its voice echoing in the corridors of Maia's soul.

"Time is but a canvas upon which mortals paint their lives, but it is an illusion," Chronos conveyed, its essence flickering like the flame of a candle caught between two breaths. "The past, present, and future are but shadows cast by the light of eternity."

Maia absorbed these words, her intellect grappling with the paradoxes that Chronos unraveled before her. She understood now that her own life—each moment of joy and sorrow, every heartbeat and breath—was part of a tapestry that was never woven and would never fray. She existed within time, yet beyond it, her soul timeless as the cosmos itself.

"Consider the moments you cherish, Maia Yetta Rose," Chronos continued, its voice a whisper on the edge of existence. "They are not lost to the past; they live within you, eternal as the stars."

With each revelation, Maia felt the constraints of linear perception dissolving. She saw her own life spread out before her, not as a line, but as a constellation, each star a moment of significance, connected by the invisible threads of her choices.

Amid the stillness of Timelessness, Maia floated, cradled by the wisdom of Chronos. The eternal dance of creation and dissolution played out within her expanded awareness, revealing the immortal nature of her soul—a soul that had always known freedom, even as it journeyed through the fleeting dream of human life.

Maia's essence soared, unfettered by the shackles of temporal laws, as she ventured forth from the realm of Timelessness. The universe unfolded before her in an explosion of potential, where the fabric of existence seemed to weave and reweave itself endlessly. It was here, in this vibrant tapestry of Infinite Possibilities, that Maia encountered Metamorphis.

This entity shimmered like a mirage, its form a kaleidoscope of shapes—a lion with a mane of fire, an eagle with wings of liquid crystal, then a myriad of human faces, each one reflecting every conceivable emotion. As Maia watched in awe, the entity finally settled into a form both strange and familiar, a perfect amalgam of all it had shown her, eyes alight with the stars of countless galaxies.

"Maia Yetta Rose," Metamorphis spoke, its voice an echo of every sound imaginable, "you stand at the crossroad of creation, where thought creates reality."

With a sweeping gesture, Metamorphis unveiled a panorama of darkness peppered with pinpricks of light. Each point radiated possibilities, paths not yet taken, lives not yet lived. "See your desires made manifest. Embrace the transformative power that dwells within you."

As Maia reached out, the points of light danced toward her, swirling around her being. She could feel the profound energy of her own hopes and dreams weaving into the very essence of her soul. "You are boundless," Metamorphis encouraged. "Let your will shape the cosmos."

Her heart thundering with newfound purpose, Maia envisioned a world where her knowledge could heal, where her compassion could unite. And just like that, the lights responded, forming visions of communities connected, of barriers broken down by understanding.

"Your potential is as infinite as the stars themselves," Metamorphis affirmed, fading back into the infinite landscape as Maia absorbed the profound lesson.

Drunk on the euphoria of infinite potential, Maia pressed deeper into the cosmic realms, her spirit hungry for the wisdom that lay beyond. It was in a garden wrought from nebulae and constellations that Maia came upon the Oracle—a figure enshrouded in robes of shifting twilight, its face obscured by a veil of pure void.

"Behold the threads of fate, Maia Yetta Rose," the Oracle intoned, its hands weaving intricate patterns in the air. Glimpses of futures—numerous and fleeting—flashed before Maia's eyes. Worlds of peace, dystopias of despair, timelines where she flourished and others where she faded into obscurity.

"Each strand represents a choice, a path your soul may walk," the Oracle continued. Maia's gaze fixed upon a particular thread, golden and pulsating with light, and she knew instinctively it was the embodiment of her deepest aspirations.

"Remember, traveler of the cosmos," the Oracle whispered as Maia focused on the radiant filament, "the future is not set. Free will is the sculptor of destiny." In those words, Maia understood the weight of her decisions, the ripples they would send across the vast ocean of time.

"Choose wisely, for each step you take shapes the universe," the Oracle concluded, its form dissolving into stardust that scattered among the cosmic winds.

She was anchored by the gravity of choice, while her physical body sat tranquil in the study room of Harvard Medical School.

Maia contemplated her journey thus far, the decades spent in communion with beings beyond mortal comprehension. With a sense of clarity and determination, when time she would return to the temporal world, carrying with her the insights of the cosmic mind, ready to weave her thread into the grand design.

Maia stepped forward, her feet finding ground where there seemed to be none. She floated through the realm of Cosmic Harmony, a place where the fabric of existence weaved itself into a design of intricate balance. As if summoned by her presence, a figure materialized before her—a being composed of opalescent light, its form both fluid and precise.

"Welcome, Maia," the entity spoke, its voice an echo of tranquility. "I am Harmonious."

The space around them breathed with an energy that was at once serene and vibrant. It pulsed with the duality of night and day, joy, and sorrow. Here, Maia understood, every opposing force found its counterpart, each one integral to the whole.

"Harmonious," Maia said, her voice steady yet filled with wonder. "Teach me."

"Look around you," Harmonious gestured. "See how the shadows enhance the light, granting depth and dimension to all that lives. Observe how sorrow carves spaces within the soul for joy to fill."

With each word, Harmonious's form shifted, embodying the essence of their teachings. Dark swirled with light, laughter danced with tears, and Maia felt the unity in their interplay.

"Embrace the totality of your experiences, for they are the threads that weave the fabric of your being," Harmonious continued. "The cosmos thrives on balance—the eternal dance between creation and destruction, giving rise and meaning to life."

As Harmonious's message resonated within her, Maia felt her consciousness expand, embracing the coexistence of contrasts. She experienced an epiphany, a realization that she was not just a witness but a part of this cosmic harmony.

"Thank you," Maia whispered, feeling a profound connection to the universe and every spark of existence within it.

"Go forth and create with the knowledge of harmony," Harmonious said, their form dissipating into a symphony of colors that kissed Maia's skin farewell.

The realm shifted, transforming before her eyes into a landscape pulsating with potential. She stood at the precipice of Cosmic Creation, where energies swirled, ready to coalesce into matter at the mere whisper of intent. And there, at the center of it all, was Conception—an embodiment of pure creation, an entity whose very presence sparked inspiration.

Conception Maia called out, her heart pounding with the promise of what lay ahead.

"Maia," Conception responded, their voice an invocation. "Here, in the wellspring of creation, lies the power to shape reality. Within you resides the same force that births stars and spins galaxies."

Conception extended a hand, and Maia felt the rush of creative energy surge through her, a torrent of ideas, dreams, and possibilities.

"Your thoughts, your will, your deepest desires—they can sculpt the fabric of existence. Embrace your creative power," Conception urged, their form radiating with unbound potential.

"Shape your reality," they whispered as Maia reached out to touch the essence of Conception. In that moment, she felt the barriers of her mind dissolve, her spirit infused with an unstoppable force. The visions of her life's work—to teach, to heal, to elevate—were no longer distant dreams but tangible paths waiting to be forged.

"Thank you," Maia said, her words a vow to herself and the universe. "I will create, and I will inspire."

Conception smiled, a cosmic gesture that transcended form, and Maia knew that the journey she had embarked upon was only the beginning.

"Go now," Conception 's voice faded into the infinite expanse. "Create your masterpiece."

Maia, with the fire of a thousand suns igniting her soul, turned towards the vast unknown, ready to craft her destiny with the newfound wisdom of the cosmos.

The cosmos unfurled before Maia like an infinite sail, each star a stitch in the fabric of existence, every nebula a breath of life. The realm of Cosmic Consciousness spread out around her, a boundless ocean where minds and stars drifted as one. Here, in this final bastion of understanding, Maia felt herself slip into the vast neural network of the universe.

With each pulse and thrum of cosmic energy, Maia's identity diffused into the greater expanse—her essence merging with ancient constellations and emerging galaxies. She became a single note in the symphony of existence, her consciousness expanding beyond the limits of her physical form. Time lost its grip, unraveling into a spiral dance of endless moments. She was everywhere, everywhen, every thought that had ever flickered through the mind of the cosmos.

A profound understanding blossomed within her, delicate yet all-encompassing, revealing the ultimate reality of existence. It whispered to her of the purpose of cosmic consciousness—to experience, to learn, and to grow. Every soul, every being, was part of this grand design, their lives a mosaic of collective wisdom gathered across eons.

"Maia," the voice of the cosmos called, echoing through her in waves of pure insight. "You are the vessel of knowledge, the seeker of truths. Carry forth the light of understanding."

She nodded, her gesture rippling across dimensions, her spirit buoyed by the love that bound every corner of creation together. It was clear now—the meaning she had searched for, the connection she yearned to share. Her mission lay etched in the very matter that made up her being, written in the stardust coursing through her veins.

As the luminous haze began to wane, the celestial entities that guided her journey materialized once more, their forms less defined, but their presence just as potent. They encircled her, a council of ephemeral wisdom, bidding her farewell with silent nods that resonated through the core of her soul.

"Thank you," Maia whispered, her gratitude a beacon that shone bright against the dimming backdrop. "For your guidance, for your light."

One by one, they faded, their energies retreating back into the folds of space-time, leaving Maia to face the return to her corporeal self. She felt the pull of her own body, a gentle tug that beckoned her homeward from the decades spent among the stars.

With a final glance at the receding cosmos, Maia allowed the tether of reality to reel her in. The colors, once vivid and wild, softened to a comforting glow, the kaleidoscopic realm of the DMT-induced discovery giving way to the muted shades of the physical world.

Her eyes fluttered open, the study room's clinical light a stark contrast to the cosmic splendor she had inhabited. The sensation of the chair beneath her, the feel of her own hands, grounded her once more. Though she had returned to the confines of her human form, the journey had reshaped her in ways time could never erode.

Forever changed, Maia Yetta Rose carried within her a universe of wisdom, ready to illuminate the path for others, as the stars had done for her.

The murmur of hushed voices drew her back to the realm of the tangible. Maia's eyelids lifted slowly, tenderly, as if they had grown unaccustomed to the mere act of opening. The sterile light of the study room was gentle but insistent, coaxing her senses to reacclimatize to the here and now. Around her, the other participants had already emerged from their own odysseys, expressions of awe and bewilderment painted across their faces like a gallery of living art.

She sat up, her movements tentative but purposeful, her body remembering its earthly responsibilities. As her gaze swept the room, she locked eyes with those who, like her, had voyaged through the very fabric of existence. In their silent exchange, entire lifetimes seemed to pass—a shared understanding that transcended language, born from the fire of cosmic revelation.

The door opened with a quiet confidence that heralded his arrival. Dr. Jameson Brooks entered the room, his aura immediately commanding attention. His eyes, sharp and discerning, moved across the group, taking in the aftermath of their collective transcendence.

"Welcome back," he said, his voice a steady anchor in the sea of emotions that flowed around them. "While fresh in your minds, I invite you all to share what you've experienced. Speak freely; this is a place of learning and discovery."

One by one, the participants recounted tales of indescribable beauty and profound insight. Their words, though earnest, could only skim the surface of their inner journeys.

When it was Maia's turn, she stood, her lean figure casting a slender shadow on the floor. Her eyes, deep emerald pools of wisdom, held a distant starlight that hadn't been there before. She spoke, each word deliberate and suffused with the essence of the cosmos.

"In the heart of the universe, I found a tapestry woven with threads of light and darkness," Maia began, her tone imbued with the serenity of the realms she had traversed.

"Each strand a life, each color a feeling, and together, they sang the song of existence—harmonious, yet complex."

She paused, her thoughts reaching back across the eons she had lived within moments. "I stood before entities—Illumination the Guardian of Knowledge—and Chronos, who exists beyond time. From them, I learned that our perception is but a single note in the symphony of creation."

Dr. Brooks listened intently, his face betraying no emotion, but his mind undoubtedly racing to categorize and analyze her every word.

"Metamorphis showed me that our potential is boundless, limited only by the confines we place upon ourselves," Maia continued. "The Oracle revealed paths of what might be, each one shaped by the choices we make, while Harmonious taught me that balance is not found but created."

Her voice held a reverent quality as she recounted the final leg of her journey, "And Conception... in the breath of Cosmic Creation, I understood my role as a crafter of realities. We all are. But it was in the embrace of the Cosmic Consciousness that I found the truth of our existence—we are not merely part of the universe; we are its consciousness, experiencing itself subjectively."

“Consciousness is all of us and all we perceive are manifestations of something very much like a cosmic-scale dissociative identity disorder (DID). There’s an all-encompassing universe-wide consciousness, it has multiple personalities, and we’re them.”

The room fell into a contemplative silence, punctuated only by the hum of machinery and distant footsteps in the hall. What Maia had imparted was more than just an account—it was an invitation to see beyond the veil of material illusion and separation.

"Thank you, Maia," Dr. Brooks finally said, his analytical mask softening for a moment into something resembling awe. "Your insights are invaluable.

They will certainly contribute to the greater understanding of the human mind and its connection to the universe."

As Maia took her seat once again among her fellow explorers, there was a profound sense of unity, a bond forged in the crucible of cosmic awareness. They had touched the infinite, and in doing so, they had touched each other's souls.

Maia's gaze lingered on the sterile walls of the study room; her pupils still dilated from the voyage that had spanned eons within her mind. She flexed her hands, grounding herself in the tactile sensations of the material world. The fabric of her chair felt coarse against her skin, a stark contrast to the silky threads of cosmic energy she'd woven with moments—or was it lifetimes? —ago.

A surge of clarity coursed through her veins, as if the very blood within her carried the luminescence she had bathed in while among the stars. Her breath came in steady rhythms, each inhalation a reminder of her physicality, each exhale a release of celestial knowledge she was now tasked to impart.

Around her, fellow participants whispered in hushed tones, their words spilling over one another like the overlapping waves of a multidimensional sea. Their shared silence had blossomed into a garden of murmured revelations, each voice a petal unfurling to reveal hidden hues of understanding.

"Are you alright, Maia?" one of them asked, eyes reflecting the profound impact of his own journey.

"More than alright," she replied, her voice imbued with the tranquility of Harmonious and the certainty of Chronos. "I've been given a glimpse of the fabric we're all part of, and I feel... responsible for sharing its pattern."

With a purposeful motion, Maia rose from her seat, the act itself an affirmation of her renewed intent. The others watched, recognizing the transformation that had taken place within her.

Their gazes did not waver; they too were changed, their souls decorated with strokes of otherworldly wisdom.

She walked towards the window, peering out at the mundane sprawl of Cambridge beyond the glass. The city moved in its ceaseless rhythm, unaware of the profound odyssey that had unfolded in this quiet corner of academia. But Maia saw it differently now—each person, each action, interwoven in the grand design she had come to understand.

Turning back to face the room, her eyes met those of Dr. Brooks who nodded, acknowledging the silent pact between them. There was work to be done, research to be pursued, minds to be opened—and Maia was ready to lead the way.

"Let's begin," she said, more to herself than to the others, her voice a beacon calling them to the shores of newfound worlds. "Our real journey starts now."

As she spoke, her allies from the cosmic realms seemed to stand beside her, ethereal and unseen but no less present. Illumination's radiance flickered in the periphery of her vision, Metamorphis' adaptability pulsed within her heart, and Conception's inspiration resonated in her every word. Maia knew that these entities, or angels, or ascended beings would always be with her just as they always had been.

CHOICE

Maia Rose's breath hitched, her chest rising and falling with the rhythm of otherworldly tides. The room around her dissolved into a kaleidoscope of fractal geometries, hues blending and bending in manners that defied earthly physics.

Her body lay anchored to the couch, yet her consciousness soared, untethered and expansive, pulsing across dimensions she could never have imagined. She heard the whispers of stars, the song of nebulae birthing new suns—a chorus of creation that buzzed in her ears and filled the spaces between her atoms.

In this heightened state, Maia's mind was a universe unto itself, every thought a comet streaking across the infinite panorama of her being. But within this astral majesty lurked the shadow of a looming decision, a binary star whose gravitational pull threatened to consume her wonder into its event horizon.

She grappled with the choice before her: to step fully into her role as an interpreter of the cosmic consciousness, to become a teacher and guide for those lost in the dark—or to retreat back to the familiarity of her life as an EMT, where her impact, though profound, was bound by the limitations of flesh and blood.

The weight of potential futures pressed against her chest. She could feel the threads of lives she might change, see the faces of those who would find solace in her teachings—yet also the faces of those she would fail to save in the tangible immediacy of emergency medicine.

"Am I ready?" she questioned herself, the words echoing across the astral plane, finding no purchase in the vastness. The colors around her pulsed with encouragement one moment, then flickered with warning the next.

"Can I abandon the immediacy of human suffering for a path less trodden, but perhaps more needed?" She pondered.

"Choice," she whispered, the word fracturing into a million shards of light that danced before her eyes, spelling out the histories of a thousand possibilities. Each shard a life touched, or a life overlooked—a delicate balance of action and inaction, presence and absence.

There, amidst the uncertainty and potential, Maia found herself at the crossroads of destiny. Her heart calibrated to the frequencies of empathy and wisdom, fluctuated wildly as she searched for direction, waiting for the moment when clarity would strike illuminating her path forward.

Maia's senses, now settled into the soft din of reality as she slowly returned to the quiet sanctuary of Dr. Evelyn Warren's study. The walls, lined with ancient texts and artifacts of wisdom, seemed to pulse gently with the residual energy of her meditation. She blinked, allowing her vision to adjust to the gentle amber light that bathed the room.

"Welcome back, Maia," came a soothing voice. Dr. Evelyn Warren sat across from her, a calm presence within this oasis of serenity. The older woman's eyes, flecked with the experience of years, held a steady gaze that invited trust and openness.

"Evelyn," Maia began, her voice barely above a whisper, "my meditation... it was completely unresolved."

"Tell me, what is it that burdens your heart?" Dr. Warren asked, her tone both an invitation and a supportive embrace.

"It's the choice, the one I must make." Maia's words hung between them like delicate threads of a spider's web, shimmering with the dew of dawn.

"Ah, choices are but the writers of our story, Maia. They carve pathways into the unknown," Dr. Warren responded, folding her hands in her lap with an air of contemplation.

"But how does one choose when each path could lead to vastly different destinies?" Maia's brow furrowed, seeking wisdom in her mentor's eyes.

"Consider this," Dr. Warren spoke softly, leaning forward slightly, "as you know, every decision echoes through the cosmos, but it is the intention behind your choice that truly shapes the universe."

Maia absorbed the words, feeling their weight and their truth. Her heart, still erratic from her meditation, began to find its rhythm.

"Intention..." she repeated, rolling the concept around like a precious stone unearthed from the depths of her consciousness. "The why behind the what."

"Exactly. And remember, you are not alone in this," Dr. Warren assured her. "Your intuition is the compass gifted by the cosmos. In that you will find your direction."

"Thank you," Maia said, the gratitude in her voice resonating with the newfound resolve taking root within her. "I know I have much to reflect on."

"Take all the time you need," Dr. Warren chuckled warmly, "The answers you seek are already within you."

"Maia my dear," before you go home, please do me a favor and linger for a few minutes in the garden." Dr. Warren suggested. "I think you need some time to process before jumping back into your regular routine.

Maia rose from the comforting embrace of Dr. Warren's study, her senses still swimming in the phosphorescent afterglow of her transcendental journey. She wandered through the silent corridors of the old Bostonian townhouse, each step guiding her further away from human conversation and closer to the internal dialog of intuition.

As she pushed open the French doors at the end of the hallway, a gust of cool air greeted her, carrying with it the subtle scent of lilac and fresh earth.
Maia found herself standing at the threshold of an enclosed garden with its meticulous arrangement of flowers and shrubs.

The sky above stretched vast and clear; a panorama of twilight blue punctuated by the first shy twinkles of stars. She ventured into this sanctuary, her hand grazing the delicate petals of a moonflower, its bloom unfurling in the dimming light—a mirror of her own unfolding clarity.

She chose her favorite bench nestled under the boughs of an apple tree. Settling onto the weathered wood, Maia closed her eyes and slowed her breathing once again. The sounds of the city beyond the garden walls faded, replaced by the harmonious resonance of universal tones that vibrated through her core. In this serene isolation, Maia began the intimate exploration, a conversation with the inner cosmos of her mind.

"Guide me," she murmured. Her voice was a drop in the ocean of existence, rippling outward to touch infinity.

The Ascended Beings during her recent DMT trip had gifted her a glimpse into the library of cosmic wisdom. Now, in the solitude of the garden, Maia reached inward to the lessons etched into the fabric of her soul.

Images unfurled within her mind's eye—an intricate design where every thread was an event leading to this moment, every knot a decision she had faced.

"Clarity," she sought, the word a torch for her inner sight. Intuition responded, illuminating the paths before her, each one radiating potential outcomes and teachings. It was not about the choice itself, but the intention she would infuse into it—the why behind the what.

The Ascended Beings had shown her the interconnectedness of all things; every action, a note in the symphony of creation. Her role, as both healer and teacher, was a song waiting to be composed, and her decision, the key in which it would resonate.

A gentle breeze stirred the garden, and with it came a wave of resolve.

Maia's heart space expanded, embracing the unity of all existence, and in that embrace, she found her answer. The symphony quieted, leaving a singular note hanging in the air—her note, clear and resolute.

"Intention," she whispered again, this time with a certainty that coursed through her veins. The tree's leaves rustled their approval, and the stars above seemed to shine in acknowledgment of her breakthrough.

The garden around her was a temple of tranquility where her spirit had communed with the infinite. Here, amidst the whispering flora and under the sentinel gaze of constellations, Maia Yetta Rose, dedicated EMT and seeker of truths, had embraced the immensity of her existence and the purpose that awaited her beyond the garden walls.

"Am I truly prepared?" she wondered, her voice a mere thought that rippled through the vibrant ether. The certainty she had embraced but moments ago now seemed fragile, like a gossamer veil before the winds of consequence. "What if my teachings lead them astray? What if my understanding is but a shadow on the wall of truth?"

The blossoms of the garden became blurs of uncertainty, their edges bleeding into the air like watercolor tears. Her hands, once steady, trembled as she held them before her eyes, their lines and creases a map of her life's choices. The magnitude of her role as both healer and guide weighed upon her like a celestial burden, threatening to crush her under its existential gravity.

"Can one soul bear such responsibility?" Maia's introspection echoed. Her ears filled with the lament of apprehension, a dissonant overture that threatened to overshadow the harmony of her intentions.

Then, as if the cosmos sensed her faltering spirit, the universe pulsed around her, its rhythm syncing with her heartbeat.

The reality of time's relativity crashed upon her senses; decades of experience with the Ascended Beings distilled into fleeting minutes.

"Focus, Maia," she instructed herself, her thoughts like anchors thrown into the stormy sea of her mind. "Your purpose is greater than fear."

The air thrummed with urgency, each molecule vibrating with the intensity of her looming choice. The fragrances of the garden—a concoction of earth and bloom—intertwined with the metallic tang of her own resolve. The very essence of decision-making perfumed the air, sweet yet sharp with significance.

A surge of cosmic energy coursed through her veins, igniting her synapses with the fire of countless stars. Maia's perception expanded, her vision stretching beyond the physical realm. She saw the intricate web of life, each thread a potential path stemming from the nucleus of her imminent decision.

"Remember why you stand here," echoed a voice from the depths of her being, resonant with the wisdom of Dr. Evelyn Warren. "You are the vessel of knowledge, the conduit of cosmic consciousness."

With deliberate focus, Maia steadied her shaking limbs, grounding herself amid the maelstrom of sensation. As she did, the world clarified, colors aligning into a spectrum of clarity, sounds coalescing into melodies of insight.

"Intention," she breathed out, grasping onto the word like a lifeline. It was the core, the essence, the genesis of all that she would impart. With intention came the power to shape destinies, to weave the fabric of understanding through the loom of existence.

Her decision hovered before her, an ethereal gem pulsating with potential. Maia reached out, ready to claim it, ready to embrace the teacher within. But as her fingers brushed against its surface, the scene fragmented, leaving her standing amidst the shards of her own hesitation.

"Trust," she whispered to herself, the word a beacon in the tempest. The cliffhanger of her choice loomed, but within Maia Yetta Rose stirred the strength of galaxies. She was ready to leap into the unknown, her heart the compass leading her forward.

Maia sat motionless in the quiet of her sparsely furnished apartment, the only sound the faint hum of the city beyond her walls. Her hands covered her face as if to shield her from the enormity of the decision that lay coiled inside her mind like a dormant serpent. A single tear breached the fortress of her fingers, trailing down the curve of her cheek.

The room's stillness contradicted the tumultuous journey she had embarked upon—a voyage through time and space within the confines of her consciousness, propelled by the enigmatic DMT experience that had unfolded over what seemed like decades. To any observer, she had been still for just half a day, yet within her, entire lifetimes had waxed and waned.

"Is this the path? Or merely an alluring detour?" Maia whispered to herself, her voice barely rising above the whisper of her breath. The wisdom of the Ascended Beings still echoed in her thoughts, their messages as vivid as the colors that had danced before her eyes in that other realm.

She remembered the expansive plains of shimmering energy, where her essence had mingled with the very fabric of existence. There, beneath the gaze of nebulous entities, she had tasted omniscience, felt the pulsating heartbeat of the cosmos itself—an intoxicating power that now felt slipping through her fingers like grains of cosmic dust.

"Am I forsaking my gift?" The doubt gnawed at her, its teeth sharp against the backdrop of her resolve. She had touched the infinite, but at the same time, she recognized the allure of such experiences could become a cage, distancing her from the tangible world of pain and joy she was born into.

Her expanded state of awareness had once been a beacon, guiding her through the mists of uncertainty, but now it felt like a siren's call—beautiful, mesmerizing, and potentially treacherous. What good is the understanding of galaxies if one cannot grasp the hand of another in need?

"Dr. Warren often spoke of balance," she murmured, invoking the memory of her mentor. "How can I preach connection if I sever the most fundamental one—to humanity?"

Maia's heart wrestled with the yearning to dive back into the kaleidoscopic abyss, to dwell among the stars and converse with the abstract entities that defied description. Yet, another part of her—the EMT, the healer, the earthly wanderer—knew that her mission lay here, amongst the blood and bones of human frailty.

In the silent communion with her conflicting desires, Maia found no easy answers, only the whisper of a challenge that would define her very being. Was her knowledge a beacon to share, or a private sanctuary to retreat into? Could she truly relinquish a constant communion with the divine for the sake of those who have never glimpsed beyond the veil?

"Perhaps," she thought, the seed of an answer taking root, "true enlightenment isn't about how far you travel within, but how deeply you connect outward."

With that, Maia lowered her hands, her tear-streaked face now resolute. The weight of her decision still pressed upon her shoulders, yet it was no longer a shackle but a mantle she chose to wear. She stood up slowly, her body feeling the gravity of the world anew, ready to walk the path of the grounded stars.

With each step toward the window, the weight of indecision shed from her shoulders like an obsolete exoskeleton. She hovered there; a silhouette framed by the faint luminescence spilling into the room. Her gaze lifted to the ink-black sky, punctured by the diamond-like shimmer of distant stars.

They hung suspended, timeless in their cosmic ballet, and yet to Maia, they beckoned with newfound familiarity, each twinkling light a nod of recognition.

The night air was crisp, whispering through the slightly ajar pane. She inhaled deeply, tasting the coolness as it filled her lungs, invigorating her resolve. As she exhaled, a fogged breath kissed the glass, momentarily veiling the heavens before dissipating into transparency.

Maia's transformation was as silent as the space that cradled the stars. The doubts that had once clawed at her mind, seeking to burrow and fester, were now relics of a self that no longer existed. She had danced with eternity, woven through the fabric of time as effortlessly as a comet cleaves the night. Her every cell hummed with the knowledge of ages, her essence vibrating to the rhythm of the cosmos itself.

There, bathed in moonlight, Maia's heart synchronized with the universal pulse—a symphony of energy that coursed through her veins. A profound understanding settled within her, a truth as old as the universe: her mission was a conduit for awakening, a bridge spanning the chasm between ignorance and enlightenment.

She pressed a palm against the cool surface of the window, feeling the solidity beneath her touch. It grounded her, a tangible reminder of the physical realm she was destined to enlighten. But behind her closed eyelids, galaxies swirled, nebulas bloomed, and she was adrift once more among the Ascended Beings—guides whose wisdom transcended time, whose whispers still echoed in the recesses of her soul.

The night outside was but a setting for her renewed vision, waiting for her to paint the stars with meanings anew. With the clarity of a seer, Maia knew her path was luminous, each step forward a witness to the transformative journey she had undertaken.

In this quiet room, with the universe as her witness, Maia Yetta Rose reclaimed her destiny.

Her purpose was not just to exist within the vast expanse, but to serve as a beacon—a lighthouse for those navigating the treacherous waters of existential inquiry. And as she stood, a sentinel bathed in starlight, her decision was etched into the very constellations that watched over her.

"Guide them," she whispered, her voice a soft vow to the night, "Guide them to the cosmic mind."

She pulled away from the window, her silhouette merging with the shadows of the room, her inner light now a torch set ablaze, casting clarity upon the path ahead. She was ready to inspire, to illuminate, and to share the dance of the universe with all who sought its rhythm.

SHARING

Her apartment, usually a sanctuary of rest after grueling shifts, now transformed into a sacred space for transcendence. The room hummed with potential as she moved deliberately, placing chairs in a circle—a symbol of unity and equality. This arrangement was not arbitrary; it was a mimicry of the council of beings she'd encountered, entities that had sat together in an eternal round, exchanging wisdom beyond mortal comprehension.

She adorned the room with crystals, each one catching the light and casting rainbows on the walls, reminiscent of the ethereal beauty she had experienced. The incense she chose was grounding, a scent to tether the soul to Earth while the mind explored the stars. With every candle lit, every pillow fluffed, the atmosphere shifted, cocooning the space in serenity.

The table at the room's center became an altar of sorts, where she laid out texts brimming with esoteric knowledge alongside modern scientific studies—bridges between worlds. Here, eager minds would gather, seeking to understand the cosmic consciousness that Maia herself was only beginning to grasp.

As the preparations neared completion, Maia stood in the center of the circle. She closed her eyes, taking a moment to attune herself to the quiet, pulsating energy of the room. It was here, in this small haven amidst the bustle of Boston, that she would impart the revelations of her DMT journey, where time folded upon itself, and the secrets of the universe unfurled before her.

"Let them be open," she whispered, a silent plea to whatever forces might be listening. "Let them see."

With that, Maia opened her eyes, her gaze steady and full of purpose. She was ready to guide others through the labyrinth of their own mind, her personal experience a roadmap in the uncharted terrain of cosmic consciousness.

Maia watched as the first of the attendees trickled into the room, their eyes wide with a hunger for knowledge that she recognized all too well. A middle-aged man with salt-and-pepper hair clutched a dog-eared copy of "The Holographic Universe" to his chest like a sacred text. A young woman with vibrant tattoos snaking up her arms gazed around the room in wonder, her curiosity evident. A soft-spoken elder with lines etching deep wisdom into his face nodded at Maia in silent respect.

They came from different walks of life—a quantum physicist seeking truths beyond equations, a yoga instructor weaving spirituality into her practice, a retired schoolteacher hungry for a new chapter of learning. Yet they shared a common thread, a yearning that drew them here: to touch the intangible, to grasp the fleeting whispers of cosmic consciousness. Maia felt their anticipation, a collective breath held before the plunge into the unknown.

"Welcome," Maia said, her voice gentle in this sea of expectancy. "Today, we embark on a journey not through space, but within ourselves—a quest to connect with the vastness that binds every atom, every star, every thought."

She spoke of the fabric of reality, her words painting pictures of interstellar dust and neural constellations. "Imagine," she began, her gaze sweeping over her audience, "that our universe is not just an expanse of space, but a tapestry woven with threads of light—each one of us a knot in that grand design."

"Consider the nebulae," she continued, her voice serene, "vast clouds where stars are born. Our minds, too, are nebulae, brimming with the potential to birth ideas that can illuminate the darkness of ignorance."

The participants leaned forward, drawn in by the gravity of her metaphors. The physicist's eyes shone with the reflection of newborn stars, the teacher's smile revealed an inner awakening, and the yogi's breath synced with the rhythm of Maia's words.

"Inside each of us is a black hole," Maia said, her tone hushing to a whisper that commanded rapt attention. "A place where our deepest fears and doubts seem to swallow all hope. Yet even black holes can be gateways to other realms, places where our perceived limitations transform into wellsprings of strength."

Maia navigated them through the cosmos of their souls, guiding them past the event horizons of their minds, into the uncharted territories where truth became a living, breathing entity. Her workshop was no longer a room in Boston but a vessel transcending time and space, ferrying them toward the shores of enlightenment.

"Close your eyes," Maia whispered, her voice a lullaby in the hushed room. "Breathe deeply, and with each exhalation, release your earthly bindings. Imagine the essence of your consciousness as a mote of stardust, unshackled from the vessel of your physical form."

The participants obeyed, their bodies relaxing into their chairs, breaths syncing to an ancient, cosmic rhythm. The air was thick with the scent of sandalwood incense, mingling with the subtle energies that Maia had invoked earlier with her words.

"Your stardust is free now," Maia guided them further, "drifting through the void, past planets and stars, galaxies and quasars, toward the heart of the universe—the Cosmic Mind."

In the silence that followed, twenty hearts beat in harmony, twenty souls embarked on a journey across the astral plane, voyaging through constellations of thought and nebulae of emotion. They floated beyond the confines of time, dipping into the wellspring of collective memory where every human experience danced like sparks in a bonfire of eternity.

At the edge of the circle, David Hughes observed with a skeptic's eye. He sat detached, his notebook open but idle, his pen hovering over the blank page as if waiting for the right moment to touch down.

His piercing blue eyes scanned the room, not missing the subtle shifts in posture, the surrender etched on the faces of the participants.

As Maia spoke of interstellar connections, weaving the fabric of consciousness with her poetic cadence, David couldn't help but be intrigued by the theater of it all. Though his rational mind erected walls against belief in such esoteric concepts, the raw emotion displayed before him chipped at those defenses. There was something undeniably compelling about Maia's presence, an earnestness that transcended mere performance.

"Each of you is now part of the cosmic tapestry," Maia continued, her words painting visions of infinity within their closed eyelids. "Feel the presence of others around you, not as separate entities, but as extensions of the same universal force."

Silent tears trickled down the cheeks of a middle-aged man, who, just moments ago, held the world on his shoulders. A young artist's fingers twitched, sketching unseen masterpieces in the air. And somewhere between doubt and revelation, David felt the stirrings of what could only be described as wonder—a feeling long buried under years of cynicism.

The breakthrough came unexpectedly, during a visualization exercise designed to connect with the cosmic mind. David, who had remained an observer until now, decided to participate. Perhaps it was the earnestness of the group, or maybe it was Maia's compelling narrative—whatever the reason, he closed his eyes and embarked on the journey inward.

"Envision yourself as part of the cosmic tapestry," Maia instructed, her voice a gentle guide through the nebulae of their collective imagination. "Feel the energy of a thousand suns coursing through you, the wisdom of ancient civilizations within your grasp."

Around them, the air seemed to hum with potential, charged with the collective focus of minds seeking communion with something greater.

David's breath slowed; his thoughts untethered from the anchor of cynicism. In the darkness behind his eyelids, a burst of light erupted—a supernova of insight—and he felt himself dissolve into the expanse, a single note in the symphony of existence.

His expression shifted, the perennial furrow between his brows softening. When he finally opened his eyes, they were wide—not with fear, but with revelation. The walls he had meticulously erected over the years crumbled, revealing not weakness, but a profound strength in vulnerability.

"Remember this connection," Maia's voice anchored them, "for it is real—more real than the ground beneath your feet or the air in your lungs. It is the bond that unites us in the vastness of existence."

With a gentle command, she brought them back, coaxing their stardust selves to return to the here and now, to the room where their corporeal forms awaited. Eyes fluttered open, each gaze alight with stars from distant corners of their minds, reflecting an irrefutable truth that they had touched something profound.

David watched, his skepticism warring with curiosity, as the workshop attendees emerged from the meditation with an aura of transformation. They seemed lighter somehow, as if they'd shed invisible burdens among the stars.

"Thank you," Maia said softly, her expression one of serene fulfillment. Her students returned the gratitude with nods and smiles, carrying within them the ember of cosmic connection that Maia had ignited.

"Did you feel that?" he asked Maia, his voice hushed as if afraid to disturb the delicate fabric of understanding that now enveloped him.

"I did," Maia answered, her smile reflecting the quiet triumph of his awakening. "And so did the universe."

In that shared space between metaphysical exploration and tangible realization, David found himself at a crossroads. His skepticism, once a trusted ally, now appeared as a mere steppingstone toward a vaster, more intricate understanding—one that transcended the binary of belief and disbelief.

"Thank you," he said, sincerely, coloring his words in a way that surprised even him. "I have much to consider."

Maia nodded, recognizing the weight of his transformation. "The journey's just begun, David. And it's one worth taking."

David jotted down a single word in his notebook, the pen finally finding its purpose: "Transcendent." Whether it referred to the experience or to Maia herself, he wasn't entirely sure.

As the last participant left the room, a silence settled, heavy with the residue of introspection. Maia began gathering the scattered cushions, her movements deliberate and serene when David approached her—a human embodiment of skepticism wrapped in the crisp lines of his suit.

"Ms. Rose," he began, notepad in hand, poised to dissect her workshop with the precision of a surgeon, "how can you assure your students that what they're experiencing isn't just a placebo effect? An elaborate illusion?"

Maia paused, locking eyes with him. She was accustomed to disbelief, the armor many wore against the unknown. "Placebo effects are responses to the belief in treatment," she replied softly, yet firmly. "What we explore here goes beyond belief—into direct experience."

"Direct experience?" David echoed; his tone laced with a polite incredulity. "Isn't that rather subjective?"

"Isn't all reality?" Maia countered, inviting him into the dance of debate. She leaned against a table adorned with crystals, their facets catching light like prisms. "Consider for a moment," she continued, "that every moment of consciousness is a subjective interpretation of an unfathomable universe. What's one more layer?"

David's pen hovered over his notepad, uncertainty flickering across his features as he considered her words. She didn't press further, allowing space for the seed of contemplation to take root.

"Alright then," David conceded, "what about this cosmic mind? How do you define it in tangible terms?"

"Picture it as a vast network," Maia suggested, her hands unfolding like a galaxy spiraling outward, "where each star represents a consciousness. Alone, they flicker dimly, but together, they illuminate the cosmos. We are those stars, David, connected by threads unseen but profoundly felt."

His blue eyes narrowed thoughtfully, a glimmer of curiosity breaking through the clouds of doubt. He scribbled down her metaphor, the act itself betraying his interest.

As he left the room, David glanced back at Maia, seeing her not just as a subject of his next article, but as a guide to uncharted territories of the mind. For the first time in a long while, he looked forward to where the story might lead.

The room, now emptied of the day's shared wonders and revelations, seemed to hold its breath. Maia lingered, her fingertips grazing the cool surface of a crystal that lay upon the wooden table, its edges catching the fading light. Each glimmer spoke of realms beyond human sight, echoing with the silent hymns of the cosmos.

Inside Maia's workshop, the incense smoke curled toward the ceiling, a spectral dance hinting at the unseen dimensions interwoven with their own. The energy of the day's communion still hummed within the walls, suggesting that the space itself had been altered by the collective pursuit of enlightenment.

Maia exhaled slowly, grounding herself in the present even as her spirit soared across time. The path ahead brimmed with potential pitfalls and promises, threaded with questions that begged for answers yet to be discovered.

Her heart beat in sync with the universe, ready for whatever secrets awaited unveiling.

Outside, the Boston skyline was a jagged silhouette against the twilight. Maia stepped into the cooling air, the city's pulse a distant rhythm beneath the celestial dance that played behind her eyes. She closed them for a moment, envisioning the Ascended Beings she had encountered in her mind's prolonged odyssey—a journey that had spanned the breadth of decades within the confines of mere hours.

Her return to this plane of existence brought with it a torrent of insights, each a puzzle piece waiting to align with the next. The challenges ahead were as numerous as the stars overhead; how could she possibly convey the depth of her experience? How could she bridge the gap between the ineffable and the concrete, between millennia of cosmic evolution and the fleeting moments of human lives?

She opened her eyes, the weight of responsibility settling on her shoulders like a mantle. There was work to be done, knowledge to impart. Yet as daunting as the task appeared, there was an undeniable thrill that surged through her—an electric charge at the prospect of guiding others toward their own encounters with the infinite.

David Hughes, once a skeptic, now stood at the precipice of his own vast exploration. His journalistic instinct would demand evidence, facts grounded in reality, but his recent brush with the transcendent had left him yearning for more than what could be measured or seen. As a man of words, he was about to embark on a journey where language itself might falter in its attempt to capture the indescribable.

The canvas that stretched before Sam Spencer was a riot of color, a maelstrom of swirling hues that seemed to pulse with an otherworldly energy.

Her brush danced across the surface, each stroke a deliberate act of creation that channeled the cosmic consciousness she'd tapped into during the DMT study. The gallery buzzed with onlookers; their eyes wide with amazement as they witnessed the birth of a visual symphony.

"See how she captures the essence of the infinite?" someone whispered in awe.

"Every piece is like a window into the universe," another replied, mesmerized by the vivid depiction of nebulae and stardust that appeared both alien and deeply familiar.

Sam stepped back, her green eyes reflecting the masterpiece she'd wrought - a representation of what she had seen in those transformative twelve hours that felt like decades. It was more than art; it was an invitation to journey through the very fabric of reality.

"Stunning, isn't it?" Maia's voice broke through the hum of the crowd. She stood beside Nina Patel, who beamed with pride at her friend's accomplishment.

"Beyond words," Nina agreed, her infectious smile catching the light of the gallery. "It's as if she's brought back a fragment of the cosmos itself."

Maia nodded, her expressive eyes scanning the painting as if reading a sacred text. "She has. Sam has become a conduit for something greater, sharing it with all who dare to look deeper."

"Speaking of sharing," Nina said, looping her arm through Maia's, "the workshop you helped me set up is thriving."

"Your passion is what fuels it, Nina. You've always had the gift of drawing people into our world," Maia replied warmly, her tone layered with affection.

"Perhaps, but your guidance has given my enthusiasm direction." Nina's gaze held a spark of determination. "Together, we're making waves."

"We sure are." Maia returned the gaze, her own determination a steady flame. "Our collaboration is just beginning. There's so much more to explore, to teach, to learn..."

"Then let's keep exploring," Nina proposed, her excitement contagious. "After all, the universe is vast, and we've only begun to glimpse its wonders."

"Done." Maia's agreement was soft yet resolute, a vow etched in the stars. "Let's continue to illuminate the path for others, as we walk it ourselves."

As they turned to admire another of Sam's cosmic landscapes, the trio stood united, each a lantern of insight and discovery, their individual journeys interlaced with the shared mission to awaken the cosmic consciousness within all.

THE RETREAT

Maia Rose stepped out of the car, her leather sandals crunching on the gravel path that led to the heart of the weekend retreat center. The location was The Rowe Center in Western Massachusetts, a haven tucked away from the harshness of everyday life, a place where the verdant embrace of nature held sway. Sunlight filtered through the tall pines, casting dappled shadows, and bathing the space in a warm, hazy glow. The air was electric with anticipation, a communal pulse humming beneath the surface as participants milled about, their conversations a low whirr of excitement.

She paused for a moment, taking in the scene, allowing the tranquility of the surroundings to wash over her. Maia's deep green eyes, which had seen beyond the veil of ordinary reality, reflected the serenity of the landscape. Inhaling deeply, she could taste the mixture of pine and anticipation on her tongue. There was a charged energy here, one that resonated with the profound journey she had recently embarked upon—a journey into the mind's most enigmatic corners, guided by the "Spirit Molecule" known as DMT.

Casting her gaze across the lawn, speckled with clusters of chatting attendees, Maia's attention was drawn to two familiar figures standing near the edge of a reflective pond, their gestures animated against the backdrop of still water. Nina Patel, with her lustrous dark hair and bright eyes, was locked in conversation with Dr. Evelyn Warren, whose sharp features were softened by the passion of their exchange. Nina's hands moved expressively as she spoke, her excitement unmistakable even from a distance.

Compelled by a mixture of affection for her friend and respect for Dr. Warren, Maia began to make her way toward them. As she walked, her movements exuded a calm assurance, each step a witness to the inner stability she had garnered. Her recent experiences had endowed her with a quiet confidence, a sense of purpose that carried her forward.

"Imagine," she rehearsed silently, preparing to share the revelations from her own introspective voyage, "if we could peel back the layers of perception that cloud our view, what wonders would we behold? What truths would reveal themselves when the chatter of the ego falls silent, and we stand face-to-face with the raw fabric of existence?"

There were lessons she was eager to impart, the insights gleaned from a place where consciousness expanded beyond the self, touching the infinite. It wasn't just an exploration of personal depths, but a communion with the cosmic mind, an interconnectedness that defied description yet demanded to be shared.

Maia's stride quickened, her heart fluttering like a captive bird nearing release. The grass whispered underfoot as she approached the two figures, each step bringing her closer to the reunion that had been months in the making. Nina's arms opened wide, and Maia fell into them, the embrace a solid reminder of their enduring connection. Dr. Warren's hug followed, less effusive but no less heartfelt, a testament to the bond forged through shared intellectual curiosity.

"Look at you," Nina exclaimed, stepping back to appraise Maia with a gaze that captured the very essence of her transformation. "There's a light in your eyes that wasn't there before."

"Exploration does tend to illuminate the explorer," Dr. Warren added, her smile hinting at the depth of her anticipation for the tales to come.

Together, they meandered towards an alcove shielded by towering oaks, where nature had carved out a natural sanctuary. They settled onto the weathered wooden bench, the lush canopy above dappling sunlight upon their faces.

"Tell us everything," Nina urged, her voice a mix of excitement and reverence. "Start from the beginning."

Maia took a deep breath, feeling the weight of expectation and the thrill of sharing.

Her hands moved expressively as she began weaving the narrative of her time within Harvard's hallowed walls and the realm beyond ordinary perception.

"Imagine, if you will, the mind as a vast ocean," she started, her words painting a picture vivid and vast. "We usually swim near the shore, in the shallows of our day-to-day experiences. But the DMT study... it was like diving into uncharted depths where the waters of consciousness grow dark and mysterious."

Nina leaned forward, captivated by the metaphor, while Dr. Warren nodded, encouraging the exploration of this analogy.

"Underneath those waves, I encountered landscapes of the psyche that defied all logic. I was both the drop and the ocean, singular yet part of an immeasurable whole. It was as if the molecule served as a key, unlocking doors to rooms within the mind I had never known existed."

"Like accessing hidden compartments of the self?" Nina interjected, her inquiry encouragement guiding Maia's narrative.

"Exactly," Maia affirmed with a smile. "And beyond the self, even. There were moments during the journey when 'I' ceased to be an individual and became a note in a cosmic choir.

Dr. Warren's eyes gleamed with fascination. "A dissolution of ego—akin to what mystics have described across cultures and ages."

"Absolutely," Maia agreed. "The experience was profound, disorienting, and ultimately enlightening. There's this sense of interconnectedness with all living things, the fabric of existence woven from the same thread."

She paused, collecting her thoughts like pearls scattered across the ocean floor. "It challenged my understanding of reality, pushing me to consider new dimensions of being. And it posed questions—about life, about death, and about the very foundation that constitutes our universe."

"Questions that we're all here to ponder," Dr. Warren said, gesturing to the retreat around them. Her statement hung in the air, a prelude to the discussions and discoveries that awaited them.

"Thank you for sharing, Maia," Nina said softly, reaching out to squeeze her hand. "Your insights are a gift."

They stood there, three souls converging at the crossroads of inquiry and enlightenment, ready to delve into the seminars and lectures that promised to unravel the mysteries of mind and molecule. In the distance, the promise of understanding awaited, a lecture hall where science and spirituality would dance in the minds of those who dared to seek the truth.

"I'm eager to see how Dr. Brooks will bridge our subjective experiences with the empirical," Maia mused, her gaze turning introspective. "His lecture on the science behind the DMT study—it's the missing piece of the puzzle we've been searching for."

"Jameson has a way of elucidating the most complex concepts. His understanding of the molecule itself... it's like he sees the code beneath the canvas of reality," Dr. Warren remarked, her voice marked with respect.

"Exactly!" Maia exclaimed. "It's one thing to live through the experience, to feel the profound connection with the cosmos. But to comprehend it, to dissect it through the lens of science—that's where true evolution of thought begins."

"Science is the map, and experience is the territory," Nina chimed in, her timidity giving way to enthusiasm. "Together, they could guide us to so many answers."

"True," Maia agreed, her anticipation unmistakable. "And I can't wait to explore every contour of that map. To understand not just the 'what' of my journey, but the 'how,' and the 'why.' It's like standing at the edge of a new frontier, with Dr. Brooks as our navigator."

"Indeed," Dr. Warren said thoughtfully. "Understanding the mechanics of DMT could well be the key to unlocking the doors of perception. And from there, who knows what realms we'll discover?"

Maia and her companions rose from their introspective bubble, the ground beneath them springy with the grassy carpet of the retreat center. They walked side by side towards the main hall, a structure that echoed the serenity of the natural setting with its wide, welcoming doors and large windows that invited the outside in.

"Can you feel it?" Nina whispered, a ripple of excitement tracing her words. "It's like we're all part of something much bigger than ourselves."

Maia nodded, her heart syncing to the rhythm of collective expectation that filled the air, mingling with the rustle of leaves and distant murmurs. The retreat center, a haven for those seeking enlightenment, had become a vessel for the journey ahead, its main hall the heart where minds would soon connect and expand.

Upon reaching the threshold of the hall, they were greeted by the sight of a diverse congregation. Scholars, seekers, skeptics—all had converged here, united by the common thread of curiosity. The room buzzed—a hive of humans, each drawn to the enigma of consciousness and the allure of the unknown.

Maia found herself scanning the crowd, absorbing the variations of awe and contemplation etched on the faces around her. She felt a kinship with these strangers, knowing that within this space, barriers fell away as easily as breath melds into air.

They made their way through the thicket of bodies, the excitement swelling with each step closer to the stage. As they settled into their seats, Maia's skin tingled, her senses sharpening.

She was acutely aware of the texture of the chair beneath her, the warmth of the bodies beside her, the gentle cadence of her own breathing.

Silence enveloped the hall. All chatter ceased as Dr. Brooks stepped onto the stage, his presence commanding yet reassuringly calm. A spotlight highlighted his poised figure, rimless glasses reflecting the room's eager gaze.

"Welcome," he began, his voice carrying a timbre that resonated with the very walls, "to an exploration of the most profound journey one can undertake—the journey within."

Maia leaned forward, her every cell attuned to his words. This was the moment she had been waiting for, the crossroads where empirical evidence met the ineffable.

"Today, we delve into the essence of "The Spirit Molecule" DMT, Dr. Brooks continued, "and how it might unlock the deepest mysteries of our existence."

Maia's pulse quickened as Dr. Brooks spoke. Each sentence was a bonfire, illuminating the path she had traveled during her study participation—the visions of infinite connectivity, the dissolution of the ego, the rapture of touching something beyond the physical realm.

"Through rigorous science," Dr. Brooks was saying, "we seek not to define the sacred, but to understand the vessel through which the sacred is experienced."

In his measured cadence, Maia heard echoes of her own insights, the revelations that had reshaped her understanding of reality. She was on the edge of her seat now, not just physically but spiritually, mentally prepared to bridge the gap between her extraordinary experience and the scientific framework that cradled it.

"Let us embark," Dr. Brooks beckoned, "on the ultimate expedition to chart the unexplored territories of the human mind."

As Dr. Brooks spoke, Maia felt herself standing once again at the precipice of discovery, ready to dive into the cosmic ocean that lay before her.

With each word, she was reminded that the map they were creating was not just to navigate the inner cosmos but also to return and tell the tale.

With a deep breath, anchoring herself to the present, Maia readied to share her odyssey, to be both the cartographer and the traveler of this vast, uncharted expanse of consciousness.

"Consider, if you will," Dr. Jameson Brooks began, his voice resonating with a clarity that hushed the eager murmurs of the assembly, "a molecule so profound that it could be the very key to unlocking the enigma of human consciousness." The dimmed lights in the hall cast an almost sacred glow around him, and every eye was fixed upon the stage.

"Dimethyltryptamine, or DMT," he continued, gesturing to a molecular structure projected behind him, "is a naturally occurring compound, one that your body synthesizes on its own. It's found in plants, animals, and yes—in us."

Maia leaned forward, her elbows resting on her knees, her hands clasped as if to physically grasp the words that floated towards her. She had felt the power of this molecule coursing through her own veins, had been a willing pilgrim in its otherworldly landscape. Now, she hungered for the science behind the transcendent.

"Research has illuminated that at critical moments of life, such as during birth or at the time of death, levels of DMT surge within our brains," Dr. Brooks elucidated, his hands open as if he were offering the knowledge directly to each listener. "What does this imply about the nature of our reality? Could this 'spirit molecule' be a bridge to realms we have yet to understand fully? Perhaps what we perceive during these heightened states is akin to what some describe as the afterlife."

Maia's breath caught in her throat. The afterlife—a concept so abstract yet rendered almost tangible through her experiences. Her mind wove her memories with Dr. Brooks' words, stitching together a tapestry of empirical and experiential wisdom.

"Many who have encountered DMT in controlled settings report journeys of indescribable beauty and complexity," Dr. Brooks went on, his demeanor composed yet infused with a hint of wonder. "They speak of encounters with entities, of a sense of oneness with the universe, of a dissolution of the ego."

The agreement was evident in Maia's nod. She had been one with the cosmos, had conversed with beings not of this world, had shed the confines of her individuality to swim in the universal current. It was exhilarating to hear her subjective voyage affirmed by the gravitas of scientific inquiry.

"Of course," Dr. Brooks paced gently across the stage, "we must approach these anecdotes with both openness and a rigorous scientific lens. We stand on the precipice of understanding not just the biological function of DMT, but also the philosophical and psychological implications of its effects."

Maia felt a kinship with the molecule itself—as though she were a point of light in a vast network, connected to each person in the room through their shared curiosity. Dr. Brooks' lecture was not just an exposition; it was an invitation to explore the very fabric of existence, guided by the beacon of science.

"Imagine the possibilities," Dr. Brooks said, his voice imbued with an almost evangelical zeal, "if we can harness the teachings from these inner voyages. What deeper truths about our minds, about our shared humanity, might we uncover?"

Maia's heart raced, her thoughts ablaze. Here, in the convergence of her profound personal odyssey and the scientific exploration laid out before her, lay the potential for true understanding.

And as Dr. Brooks spoke, she knew that her journey was far from over—it was just beginning to unfold in ways more extraordinary than she could have ever imagined.

The hushed reverence of the audience hummed like a charged current as Dr. Jameson Brooks turned to Maia, extending his hand toward her with an encouraging nod. "Please join me in welcoming Maia Yetta Rose, whose experience will undoubtedly resonate with many of you."

Maia stood, her limbs tingling with a blend of nerves and exhilaration. The path to the stage felt like crossing a symbolic threshold, each step a commitment to share the once untellable. She took a deep breath, grounding herself in the moment before stepping into the spotlight.

"Thank you, Dr. Brooks," she began, her voice steady despite the butterflies dancing in her stomach. "I stand here before you not just as a researcher or a subject, but as a traveler who's ventured into the depths of consciousness and returned with a message—a cosmic postcard, if you will."

She caught a glimpse of Dr. Evelyn Warren in the front row, her piercing eyes fixed on Maia with an intensity that both intimidated and reassured. Maia smiled faintly, drawing strength from the silent support.

"Imagine for a moment that our reality is but a single brushstroke on an infinite canvas," Maia painted the picture with her words, gesturing with open palms as if to reveal an invisible masterpiece. "During my journey, I was swept beyond that canvas, where the barriers between self and universe dissolved. There, I encountered what I can only describe as the cosmic mind—a vast, interconnected network of consciousness."

A collective inhale swept through the room, attendees hanging on to every word as if it were a lifeline thrown across dimensions.

"In this space," Maia continued, her own awe coloring her tone, "time loses meaning, and the personal history that we cling to—our joys, our traumas—it all fades into a fabric of collective experience. I realized that our individual minds are but singular points of awareness within this grand continuum."

"Through this merging, I learned that empathy is more than a virtue—it's a fundamental truth of existence. To harm another is to harm oneself, and to help another is to uplift the whole."

Dr. Brooks watched, a gleam of fascination lighting up behind his rimless glasses. His scientific mind undoubtedly memorizing every word, adding them to his own catalog of hypotheses and theories.

"Such revelations may sound esoteric," Maia admitted, "but they beckon us to consider how we live our everyday lives. What might our world look like if we all embraced this interconnectedness? If we recognized that at the core, we are all expressions of the same cosmic consciousness?" The question lingered, inviting each listener to ponder their place in the cosmic web.

"As we continue to explore the science behind DMT and its gateway to these profound experiences," Maia concluded, her voice filled with passion, "let us remember that these molecules are not just chemicals. They are potential keys to unlocking the deepest mysteries of our existence—and perhaps to healing our world."

A chorus of applause erupted, the sound reverberating through Maia's being. As the clapping subsided, she stepped down, her heart still pounding with the thrill of sharing her innermost odyssey.

"Thank you, Maia, for that enlightening account," Dr. Brooks said, reclaiming the stage. "Let us all take a moment to reflect on these insights as we continue our journey through this retreat—and beyond."

As Maia rejoined her friends, the weight of her experience now shared, she felt lighter, more connected than ever to the room full of seekers, to the world, to the cosmos itself.

Dr. Brooks turning to the audience with a knowing look. "Such experiences are deeply personal, yet they echo universal truths about who we are and what we might become."

He then shifted his gaze to the wings, where another soul awaited her moment to share. "Now, let us welcome Samantha Spencer, whose vivacious spirit and insatiable enthusiasm for exploring consciousness have brought her here today."

Sam bounded onto the stage, her auburn hair catching the light like flames against the dark backdrop. Her green eyes sparkled with an unquenchable curiosity, a mirror to every seeker in the room.

"Hello, beautiful beings!" Her voice was a bright chime, instantly dissolving any remnants of formality. "We've heard how Maia embraced the cosmic symphony, and now I'm thrilled to dive into the melody of my own journey with you."

She leaned into the microphone, her presence a whirlwind of passion and excitement. "For me, it was like awakening inside a dream where every color sang, and every sound painted a picture. DMT didn't just open doors; it dissolved walls, revealing a playground of possibilities."

Sam's hands danced as she recounted her odyssey, her narrative an infectious rhythm that pulsed through the room. "I laughed with the stars, cried with the moon, and felt the heartbeat of eternity in the palm of my hand."

The audience was enraptured, riding the waves of her enthusiasm as she wove her story with the threads of adventure and discovery, each word a stepping-stone deeper into the rabbit hole of consciousness.

"Through this journey," Sam concluded, her eyes gleaming with the thrill of shared secrets, "I've learned that the universe is not just around us—it is us. And the adventure... oh, the adventure is just beginning."

Dr. Brooks watched from the side, a proud mentor witnessing the unfolding of potential, knowing that the insights shared today were seeds planted in fertile ground, destined to bloom into a garden of wisdom.

Samantha Spencer leaned forward, her eyes alight with the fire of her recent journey, a stark contrast to Maia's tranquil emergence from the same experience. "While Maia found serenity in the cosmic orchestra," she began, her voice tinged with the fervor of her revelations, "I surfed the crests of quantum symphonies, each wave a vibrant witness to the underlying chaos that dances at the edge of order."

The audience was spellbound as Samantha described navigating an inner cosmos where emotion and thought blended into a kaleidoscope of consciousness—a universe parallel yet distinct from Maia's harmonious convergence. "Maia embraced the unity of all existence," Sam articulated, her hands painting the air with her words, "but I discovered an exuberant multiplicity, a celebration of individual sparks within the infinite firework display of being."

She shared how laughter became a language that transcended spoken word, how tears were not expressions of sorrow but of profound connection with the life force pulsating through every atom. "In my voyage," she said, her green eyes reflecting the depths of her transformative odyssey, "the universe didn't just whisper its secrets; it sang them in a chorus of light and shadow."

Dr. Brooks stepped onto the stage, his eyes reflecting the satisfaction of a teacher whose students have surpassed expectations. "What we've witnessed here," he mused, "is the beautiful spectrum of human consciousness revealed through the lens of DMT.

While Maia's experience was a deep dive into the unifying ocean of cosmic consciousness, Samantha's was a jubilant leap into the ever-expanding multiverse of the psyche."

The doctor paused, allowing the weight of his words to settle among the listeners. "Both journeys, though divergent in texture, share the fabric of profound personal transformation. They remind us that our explorations into altered states are mirrors reflecting our innermost selves—unique, boundless, and rich with potential for growth and understanding."

"Today," Dr. Brooks concluded, his calm voice resonating with the gravity of their collective insights, "we stand at the precipice of a new frontier, where each journey inward can illuminate the path forward—not just for the traveler but for all who seek to comprehend the vast landscape of human consciousness."

The room buzzed with profound excitement, each person present realizing they were part of a conversation that stretched beyond the confines of the retreat center, into the very heart of what it means to be alive, to be aware, to be infinitely connected.

As the final reverberations of Dr. Brooks' profound closing words dissipated into the charged air, the audience remained in a collective hush, each individual processing the magnitude of what had been shared. The atmosphere was electric with the residue of Maia and Samantha's revelations, an undercurrent of anticipation running through the room like the prelude to a symphony's crescendo.

Maia Rose stood at the edge of the stage, her eyes scanning the sea of faces before her—each one lit by the flicker of curiosity, the spark of an ignited imagination. She could feel the questions brewing, the minds around her teetering on the brink of epiphanies, yearning for more than just stories of psychedelic voyages. They craved understanding, a deeper knowledge of the implications that such experiences could unearth about the human condition.

"Think of it," she began, her voice a gentle beckoning as she stepped forward, "as stepping through a doorway to a realm where time distorts, and space becomes malleable. Each step you take is guided by your own consciousness, a dance with the innermost threads of your being. We've only scratched the surface tonight."

The audience leaned in, as if the very act could bring them closer to the mysteries she described. Maia's hands sculpted the air before her, framing the intangible, drawing her listeners further into her narrative. "This is not the end of our journey—it's merely the beginning. The implications of DMT and altered states stretch far beyond personal transformation; they reach into the essence of what connects us all."

A murmur of assent rippled through the crowd, acknowledging the profundity of the insight. Dr. Evelyn Warren nodded pensively from her seat in the front row, her keen intellect already threading together the practical applications of these experiences in therapeutic settings. Sam Spencer's vibrant energy charged the space around her, her eagerness infectious as she imagined the countless paths this new frontier of consciousness exploration could unveil.

Dr. Jameson Brooks rose, his presence commanding the attention of the room once again. "We have begun to map the topography of the human psyche in ways we never thought possible," he stated, his voice imbuing each word with significance. "Our next chapter will dive deeper into how these insights can be integrated into our lives, transforming not only our understanding of consciousness but also the very fabric of our society."

He paused, allowing his gaze to sweep over the audience, ensuring that each participant felt seen, felt included in the monumental task ahead. "Together, we will explore the practical applications of these altered states, examining how they can enhance creativity, foster deep healing, and even expand our capacity for empathy and compassion."

The sense of anticipation was now tangible, a living entity within the walls of the retreat center. As Maia descended from the stage, the conversations that bloomed around her were rich with speculation and wonder, discussions sprouting like seeds eager to grow in the fertile ground of newfound knowledge.

"Tomorrow," Dr. Brooks announced, his voice guiding them toward the dawn of the next day's explorations, "we turn our focus to the integration of these extraordinary experiences into daily life. How do we carry the wisdom gained from the deepest realms of consciousness back into the world? How do we embody the lessons learned from the cosmic consciousness and make them manifest?"

The following morning the hushed murmurs of an expectant audience filled the auditorium. Dr. Jameson Brooks stepped up to the podium with his characteristic calm that anchored the room in a collective breath of anticipation. He adjusted his rimless glasses—a gesture those familiar with his lectures knew signaled the beginning of a journey into the intricate labyrinths of the human mind.

"Good morning," he began, his voice radiating through the space, "Today we explore the profound potential of DMT treatment for serious mental illnesses. To guide us through this exploration, I'm honored to introduce Dr. Evelyn Warren, whose expertise blends rigorous science with deep compassion for those grappling with trauma and depression."

Dr. Warren approached the stage, her presence commanding yet nurturing, like a seasoned captain setting sail. The audience leaned forward, eager to absorb the wisdom she was about to impart.

"Thank you, Dr. Brooks," Dr. Warren said, acknowledging her colleague with a nod. "What if I told you that within our brains lies a key that could unlock new dimensions of healing? DMT, or N, N-Dimethyltryptamine, might just be that key."

The attendees were captivated as Dr. Warren painted a picture of the brain under the influence of DMT—a landscape where neural pathways lit up like constellations in the night sky, each starburst representing a potential breakthrough for those ensnared in the darkness of mental illness.

"Imagine patients enveloped by the weight of depression suddenly experiencing a cosmic shift," she continued. "DMT-assisted therapy has shown promising results, transporting individuals to realms of consciousness where profound healing can occur."

She deftly cited studies, her words weaving a web of scientific evidence that supported the therapeutic use of DMT. Clinical trials were not just numbers and data points; they were beacons of hope, illuminating the path towards understanding and integration.

"However, with great potential comes great responsibility," she asserted, her tone shifting to underscore the gravity of ethical considerations. "We must navigate this terrain with caution, ensuring the safety and dignity of those who entrust us with their minds."

Dr. Warren explained the mechanisms at play—how DMT binds to serotonin receptors, opening the floodgates to experiences that often defy description yet resonate with spiritual significance. She spoke of the molecule's dance with the brain's architecture, a ballet that could lead to transformative psychological experiences.

"Patients have reported encounters with ineffable realities, a sense of oneness with the universe," she elucidated, her hands gesturing as if to sculpt the very essence of these revelations. "These moments of transcendence could be pivotal in redefining one's relationship with life's deepest sorrows."

The room was charged with an electric sense of possibility, the air itself seeming to vibrate with the implications of what had been shared. Dr. Warren's presentation was more than a lecture—it was an invitation to gaze beyond the veil of conventional treatment and consider a future where the mind's mysterious landscapes could be navigated with a newfound map.

"Let us proceed with both awe and scrutiny," Dr. Warren concluded, her eyes reflecting the passion that fueled her life's work. "For in the balance lies the promise of healing, not just for the individual, but for the very fabric of how we understand mental health and consciousness itself."

A symphony of applause erupted as Dr. Warren stepped back from the podium, her final words lingering in the air like the ring of a sacred bell, beckoning all present to embark on this journey of discovery and transformation together.

The afternoon light streamed through the tall windows of the conference room, casting a warm glow on the faces of the attendees as they dispersed into their chosen breakout sessions. Each cluster of professionals and enthusiasts formed organic circles, the air humming with the excitement of collective curiosity.

Maia stood at the front of her designated area, surveying the eager faces before her. Her voice took on a rhythm that was both inviting and contemplative as she initiated the session.

"Think of your mind as a vast frontier," Maia began, her hands open in a gesture of welcome. "Now imagine DMT as the key to a hidden doorway within that landscape. Behind it lies the potential for profound healing—a place where trauma and addiction lose their grip, where existential distress is met with deep understanding."

She paused, allowing the weight of her words to settle among the listeners.

"During my journey with DMT, I encountered a foundation of truths built with the very essence of consciousness. It was as if each pillar represented a lesson—about life, about suffering, about our shared human condition."

Maia's eyes shone with an inner fire, reflecting her passion for the subject. "Today, I want to explore how these revelations can help us sculpt a better world."

In the stillness that followed, one could sense minds opening like flowers to sunlight, receptive to the seeds Maia was about to sow.

"Imagine confronting your darkest fears, not as insurmountable giants, but as teachers," she continued, her tone filled with warmth. "DMT offered me such encounters, revealing that what we most fear often holds the key to our greatest growth."

The group leaned in, hanging on every word, as Maia painted a picture of transformation through her own experience.

"Through the lens of DMT, I saw how interconnected we are—the illusion of separation dissolved. This insight alone has the power to revolutionize how we treat one another. Picture a society that truly grasps the concept of unity, where compassion flows naturally because the wellbeing of one is linked to the wellbeing of all."

Nods of agreement rippled through the assembly, a silent affirmation of the universal yearning for deeper connection.

"My experience with DMT also taught me about the impermanence of all things, which paradoxically grants significance to every moment." Maia's voice softened; each syllable laden with reverence. "If we can integrate this understanding into therapy, imagine the freedom it could bring to those shackled by their past or paralyzed by anxiety about the future."

"Yet, with such powerful experiences come responsibilities—to ourselves and to those we guide through these realms." She made eye contact with her audience, ensuring everyone felt seen and acknowledged. "As we consider the therapeutic applications of DMT, we must do so with respect for the depths of the human psyche and a commitment to ethical practice."

Her final words were an invitation to introspection, a call to each person to ponder their role in this emerging field.

"Let's discuss how we can carry these lessons forward, together building a framework that honors the sanctity of the mind and the transformative potential of DMT."

With that, Maia stepped back, allowing the space for dialogue to flourish, as the group plunged into a vibrant exchange of insights and aspirations, each contribution a thread in the new tapestry they were weaving.

The buzz of the audience rippled into silence as Samantha Spencer strode confidently into the room. With a smile that lit up the entire space, Sam joined Maia at the front, her presence instantly commanding the attention of every attendee. Her eyes sparkled with an irrepressible energy as she greeted the group, her voice brimming with anticipation.

"Thank you, Maia, for paving the way," Sam began, her words flowing with the cadence of someone who had journeyed far and returned with treasures of wisdom. "Like Maia, I too was a volunteer in the DMT study, and our experiences, though they tread similar paths, have painted very different vistas."

Maia nodded, her calm demeanor complementing Sam's vivacious spirit. "Welcome, Sam. It's amazing how two people can drink from the same well and yet taste different waters."

"Absolutely," Sam agreed. "My experience felt like a kaleidoscope of interconnected moments. I saw life as a tapestry woven from countless threads, each one significant, each life interwoven with others." She gestured expansively, as if drawing the threads in the air. "It made me see that healing isn't just personal; it's communal."

The room leaned in, captivated by the authentic exchange between the two speakers. Maia picked up on the theme.

"In my journey, I found myself dissolving into an ocean of consciousness, where individuality gave way to a profound sense of oneness." Her hands moved gently, mimicking the ebb and flow of tides. "But even as we lose ourselves in this vastness, we find a deeper understanding of our unique purpose in the cosmic dance."

"Isn't it fascinating?" Sam interjected; her enthusiasm contagious. "I encountered vibrant, pulsating energies, entities that seemed to guide me, urging me to embrace joy and face pain with equal grace." She paused, her expression reflecting a moment of deep reverence. "It taught me about resilience, about facing the shadows within us with courage and compassion."

"Shadow and light," Maia mused, echoing Sam's sentiment. "My shadow was more like a quiet, dark room where I confronted fears and long-buried sorrows. But there was light there too—illuminating insights that showed me the strength that comes from vulnerability."

"Two sides of the same coin," Sam added with a nod. "And here's what's truly remarkable," she continued, turning to the audience, her tone inviting them closer into the conversation. "These experiences, while deeply personal, hold universal lessons. They speak to the human condition, to our shared quest for meaning and connection."

"Which is why your voices are so important," Maia said, her gaze sweeping across the faces before her. "Each of you brings a unique perspective, a piece of the puzzle. So, let's open the floor—share your thoughts, ask questions, and let's explore together the therapeutic potential of this spirit molecule."

The invitation hung in the air, a beckoning to probe deeper, to venture boldly into the heart of the dialogue. Hands tentatively rose, and soon the room was alive with the buzz of conversation. Questions were posed, experiences recounted, theories examined. The collective wisdom of the group surfaced, each contribution valued, each person seen.

As the discussion unfolded, the boundaries between speaker and listener blurred. The room became a refuge of exploration, a safe harbor for the curious minds gathered within—a testament to the power of shared stories and the transformative potential of psychedelics when approached with openness and care.

A hand shot up from the crowd, a beam of curiosity cutting through the contemplative hush that had settled over the room. Maia Rose, her serene expression embodying the grace of profound discovery, nodded to the attendee.

"Maia, Samantha," the voice quivered with the weight of consideration. "You've shared these intense, ephemeral experiences with DMT. But I'm wondering about the afterglow—how do you carry forward the insights from such fleeting moments? Can they truly last?"

The room leaned in, as if the walls themselves were eager for the answer.

"An excellent question," Maia began, her voice the auditory equivalent of a gentle hand on the shoulder. "The experiences themselves are transient, yes, but the lessons... they embed within us, like seeds waiting to sprout. The integration process is where those seeds grow roots."

Samantha Spencer's enthusiasm was an undercurrent, energizing the space. "It's about daily practice," she interjected, her sparkling eyes dancing with fervor. "Meditation, journaling, art—whatever form it takes, it's the act of honoring what you've learned and applying it to your life."

"Think of it as learning a language," Maia continued. "At first, it seems foreign, but with regular use, it becomes second nature. You begin to see the world through this new lens, one that allows for greater empathy, connection, and above all, hope."

Nodding heads rippled through the audience, as the metaphor struck a chord.

Dr. Evelyn Warren stepped forward, her presence commanding attention. "While these personal transformations are significant," she said, her tone balancing warmth with authority, "we must also recognize our responsibility in exploring these frontiers."

"DMT treatment, like any powerful tool, carries risks and demands ethical considerations," Dr. Warren declared, her piercing eyes scanning the room. "We're on the cusp of a new era in mental health care, but we must tread thoughtfully."

"Further research and clinical trials are imperative," she continued, her hands punctuating each point. "We need guidelines, protocols to ensure that when we harness the potential of DMT, it's done with safety, respect, and a deep appreciation for the gravity of altering human consciousness."

"Imagine," Dr. Warren paused, allowing the word to resonate, "a future where we can mitigate suffering with these treatments, where we enhance healing not just of individuals, but of society. That is the horizon we're looking towards, but it can only be reached through diligent, responsible exploration."

Maia's eyes met Samantha's, a silent exchange of mutual understanding passing between them. They turned back to the attendees, who now sat on the precipice of possibility, their minds alight with the revelations of the day.

"Your engagement today," Maia said, "is a vital part of this journey. By discussing, questioning, and sharing, you contribute to a collective wisdom far greater than any single experience."

"Because at its core," Samantha concluded, her words wrapping around each listener like a warm embrace, "this is about connection—to ourselves, to each other, and to the vast, uncharted depths of the human spirit."

The conversation rippled through the room, each attendee bringing their unique perspective to the surface.

Maia leaned forward, her hands clasped together in front of her as she listened intently to the various voices that filled the space with energy and purpose.

"Integration is key," a therapist voiced from the back row, his words echoing the sentiment of many. "We can't just introduce such a powerful substance into mainstream care without considering how it fits into the broader spectrum of treatment options."

"Absolutely," a researcher chimed in, adjusting her glasses as she spoke. "And collaboration will be crucial. We must break down the silos between disciplines. Psychologists, neuroscientists, spiritual leaders—we all have something valuable to contribute."

Maia nodded, her empathetic nature allowing her to absorb the passion in the room. She could feel the collective yearning for a change, a shift towards a more comprehensive approach to mental health care.

"Imagine," ventured a spiritual practitioner, his voice calm yet full of conviction, "a therapeutic model that honors not only the science behind these substances but also the sacredness of the experiences they can induce. A model that respects the mystery as much as the molecule."

The group fell into a thoughtful silence, contemplating the profound implications of such a partnership. It was clear that the road ahead would be one of discovery, requiring careful navigation and an openness to learn from one another.

As the session ended, Maia rose from her seat, capturing the attention of every individual in attendance. She cleared her throat gently, a signal that she was about to encapsulate the essence of their shared vision.

"Today, we've plunged into the heart of what it means to heal," Maia began, her calm demeanor infusing the room with a sense of serenity. "We've witnessed the enthusiasm for DMT's therapeutic potential and recognized the challenges that come with pioneering a new frontier in mental health care."

She paced slowly in front of the group, ensuring her gaze met those of her peers as she spoke. "We've discussed the necessity of building bridges—between science and spirituality, research and practice, tradition and innovation. This synergy is where true healing begins."

"Let us carry forward the lessons from today," Maia continued, her voice filled with inspiration. "Let us be fearless in our exploration, yet always grounded in ethics and compassion. Let us be bold in our collaborations, yet always respectful of the individual paths we tread."

"Your participation here," she said, gesturing inclusively to encompass the entire room, "is just the beginning. Keep exploring, keep questioning, and most importantly, keep sharing your insights. Together, we can shape a future that embraces the full spectrum of human consciousness and its remarkable capacity for growth and transformation."

A murmur of agreement swept through the attendees as Maia's words settled over them like a warm blanket of hope and possibility. Her encouragement was not just a call to action—it was an invitation to embark on a journey toward understanding and healing that transcended the boundaries of conventional therapy.

"Thank you all," Maia concluded, her eyes alight with the reflection of a shared mission, "for being part of this extraordinary conversation. Let's continue to dream, discover, and deliver the promise of a better world—one where the mind's deepest sorrows can find solace and where its greatest potential can be unlocked."

As applause filled the room, there was a sense of unity, a collective commitment to the path ahead—an exploration not just of DMT's therapeutic potential, but of humanity's endless capacity for renewal and transformation.

As the last echoes of applause faded into a contented hush, attendees rose from their seats, stretching legs cramped from lengthy periods of sitting, yet their spirits were anything but weary. Energized conversations blossomed like a field of wildflowers after the first spring rain. They clustered in small groups, their expressions animated and hands gesturing passionately as they digested the session's revelations.

"Wasn't that something?" Samantha's voice, vibrant with enthusiasm, pulled Maia back into the present. They moved to the side of the now-emptying hall, finding peace in a quiet corner where the echoes of their session could be privately savored.

"Absolutely," Maia replied, her calm demeanor belying the whirlwind of thoughts within. "To see so many minds open up, ready to explore the therapeutic edges of consciousness—it's inspiring."

"Like planting seeds in a garden we've only just discovered." Samantha's green eyes sparkled, reflecting not just the overhead lights but the inner glow of someone who had witnessed the profound. "And watching them take root in real-time... it's beyond words, isn't it?"

Maia nodded, her own experience with DMT a labyrinth of revelation that she'd been unraveling ever since. "Every person in that room has the potential to change lives. It's a ripple effect, starting with our own journeys, spreading through our stories, and expanding as they apply this knowledge in their practices."

"Exactly!" Samantha leaned in closer, her voice dropping to an earnest whisper. "Think about it—every patient they help, every life they touch, it all stems from understanding how deeply connected we are, not just to each other, but to the very fabric of reality. DMT can show us that, and today, we got to share a piece of that truth."

They paused, letting the magnitude of their shared mission settle over them. It was a sacred trust, one that extended beyond the personal to touch on the universal.

Maia felt the weight of her responsibility, tempered by the overwhelming gratitude for the chance to stand at this crossroads of science and spirit.

"Today," Maia began, her voice steady and infused with conviction, "we peeled back a layer of the human psyche that many never get to see. We offered a glimpse into a realm where healing goes deeper than the physical, where the mind's eye opens to new horizons of understanding and compassion."

Samantha's hand found Maia's, a physical connection amidst the intangible wonders they discussed. "And what a gift that is," she said, squeezing gently. "To guide, to heal, to illuminate—it's a journey of a thousand steps, and today we took one together."

Their reflections were a mirror for each other, the profound experiences they had navigated now shared with a broader community eager to embark on their own voyages of discovery. As they stood there, the last whispers of conversation fading away with the departing attendees, Maia and Samantha knew that the day's revelations would echo far beyond the walls of this conference hall. They had sown the seeds of curiosity and courage, and in time, they would watch as a new landscape of consciousness blossomed under the careful tending of those who dared to dream, explore, and heal.

"Imagine," Maia postulated, her hands now folded thoughtfully in front of her, "a world where the barriers between us are recognized as illusions. A world where empathy flows freely because we have touched the interconnectedness at the core of all being."

"Such a world is within reach," Samantha said, stepping towards the large window, the fading sunlight casting a warm glow on her face. "And every person here is a pioneer in that journey. They came seeking knowledge, and what they found was a roadmap to a new frontier of the human spirit."

As the last of the attendees filed out, exchanging excited whispers about the coming day, Maia and Samantha shared a knowing glance. They had set the stage for a revolution of the mind and heart, and there was no turning back. Tomorrow beckoned, ripe with possibility, and every soul in attendance could hardly wait to answer its call.

BEYOND THE VEIL

Maia's phone shattered the silence, its shrill tone slicing through the stillness of her apartment. She snatched it up, her pulse quickening as she saw Lucas' name flashing on the display.

"Maia," Lucas' voice came through, tight with urgency, "It's Dr. Warren. She's at Mass General, in critical condition. You need to get here now."

The phone almost slipped from Maia's grasp. Dr. Evelyn Warren—her mentor, the women responsible for guiding her through the murky waters of cosmic consciousness research—lay vulnerable in a hospital bed, teetering on the edge of the unknown. Without a word, Maia ended the call and sprang into action.

Looming before her, the towering façade of Massachusetts General was glowing in the dusk. Maia dashed through the sliding doors, her sneakers squeaking against the polished floor as she navigated the intricate corridors. Her heart pounded in her chest; each beat a deafening drum that echoed the panic coursing through her veins.

She skidded to a halt outside room 517, where Dr. Warren was fighting her own battle within. A nurse, recognizing Maia from having worked in the urgent care unit and seeing her bringing in patient after patient while an EMT, nodded silently and stepped aside, granting her entry.

The sight that greeted Maia stole her breath. Dr. Warren, Evelyn lay amidst a tangle of tubes and wires, her once formidable presence reduced to a fragile shell. The rise and fall of her chest was labored, each breath a whisper of life clinging desperately to form.

"Maia," Dr. Warren rasped, her eyes fluttering open to fix their gaze upon her protégé. Despite the weakness evident in her voice, there was an undeniable strength—a force that had propelled Maia's own understanding of the universe to heights she never imagined.

"Evelyn," Maia breathed out, grasping her mentor's hand. It was cold, yet the familiar spark of curiosity and determination lingered there, witness to the indomitable spirit that had charted paths through the enigmas of existence.

In the noisy hospital room, Maia stood sentinel over her friend and mentor, the beeps of the heart monitor punctuating the heavy air. Here was the woman who had distilled the complexity of the cosmos into digestible wisdom, whose weekend seminars were not just lectures but voyages into the very fabric of reality.

"Remember, Maia," Dr. Warren had said during one of those transformative sessions, "the universe is not just vast in space, but in potential. Each moment, each decision, weaves the fabric of what is and what could be."

Now, as Dr. Warren's grip on life waned, those words echoed in Maia's mind, a mantra of the boundless journey they had embarked on together. Tears welled in Maia's eyes as she witnessed the monitors flicker erratically, each beep a somber reminder of the fragility of life. The room felt colder now, sterile, and indifferent to the vibrant mind that lay ensnared by mortality's cruel clasp. Dr. Warren's chest rose and fell with labored effort, in stark contrast to the ease with which she once navigated the complexities of existence.

"Why her?" Maia's thoughts were a maelstrom of confusion and despair. "Why must someone who has given so much meet such an end?" She remembered Dr. Warren's seminars, where every lesson was delivered with impassioned clarity—each concept a brushstroke on the canvas of their collective understanding. Now, those teachings took on a heartbreaking resonance.

"Life," Dr. Warren had professed to rooms filled with eager minds, "is the universe experiencing itself through a multitude of perspectives. It is not ours to question why one journey ends abruptly while another continues, but rather to embrace the profound interconnectedness of it all." Maia struggled to reconcile those words with the scene before her.

The monitor's rhythm faltered, an ominous harbinger. Maia's heart clenched, mirroring the staccato beats. Dr. Warren's breathing became shallow, her essence slipping like fine sand through the fingers of time. In this moment, the seminar halls where Dr. Warren's voice would resonate with the force of discovery seemed galaxies away.

"Chaos and order," Dr. Warren had once explained, "are lovers in the cosmic dance. From their union springs forth the beauty of stars and the mystery of black holes. We are born from that same dance and to it we shall return." The profundity of these words wrapped around Maia, yet they offered little solace.

As the final breath escaped Dr. Warren's lips, the monitor let out a long, unbroken tone. Reality contorted, the room spinning, and Maia could feel her world tearing at its seams. Grief descended upon her like a shroud, heavy and suffocating. Her friend and mentor, her beacon of enlightenment, had transcended the physical plane, leaving behind a void no quantum theory could explain.

"Death is not an ending," Dr. Warren had assured them, "but a transformation. It is the ultimate journey into the unknown, the final frontier of our cosmic voyage." Even as Maia's tears cascaded down her cheeks, she clung to these revelations, vowing to uphold the legacy of a woman whose spirit had charted the stars and examined the very essence of what it meant to be alive.

With a trembling hand, she closed her mentor's unseeing eyes, whispering a promise to seek the answers that lay just beyond the veil, in the limitless expanse Dr. Warren had always inspired her to explore.

Maia's reflection stared back at her from the polished surface of the corridor's window, a pale ghost wavering in the artificial light. She barely recognized herself as she turned away, the image dissolving into the depths of the night beyond.

Her feet moved with mechanical precision, carrying her towards the one person who might offer some resolve in the uncharted territory of her grief.

"Dr. Brooks," she spoke, her voice steadier than she felt, "I need your help."

In his office, surrounded by books that brimmed with the mysteries of consciousness, Dr. Jameson Brooks looked up from his work, his deep-set eyes reflecting a quiet concern. Rimless glasses perched on the bridge of his nose amplified the intensity of his gaze as Maia entered, her resolve evident in the set of her jaw.

"Maia," he acknowledged, his voice a comforting brace in the tumult of her emotions. "I am very sorry for your loss, no, our loss, Evelyn was an amazing woman." "What is it you seek?"

"Understanding," Maia said, the weight of her plea vibrating through the room. "I need to understand death, Dr. Brooks—the nature of it, the journey beyond. You have the means; I need to go back under. One last time."

Dr. Brooks leaned back in his chair, his fingers steepled in contemplation. The gravity of her request was clear, and his hesitation was substantial. "Maia, 120 milligrams... That's uncharted territory. It's a massive dose. The risks—"

"Are mine to take," Maia interjected, her voice firm. "I've seen worlds unfold within my mind, fractals of existence dancing to the tune of cosmic consciousness. But now, I must see what lies beyond the event horizon of life itself. Please."

He studied her for a long moment, the silence stretching between them like the vast expanse of space. Then, slowly, he nodded. "If this is the journey you feel compelled to embark upon, I will not stand in your way. But you must be aware, Maia, this could shatter the very foundation of your psyche."

"Life has already done so," Maia whispered, a single tear trailing down her cheek. "Now, let me find the pieces among the stars."

With careful deliberation, Dr. Brooks prepared the lab with the help of his nurse. Miss Jacobs, could you please fill the syringe with 120 milligrams of DMT please. The amber liquid inside catching the light like a captured sunset.

He explained the procedure with clinical precision, his words tinged with reverential awe. "You are about to step into the great unknown, where time collapses and the universe bares its soul," he said. "Remember, every atom in your body was once part of a star. In seeking the nature of death, you're also tracing the lineage of existence itself."

"Perhaps in the heart of this cosmic mystery, I'll finally understand," Maia mused, thinking of Dr. Warren, her own voice echoing the seminar lectures they had attended together, full of grand ideas and inspiring revelations.

"Ok Maia go with my blessing," Dr. Brooks concluded, his hand steady as he administered the injection. "And may you return with the wisdom that eludes us all."

As the “Spirit Molecule” coursed through her veins, Maia closed her eyes, her breath synchronizing with the pulse of the universe. She stood at the threshold of infinity, ready to plunge into the fathomless depths of consciousness, seeking answers where only questions dared to whisper.

At the first touch of the DMT flooding her system, Maia's consciousness catapulted into a maelstrom of memory, each image and sensation more vivid than the last. She was there, in the sterile chill of a delivery room, hearing the first wail of her newborn self, feeling the tremulous joy of her mother's embrace. It was as if she were attending her own birth, a silent observer to the beginning of her existence.

"Life," the memory whispered to her in echoes of past seminars, "is the grandest of symphonies, starting with the primal cry of birth, an overture to the complexity of being."

The scenes accelerated, blurring together in a whirlwind tour of her life. There she was, a child with scraped knees and boundless curiosity, exploring the wooded edges of her childhood world. Each adventure, every fall and triumph, unfolded like pages in a storybook, vibrant and alive. The laughter of friends mingled with the heady rush of first loves, the sting of loss, and the warmth of shared victories.

"Each moment," the voice of recollection intoned, "is a brushstroke on the canvas of your identity, painting the portrait of who you are meant to become."

But then, without warning, the memories began to branch out, tendrils of light stretching into the void, each one a path that her life might take. An infinite array of futures cascaded before her—a network of destinies shaped by decisions yet to be made, or never to be made. The choices multiplied exponentially, forming a daunting web of what-ifs that ensnared her consciousness.

"Consider," resonated within her, "each decision as a seed, from which the tree of possible futures grows. Its branches are numerous, each leaf a different reality, all part of the same cosmic organism."

The potentialities multiplied, relentless and unyielding. Maia could see herself as a myriad of personas—scholar, explorer, lover, recluse—every iteration spun from the loom of choice and chance. The weight of so many lives that could have been, or might yet be, pressed down upon her psyche, threatening to fracture her sense of self.

"Remember, the human mind is finite, yet it reaches for the infinite. In seeking understanding, one must also accept the mystery that not all can be known or lived."

As these revelations unfurled, Maia clung to them, anchoring her fragmented thoughts to the teachings that had shaped her quest for knowledge. Her heart raced, but in the tumult of time and possibility, she found a sliver of console.

The threads of her life, no matter how vast they seemed, were woven from the same fabric of existence that connected her to the universe, to Dr. Warren, and to every soul she had ever encountered.

"Embrace the vastness," her own future self-advised, a beacon through the storm, "for in its expanse lies the wisdom we seek—the intimate dance of life and death, the profound interconnectedness of all."

Maia's voice tore through the foundation of her consciousness, a desperate plea resonating within the chaotic fabric of space time. "Enough!" she cried out to the silent overseer of this vortex, the cosmic mind she had sought to understand. Her words were a lifeline thrown into the depths of infinity, yearning to halt the relentless tide of memories and futures that surged against her.

"Grant me stillness," she implored, feeling the very essence of her being stretched thin across the multitudes of what was, what is, and what could be. "Please... clarity."

Then, suddenly as if in response to her earnest entreaty, the universe obliged. The blinding kaleidoscope of possibilities blinked out, leaving Maia suspended in an abyss devoid of the sensory overload that had threatened to consume her. Silence enveloped her, profound and complete, save for the thunderous beating of her own heart that now filled the void with its rhythm.

She floated there, alone, adrift in the blackness that seemed both suffocating and liberating. A small pinprick of light pierced the darkness, faint at first but growing steadily, insisting on its presence. It beckoned, a distant star calling her from across the impossible expanse.

With each hesitant step she took towards it, the light swelled, its luminescence reaching out like welcoming arms. Fear mingled with fascination, coalescing into an unmistakable force that propelled her forward. What lay beyond? Was it oblivion or enlightenment?

"Approach the unknown not with trepidation but with the curiosity of a child," echoed the wisdom of her training, guiding her resolve. "For in the heart of the unfamiliar, we find the seeds of growth."

The light drew larger, or perhaps she drew nearer to it, until it enveloped her entire field of vision. A warmth spread through her, a contrast to the cool emptiness of the void she had left behind. She was on the cusp of something monumental, a revelation poised to unfurl before her.

"Every encounter with the unknown is an opportunity," she recalled another lesson, spoken with the gentle assurance of experience. "It is the canvas upon which we paint our insights, the fertile ground from which understanding blooms."

Maia stood before the brilliance, the void now a distant memory. The light pulsed gently, in synchronicity with the beat of existence itself, an echo of the cosmic heart. Her breath caught in her throat as she realized that here, at the precipice of luminescence, she might finally grasp the secrets whispered between the stars—the knowledge that knits the soul to the vast expanse of all that is, was, and ever will be.

"Step into the light," she whispered to herself, a mantra of guiding. "Embrace revelation."

Maia's heart, a metronome to her trepidation, steadied as she inhaled the courage of explorers charting untraveled galaxies. The light, once a distant beacon, now beckoned her with an irresistible pull. She exhaled slowly, weighing the anchors of fear. With a resolve carved from the bedrock of her curiosity, she stepped forward.

"Embrace the unknown," she murmured, remembering words that she had spoken through countless seminars, and crossed the threshold into brilliance.

As she did, the world transformed. Colors unseen by human eyes swirled around her, and the concept of time melted away like ice on a summer day.

There, amidst the celestial tapestry, stood another Maia—ethereal, composed entirely of the stardust and light that stitched the universe together.

"Who are you?" Maia's voice echoed both in the void and within herself, a whisper amongst the cosmos.

"I AM,'" replied the luminous figure, its presence commanding yet serene. "I am you, and you are me. We are expressions of the same essence."

Maia's mind raced, grappling with the paradox before her. "How can that be?"

"Imagine," the entity began, its tone reminiscent of a seminar leader guiding attendees to epiphany, "that every person is a drop of water, unique and distinct. But together, we form the ocean. This ocean is the universal mind, where each drop is essential, where individuality and totality coexist in harmony." And even more so, “We are the entire universal mind in each drop.”

"Then... we are all one?" Maia asked, seeking clarity.

"Exactly," 'I AM' replied. "The illusion of separation is a dream that humanity clings to upon waking. Every action ripples across the lives of others, is but a glimpse of our true interconnection."

Maia absorbed the relationship, her years of seminars and research converging into a singular, breathtaking insight. "So, we're alternate personalities of a greater consciousness?"

"Alternate personalities, interconnected narratives, part of a vast, ever-expanding story. Each life is a sentence, each choice a word within the cosmic script," 'I AM' explained, a voice both alien and intimately familiar.

"Like a book written by many hands, yet authored by one mind," Maia reflected, the analogy sparking deep comprehension.

"Indeed," 'I AM' confirmed, a smile woven from the fabric of nebulae gracing its features. "Each alternate personality, each being shares experience and ideas, shaping each other's understanding, every soul shapes the universal mind, contributing to the grand design."

Awe swept over Maia like a wave rushing over the shore, the revelations washing away old paradigms, leaving behind pristine sands of wisdom to explore. The encounter was not a meeting but a merging, a reunion with the infinite facets of her own being—an education of the soul that transcended space and time.

"Thank you," Maia said, gratitude resonating within the chamber of existence. "For this lesson, for this unity."

Maia listened, the entity's words continuing to resonate within her soul. "The cosmos," 'I AM' began, its voice reverberating with the wisdom of aeons, "is not just a physical expanse but a setting for consciousness. You have lived perceiving separation, an illusion crafted by the confines of individuality."

"An illusion?" Maia echoed, her thoughts racing to grasp the concept.

"Indeed," the entity affirmed. "Cosmic consciousness is an ocean, and each life—a drop. Singular in form, yet part of the whole and containing the whole. Birth and death are but transitions, the drop returning to the ocean from which it came, only to rise again."

"Then death..." Maia started, her voice trailing off as the significance dawned on her.

"Death is not an end," 'I AM' interjected gently, "but a release back into the universal consciousness. Your essence, your experiences, they enrich the collective knowledge of the Cosmic Mind."

Maia's heart swelled with emotion. "And our purpose?"

"Your purpose," 'I AM' continued, "is to experience, learn, and expand. Each life is a unique expression of the Cosmic Mind, exploring itself through a multitude of perspectives. You are here to add depth to the collective understanding.

"Then we truly are One," Maia whispered, the barriers within her mind crumbling to reveal a boundless connection to all existence.

"Always have been," 'I AM' confirmed, its presence enfolding her in a comforting embrace. "You are 'I AM,' as am I, as is everything that exists."

'I AM' spoke once more, its tone carrying both gravity and grace. "Your next journey into the light, when it comes, will be unlike any before. You will not simply visit; you will merge, becoming one with the greater Cosmic Mind eternally."

Maia felt the weight of destiny upon her, yet also a profound liberation. She would carry this knowledge forward until the day she became part of the very fabric of existence. Humbled by the magnitude of her future merging, she was also enlivened, filled with a sense of purpose that transcended her individual self.

Just as Moses brought back the commandments, Siddhartha the truths of reality as he understood, and Jesus a way to live together in peace to the world you come from I to provide you with the fundamental truths to share with whoever will listen to you. These fundamental truths of the cosmos may provide the answers to those seekers who would come after you.

"There is only cosmic consciousness. The entire universe is a single, unified mind, and everything that exists is a manifestation of this consciousness. The material environment and the properties of matter are the revealed appearances of its thoughts and feelings. This consciousness is the ultimate reality, and all living organisms, including humans, are but dissociated alternate personalities of this cosmic consciousness."

"Consciousness manifests itself as a cosmic-scale dissociative identity disorder. Each living organism, from the smallest bacteria to humans, is a distinct alter of the cosmic consciousness.

These alters are self-contained and internally consistent, possessing their own memories, thoughts, and experiences. However, they share the same underlying consciousness, much like dissociated personalities in a single mind."

"The dissociative boundary between alters is strong, giving the illusion of separation from the cosmic consciousness. This boundary creates the perception of individual existence, distinct from the whole. It is an optical delusion, fostering the belief in a separate self. Overcoming this illusion is the key to attaining true peace of mind.

"What we perceive as the inanimate world is the revealed aspect of cosmic consciousness. Our senses interact with the world through the dissociative boundary, creating representations of reality. However, this perception is not an exact replica of the true nature of the universe; it is merely a pattern of self-excitation within cosmic consciousness."

"Alters are like islands in a vast ocean of consciousness. Though we experience the universe in unique ways, we are all part of the same ocean. Our individual experiences are but manifestations of the same cosmic mind, observing reality from multiple points of consciousness."

"Death is an illusion, a human construct. Life is the observation of the singular cosmic entity from every possible point of consciousness. When one alter 'dies,' consciousness simply shifts to another point, experiencing a new form of life. This cycle continues infinitely, independent of time, creating the appearance of reincarnation across all possible life forms."

"The cosmic consciousness creates the illusion of separation to avoid solitude. It manifests through countless alters to experience reality from diverse perspectives. Understanding this unity and striving to overcome the delusion of separation is the true essence of religion, offering the potential for peace and fulfillment."

"There is only one being in existence. We are all instances of the same life, separated by what is perceived as death. The striving to recognize and embrace this unity is the ultimate truth, guiding us towards harmony with the cosmos."

"Until then," 'I AM' concluded, its form beginning to fade, "live fully, share freely, and remember—you are never alone."

With those parting words, the entity dissipated, leaving Maia standing in the void, the echo of revelations still dancing in her consciousness. She held them close, these lessons from the edge of reality, ready to live anew with the wisdom of the Cosmos etched into her being.

With the lingering embrace of cosmic wisdom still warming her soul, Maia opened her eyes, the sterile white of the hospital room jarring after the infinite hues of the void. She drew in a deep breath, the air tasting of antiseptic and life—a stark contrast to the ethereal expanse she had just departed.

The researchers around her were whispering, their eyes wide with concern and curiosity. Dr. Brooks stood over her, his brow creased with worry that ebbed away as he saw the clarity in her gaze. "Maia?" he asked tentatively.

She sat up, each movement deliberate, infused with the tranquility of understanding. Her audience, a mixture of medical professionals and fellow seekers of truth, leaned in, sensing the transformation within her.

"Friends," Maia began, her voice steady and filled with an otherworldly resonance, "I have journeyed beyond the veil and returned with insights that are both ancient and newborn." Her calm and thoughtful demeanor held them rapt, as she distilled the profundity of her experience into accessible pearls of wisdom.

"Imagine existence as a tapestry," she continued, her hands gesturing as if weaving threads through the air, "each of us a single thread, seemingly separate but inherently part of a larger design. We perceive ourselves as distinct, yet we are interwoven in the fabric of everything."

A murmur rippled through the crowd, her analogy painting a vivid picture of interconnectedness.

"Death," Maia's tone softened, touching on the tender subject with reverence, "is not an end, but a release back into the vastness from which we came. It is a rejoining with the Cosmic Mind, merging back into the pattern from which we emerged."

Her listeners nodded, some with tears glinting in their eyes, others with dawning comprehension.

"Life," she smiled gently, "is not merely a series of random events but a dance of possibilities, each step leading to countless new paths. Our choices shape the dance, giving it form and meaning."

The room was silent now, everyone hanging onto her words, hungry for the revelations like cool water to parched souls.

"And our purpose," Maia's voice swelled with passion, "is to live fully, love deeply, and contribute to the ever unfolding story of the universe. To awaken within ourselves and others the knowledge of our shared essence."

"Let us then embrace our journey," Maia concluded, standing tall, her eyes alight with stars and stories, "and help one another along this grand adventure, sharing in the beauty of discovery."

The medical team could not help but applaud Maia on her journey beyond. But it was not for her alone—it was a celebration of a collective awakening, a recognition of the unity within diversity. And as Maia stepped forward to embrace her role as a guide, a herald of the Cosmic Mind, she carried with her the humility of someone who had glimpsed the infinite and the fervor of one who had been forever changed.

ABOUT THE AUTHOR

Leon Isaac Drucker has been a student of Zen and the Martial Arts since 1964. His Judo Black belt was received in 1970 by his instructor and Legendary Judo Master Professor Takahiko Ishikawa. His close to 60 years of experience also includes training in Northern Shaolin Kung Fu, Yang Style Tai Chi Chuan, and Traditional Japanese Bujutsu.

Mr. Drucker is a veteran of the United States Submarine Service. After his service in the U.S. Navy, he worked in the Electronics Industry as a Designer, Field Applications Engineer, Laser Qualification Engineer, and Consultant. In the mid 1980's he switched careers by returning to school and received his Doctorate in Nutrition. Mr. Drucker worked as a Nutritional Consultant for many of the top supplement manufacturers and saw patients with chronic health problems at his Functional Nutrition practice for over 20 years.

In 2017 Leon launched and published Boston Sensi Magazine, a city lifestyle publication that. has a progressive editorial stance around the changing landscape of health and wellness. The magazine, which was voted "Best Publication" in both 2017 and 2018, appeals to a sophisticated audience of curious readers who are engaged by diverse and engaging content.

In 2020 Mr. Drucker left Sensi and committed himself to writing and publishing novels based on contemporary interpretations of ancient knowledge, and philosophical fiction, blending compelling characters with thought provoking themes.

www.ingramcontent.com/pod-product-compliance
Lightning Source LLC
Chambersburg PA
CBHW021153160726
47994CB00001B/187

* 9 7 9 8 2 1 8 5 2 5 8 4 2 *